TA

TANTALUS

Louise Brindley

This first world edition published in Great Britain 1999 by
SEVERN HOUSE PUBLISHERS LTD of
9–15 High Street, Sutton, Surrey SM1 1DF.
First published in the USA 2000 by
SEVERN HOUSE PUBLISHERS INC., of
595 Madison Avenue, New York, NY 10022.

British Library Cataloguing in Publication Data

Brindley, Louise
        Tantalus
        1.   Detective and mystery stories
        I.   Title
        823.9'14 [F]

        ISBN 0-7278-5497-6

Typeset by Palimpsest Book Production Ltd
Polmont, Stirlingshire, Scotland.
Printed and bound in Great Britain by
MPG Books Ltd, Bodmin, Cornwall.

Especially for Jim

One

Throughout the long hot summer, Geraldine Frayling had written at an open window overlooking the steep and leafy garden of her Hampstead residence, clad in her heatwave gear – a green bath-sheet worn sarong fashion, feet, legs and plump shoulders bare, hair scraped back and fastened with a rubber band, forehead girdled with a kind of John McEnroe sweat band to prevent her glasses sliding down her nose with perspiration.

Not that the device worked very well. Her glasses continued to slide as she got to grips with the latest exploits of her uppercrust sleuth, Virginia Vale – a female version of Lord Peter Wimsey, with a penchant for finding bodies in unlikely places, from Wapping to Wandsworth.

Frayling was not her real name, it simply looked better on her book jackets. Her family name was Mudd, and her parents invariably referred to her as Gerry, never Geraldine.

When her agent tactfully advised her that Gerry Mudd was not an ideal name for an authoress to be stuck with unless she had a publishing death wish, she had adopted the surname Frayling – that of her mother's new husband – thus providing a satisfactory solution to the problem. Not that her father was best pleased. But then, Fred Mudd was never best pleased about anything, much less his ex-wife's new partner in life. 'Poncy', in his view.

Virginia Vale had provided the wherewithal to purchase

the Hampstead house, Gerry reflected, pausing momentarily from her labours to wipe her face with a damp flannel. Not that she'd been overly impressed with it at first sight, the state it was in. 'In need of modernisation', according to the estate agent's blurb. The understatement of the decade so far as she was concerned, on the day she had come to view the property.

Even so, she had realised its potential, what she thought of as the happiness factor: nothing whatsoever to do with grotty paintwork, inches thick dust and peeling wallpaper, everything to do with the foot-deep skirting boards, ceiling rosettes, solid staircases and mahogany banisters.

Above all, she had loved this long attic room with its jutting dormer window overlooking the steeply plunging garden, a room in which she could write to her heart's content, in splendid isolation.

The estate agent had been more than a little edgy and impatient with her that day, Gerry recalled, wanting her to make a snap decision as she wandered from room to room trying to work out how much it would cost to carpet and furnish the house, let alone have it redecorated from top to bottom and create the modern kitchen she had in mind.

Eventually, glancing pointedly at his wristwatch, he had dangled the carrot of a possible price reduction of, say, five thousand pounds, if his client proved amenable to the suggestion.

"Make it ten, and you're on," Gerry advised him cannily. "It'll cost me all that, and more, to make the house fit for human habitation."

"Very well, then, I'll see what I can do!"

The trouble was, Gerry had never been rich enough before to think in terms of owning even a modest flat of her own, much less a detached Victorian villa in a posh area of London, but she had fallen in love with this house, despite its defects, and she had wanted it more than she had wanted anything in her life before. A home of her own, with lots of space. A kind of haven, a caravanserai . . .

Now it was hers, thanks to her alter ego, Virginia Vale, her attractive super-sleuth whose exploits had captured the readers' imaginations and launched her creator into the ranks of bestselling authors, with royalties, TV contracts and film-rights rolling in at a rate of knots. A far cry from the past.

Gerry's parents regarded writers as odd-bods, and they had done nothing whatsoever to encourage her to become one, even saying that she'd be far better off stacking shelves in a supermarket, when she left school, than wasting her time on further education at the local Tech.

"Look here, my girl," her father had warned her succinctly, "the sooner you get those 'pie-in-the-sky' notions out of your head and start earning your keep, the better! What your ma an' me need right now is cash in hand to pay for your board and lodging, an' don't you forget it!"

And so the beleaguered Gerry had taken a boring day-time job stacking shelves in a local branch of Tesco to pay her parents for her upkeep, before dashing off to evening classes to attend courses relevant to writing – mainly touch typing, English literature, basic English for beginners, plus elocution lessons to tone down her strong regional accent.

Arriving home around nine thirty in the evening, she would hurry upstairs to her room to scribble away at her first ever novel, *Virginia Vale Investigates*, stuffing her ears with cottonwool to deaden the sounds of verbal warfare from the rooms below, the banging of doors and the occasional shattering of china when her ma and pa were engaged in a quarrel bearing the hallmarks of a 'shout-out' at the OK Corral.

Frankly, it had come as a relief when her parents had finally parted company to take up residence with their new partners until they were free to remarry – 'Poncy' versus 'Tarty', at which point, refusing to take sides, Gerry had found herself a bedsit in Clapham, in which she'd felt free to get on with her life in her own way. Not that her ma and da had raised objections to her going it alone, she'd thought wistfully – it was almost as if they were glad to see the back of her.

Her manuscript completed, she had typed it painstakingly on a wonky second-hand typewriter and sent it to an agent whose name she had discovered in the pages of *The Writers' and Artists' Yearbook*, fairly certain that it would come crashing down on her doormat one fine morning, accompanied by a 'Thanks, but no thanks' rejection slip.

To her amazement, the agent had retained the manuscript and requested a meeting. The book had its faults, of course, but he liked the racy style of writing, and he was prepared to offer it to various publishing houses to gauge their reaction.

Thereafter, the agent, William Bentine – 'Call me Bill,' he'd said, with more than a touch of Robert Redford about him – had treated her to lunch at a Greek restaurant near Red Lion Square. It was dim and noisy, and he had ordered a dish of meat wrapped in vine leaves which Gerry had regarded with dismay, not knowing what to do with the vine leaves. Lacking sophistication, she'd have infinitely preferred to have had steak pie and chips.

So had been launched the career of the crime novelist Geraldine Frayling, and when her new abode had been refurbished, she had engaged the services of a cook-housekeeper and a part-time gardener who, she fondly imagined, would keep the household cart on the wheels while she and Virginia set about discovering more bodies in the London area.

She might have known things wouldn't work out as planned. Her own fault entirely for hiring a volatile Frenchwoman as housekeeper, and lumbering herself with a young alcoholic

Irishman who knew as much about gardening as she knew about sheep-shearing.

To add to her problems, her housekeeper Anna Gordino, until recently married to an Italian innkeeper, tri-lingual as a result, pidgin English being her third language, would insist on breaking her concentration at regular intervals throughout the day, so as to impart the latest bad news from the kitchen, whilst her alcoholic gardener, Liam McEvoy, appeared to spend most of his time in the shed picking losers from his *Sporting Pink* newspaper instead of lopping overhanging branches from the maze of paths leading down to the boundary wall of her domain, burning rubbish, or whatever else gardeners were supposed to do if they knew their onions.

Onions! Gerry doubted if Liam, put to the test, would be able to differentiate between pickling onions and crocus bulbs. So why not fire him and have done with it? Because she liked the Irish cheek and charm of the man, his quirky sense of humour and lack of pretension. Above all, because he, like herself, was a survivor in the battle of life.

One hot Friday morning in August, Anna Gordino appeared on the threshold of Gerry's sanctum complaining that the extractor fan in the kitchen had gone 'pouf', that Liam had not turned up for work as usual, and what should she do about it?

Apparently the voluble Anna with her smouldering eyes and Edith Piaf haircut – home-butchered gamine for want of a kinder description – had still not cottoned on to the idea that she had been hired to look after her employer, not the other way round, or so Gerry thought resignedly, pausing in the middle of a blizzard in which her alter ego, Virginia Vale, was about to track a serial killer by his footprints in the snow.

Sighing deeply, tightening the rubber band holding back

her hair, and wiping her glasses on the bath-sheet, "You'd best send for the electrician," Gerry advised Anna. "His number's on the pad. As for Liam, he's bound to turn up sooner or later. He's probably been out on the tiles all night."

Anna looked shocked.

"You mean he sleepa on ze roof when ze 'eat is on?"

"I shouldn't be a bit surprised! Now really, Anna, you must let me get on with my work. All I want for lunch is a sandwich and a glass of orange juice. I'll have dinner on the patio around seven thirty." (The patio, Gerry's pride and joy, created from a once dreary dustbin area adjacent to the back door of her Hampstead eyrie.)

"Ah," Anna cried triumphantly, "thees ees why I come! You are invited to eata weeth Monsieur Berenger and ees wife thees evening! 'E say, on ze phone, zey go on 'oliday tomorrow."

"Really?" Gerry beamed.

She liked the Berengers enormously, her charismatic fellow-writer and his attractive Austrian-born wife Lisl – a talented artist – with whom she had struck up a rewarding friendship shortly after moving into the 'eyrie' and finding that they were living next door to one another.

Overwhelmingly kind and hospitable, they had at once taken under their wing a newcomer to the ranks of bestselling authors, which Maurice, by reason of his many brilliantly crafted crime novels, had graced for the past decade.

She had the Berengers to thank for introducing her to their many distinguished and influential friends – artists, actors and TV producers, and also to members of their family circle. There was Maurice's nephew Tim Bowen, for instance, a somewhat colourless young man, owl-like in appearance, wearing enormous, thick-lensed glasses, who taught history at a public school near Reading, and his sister

Cassie – short for Cassandra – a statuesque blonde who worked for a man called Christian Sommer at his antiques gallery in Chelsea. Last, but by no means least, Christian Sommer himself, who had made more than a small dent in the heart of Miss Geraldine Mudd.

On the occasion of that first dinner party she'd attended, chez Berenger, she had scarcely been able to drag her eyes away from his chiselled features and thatch of Viking-blonde hair, his lean, broad-shouldered body fairly welded into a faultlessly tailored evening dress suit in which he appeared entirely at ease and uninhibited, despite the figure-revealing lines of his apparel.

By the same token, Sommer had seemed incapable of dragging his eyes away from Cassie Bowen, and who could blame him? She really was a joy to behold in her black lace evening gown, her blonde tresses piled up, in a kind of pyramid, above her piquant, heart-shaped face. But such a radiant vision was spoilt when she laughed, in Gerry's opinion, by its display of far too many front teeth embedded in too large an area of gums, reminiscent of a racehorse at the starting-gate of the Grand National, snickering, to put it mildly.

Returning home when the party was over, Gerry had thought despondently that such was the way of the world, fat women didn't stand a chance compared with nature's skinny lizzies who, despite the massive extent and awful pinkness of their gums, had it made so far as their boobs and waistlines were concerned.

She was fat, and she knew it! Lying on her bed like a beached whale, she wondered if liposuction would work. Alternatively, she might try having her jaws wired together, or book in for a month at one of those health farms where the inmates existed on carrot juice and celery sticks.

What? Starve herself? No way! If people didn't like her the way she was, they must lump her, and yet . . . One

7

thing for sure, if Virginia Vale had been a guest at that dinner party, she would have had Christian Sommer's scalp on her belt with one cool, appraising glance from those hazel green eyes of hers. Cassandra Bowen wouldn't have stood an earthly. But then, neither had Gerry Mudd, who didn't show her gums when she smiled!

Now, on this hot August day, slipping into a pair of espadrilles, Gerry quitted her attic studio by the fire-escape door and wandered down the curving iron steps to the garden, hitching up her bath-sheet as she went, feeling like an item of Italianate sculpture in her swathed drapery and with her mouse-brown hair gathered into a Hebe-like knot at the back of her head: a far cry from her fictitious heroine, who would not be seen dead in such a get-up, unless she had just stepped out of the shower.

Virginia Vale appeared on the pages of her novels as a sylph-like redhead whose favourite gear included tartan trews, Indian moccasins, camouflage jackets, shapeless sweaters and baseball caps unless, as the text suggested from time to time, off duty from her crime busting capers, she would dine at The Savoy or Quaglinos with one or another of her wealthy admirers, stunningly dressed, with emerald earrings the size of mini-chandeliers brushing her shoulders.

Crossing the stone-flagged patio to the strains of 'La Vie en Rose' from the kitchen, croaked by Anna Gordino doing her Piaf impersonation, Gerry mused that she had imbued Virginia Vale with the qualities she most admired in other women – slenderness, beauty, courage and resourcefulness – allied to a family background of the kind she had never known. And it had not been easy finding out how the other half lived, to think her way into an upper class scenario.

She had started by reading, from cover to cover, those glossy magazines in which the gentry discreetly advertised their ancestral piles, manor houses, riverside residences – or whatever they wished to part with in a hurry – accompanied by photographs, plus details of heated swimming pools, stabling, servants' quarters, acreage and the asking prices, at which her mind had boggled initially.

Even so, she had read on, building a composite picture of the kind of house that Virginia and her parents, Sir William and Lady Letitia Vale, would inhabit: an Elizabethan residence with mullioned windows; a minstrel gallery; drawing room the length of a tennis court; spacious lawns dotted with stately elms and spreading cedars; secluded rose gardens; herbaceous borders; a walled kitchen garden; and a lodge-keeper's cottage near the main entrance of the estate.

Fondly, in imagination, Gerry had given birth to Sir William and Lady Letitia breakfasting on bacon and eggs, kidneys and kedgeree from the chafing dishes on the Sheraton sideboard; they would be calling one another 'darling', not 'you lazy, good-for-nothing slob' or 'you fat, miserable cow', as her own parents had done over burnt toast and Robertson's Golden Shred marmalade in the kitchen of a council house in Clapham.

All in the past now, Gerry reflected, drifting beneath the trees in her bath-sheet and espadrilles, safe in the knowledge that she was hidden from prying eyes by the density of the vegetation sloping down to the high brick wall bordering her domain, deriving pleasure from the thought that she had achieved all this by her sheer determination to succeed, despite the odds stacked against her at the outset, what with her parents' opposition, and a sketchy education in overcrowded classrooms in which the pupils had exerted a reign of terror over the teachers.

Little wonder she had headed towards the nearest public library when school was over, to borrow crime novels by her favourite authors – Agatha Christie, Ngaio Marsh and Dorothy L. Sayers in particular – whose supersleuths,

Hercule Poirot, Chief Inspector Roderick Alleyn and Lord Peter Wimsey, had made a deep and lasting impression on her, to the extent of wanting to write detective stories of her own, each featuring a female sleuth as unlike herself as possible.

Now she was trying to figure out the ending of her current novel, *The Blasted Heath*, and she needed to think fast, because the book was due for completion by an end of September deadline: the penultimate chapter leading to the nail-biting denouement, which would have Virginia Vale's legion of admirers too scared to sleep by the last page.

Nothing in the world was more frightening or disturbing, Gerry figured, than the dawning realisation that someone regarded as a friend was nothing of the kind after all, but rather a deadly enemy, a demon face hidden behind a smiling mask. A potential killer.

Truth to tell, she felt physically exhausted. Perhaps she needed a holiday? Come October, why not take a trip to Venice aboard The Orient Express – the fulfilment of a long-held ambition? She could easily afford such a luxury, so what was stopping her? Lack of self-confidence for one thing, due to her appearance: all bust and bum, no waistline to speak of. Right now, lacking the support of bra and girdle because of the heat, she felt herself to be 'swelling wisibly' like Sam Weller's turkey.

In any event, the money would be better spent on bringing the garden under control. Not that she disliked the idea of a wooded estate, but whoever had planted the trees way back in the 1890s had made no allowance for their growth. Now their convoluted roots had begun buckling the paths, requiring the attention of a tree-surgeon to tackle the overcrowding problem before Tarzan and his mate took up residence in her jungle. Besides which, she fancied a small clearing here and there, a rose garden, a lily pool, a gazebo.

*   *   *

Tripping over a tree root thrusting up from buckled asphalt, she regained her balance near the garden shed in which, Liam kept his tools, thinking it odd that he had not turned up on pay-day to collect his wages. "Come day, go day, God send pay-day," she'd heard him say often enough in that devil-may-care way of his, the cocky young so and so.

It was then that she noticed that the door of the shed was not closed and padlocked as she had imagined it would be, but slightly ajar. So Liam must have come to work after all, despite Anna Gordino's assurance that he had not. Hmm, well, that figured. Knowing he was late, he'd have sneaked in the back way to avoid a penny lecture from the housekeeper on his errant ways so far as timekeeping was concerned.

Come to think of it, a word in his ear on the same subject might not come amiss from herself, Gerry considered. Not a 'telling off' as such, merely a reminder that, since she was paying his wages, she had the right to expect that he would come to work on time to earn his weekly pay-packet.

Approaching the shed, she called out, "Liam, are you there? I want a word with you!"

No response. No sign of life, of movement. Just silence. Complete and utter silence.

What caused her to hang back before entering the shed, Gerry had no clear idea at the time, or afterwards. No way could she have put into words the gut feeling she had that something was terribly wrong. How to explain a sudden sense of danger, an emanation of evil? Possibly it had been the sickly sweet smell of death issuing from the door of the shed that had so unnerved her.

Crossing the threshold, Liam had obviously been dead for some time, she registered bemusedly, hence the odour of putrefaction and the swarm of bluebottles buzzing about the corpse, beside which lay an empty whisky bottle and the half consumed contents of a bottle of pain-killing tablets.

Sickened and shaken by her discovery, backing away from the body, her mind in a turmoil, Gerry stumbled back to the house to phone the police – the only option under the circumstances – and report an unnatural death on her premises.

What she could not understand, or come to terms with, was that Liam McEvoy, a survivor in the battle of life, had chosen to do away with himself in a garden shed, of all places. It didn't make sense.

Something was wrong with the set-up. Something she had witnessed didn't ring true. Some detail she had noticed had sounded a warning bell in her subconcious mind. But what?

Suddenly she remembered!

Of course! Would a man in the final stages of unconsciousness, washing down pain-killing tablets with whisky in an attempt to commit suicide, have taken the trouble to replace the lid of the bottle of tablets so tidily?

Obviously someone had. If not Liam, then – who?

Two

Writing about the police, Gerry discovered, and watching episodes of *The Bill* on TV, had little bearing on their presence in her home and garden. They seemed to be everywhere, and they looked enormous, somewhat threatening – especially the Detective Inspector in charge of the enquiry, a very tall man, brisk in manner, who fired questions at her like bullets from a gun.

"Tell me, Miss Frayling, when did you last see your gardener alive?" Detective Inspector Clooney wanted to know.

"Last Friday, when he came to collect his wages. I happened to be in the kitchen at the time," Gerry said unhappily.

"What were his hours of employment?"

"Mondays, Wednesday and Fridays, from ten to four o'clock."

"Today is Friday," Clooney reminded her.

"Yes, I know it is."

"According to your housekeeper, you knew that McEvoy had not turned up as usual, this morning. Didn't that alarm you?"

"No, not really. He wasn't a very good timekeeper. I felt sure he'd come sooner or later to collect his wages."

"How long had he been in your employ?"

"Since last April, when I came here to live."

"How did you come by him? Via an employment agency, or did you place an advert in the local paper?"

"Neither," Gerry uttered dejectedly. "He simply turned up on the doorstep one day; said he'd been employed as a gardener by the former owner, and asked if he could have his job back. I saw no reason to refuse his request. Well, you've seen my garden, the state it's in?"

"Quite! And the name of the former owner?"

"Oh lord, let me think!" Gerry puckered her forehead. "Constantine! Yes, Constantine – a retired archaeologist or some such. We never met. You'd best ask the estate agent about that."

"The name of the estate agent?"

"Lance Bellingham, of Charters and Bellingham. They're in the Yellow Pages."

"Now, tell me, Miss Frayling, what prompted you to look in the shed?"

"Because the door was open when it shouldn't have been. Not if Liam hadn't turned up for work this morning. He would have closed and padlocked the door when he went home at four o'clock on Wednesday."

"Quite so, which suggests that Mr McEvoy did not leave the premises on Wednesday. A fact substantiated by his common-law wife's phone call to the police station on Thursday morning, reporting him as a missing person."

"His common-law wife? I didn't know he had one," Gerry said, feeling sick, remembering the smell inside the shed, and the bluebottles.

"Oh yes. A Miss Zoe Smith, apparently. Now, tell me, were you satisfied with McEvoy's work on the whole? You had not warned him, for instance, that he might well lose his job if he didn't mend his ways?"

On the defensive, tired of being questioned, "Meaning what, exactly?" Gerry said stubbornly.

"Oh come now, Miss Frayling, you have already admitted that the man was a bad timekeeper, and we gleaned from

14

Miss Smith that he was an alcoholic. Not the happiest of scenarios, wouldn't you agree?"

"No, I damn well wouldn't!" exclaimed Gerry, who had changed into a dirndl skirt and sloppy sweater when she knew the police were coming, and who now rose to her feet, quivering from stem to stern.

"Now you listen to me, Inspector! I liked Liam McEvoy enormously. So he was a bad timekeeper, an alcoholic, but above and beyond all that, he was a likeable human being, and I'm sorry he's dead! The thing is, did he commit suicide, or was he murdered? Think about it, Inspector! Think about that bottle of painkillers with the lid neatly in place. Or hadn't you noticed?"

"No need to adopt that attitude," Clooney said coldly. "We cannot arrive at the truth of the matter until the stomach contents of the deceased have been analysed." He paused momentarily. "If the stomach contents contain no trace of barbiturates, one would naturally assume that the bottle of tablets had not been opened in the first place. Agreed?"

"Yeah, I guess so," Gerry acknowledged, feeling deflated. "The truth is, I can't bring myself to believe that Liam committed suicide. He was a happy alcoholic, not a sad one." Tears filled her eyes. "On the other hand, who on earth would have wanted him out of the way? He was such a harmless kind of person."

Clooney drew in a deep breath. "You've made your point, Miss Frayling," he said less forcefully, "now I suggest that you leave this investigation to the professionals." He added briskly, "There will be an inquest, of course, which you will be required to attend to give evidence."

"Not to worry, Inspector, I'm not thinking of skipping the country, if that's what's bothering you," Gerry assured him sarcastically, heading towards the door with as much dignity as she could muster.

*   *   *

15

When she had gone, Clooney walked down to the garden shed to supervise the removal of the deceased to the mortuary van parked near the back entrance of the premises.

Deep in thought, he pondered the significance of that bottle of barbiturates with the lid neatly in place – a second flaw in the suicide theory, in his view.

The first was that few suicides, in his experience, and according to statistics, quitted the world without leaving a farewell letter of some kind, at least a hastily scrawled note addressed to their nearest and dearest, explaining their reasons for wanting to end it all. In this case, no such message had come to light.

Oh damn and blast, he thought sourly, the last thing he needed right now was a full-scale murder enquiry, necessitating the postponement of his long awaited summer holiday in Cyprus until the mystery was solved to the satisfaction of the powers-that-be at Scotland Yard.

"Well, get a move on, Constable," he said abruptly to the driver of the mortuary van, when the remains of Liam McEvoy were aboard, "we haven't got all day!"

"Sir!" Getting a 'move on' indeed, the constable wondered who had rattled Clooney's cage. Not that it took much rattling anyway. Some kind of male menopause, he reckoned, or, more than likely, he'd had another flaming row with his wife. If so, it wouldn't be the first, nor probably the last!

Struggling into a corselette, and wondering what the hell to wear that evening, it had crossed Gerry's mind to cancel her supper date with the Berengers. On the other hand, she felt in need of company, and Anna Gordino had already gone upstairs to her room, locking the door behind her.

In the event, Gerry turned up at the Berengers' half an hour late, wearing the latest addition to her wardrobe – a red trouser suit in which she felt as hot and uncomfortable as a greenhouse tomato.

What had possessed her to buy the damn thing in the first place, she would never know. She hadn't liked it that much in the shop; she hated the sight of it now.

The Berengers' housekeeper, Mrs Temple, a prissy little woman with dyed brown hair and gold-framed glasses, answered the doorbell, smiled thinly, and led her through to the terrace, where a buffet supper was set out on a table near the balustrade overlooking the immaculately kept garden beneath, Chinese lanterns glimmering between the branches of a cedar tree at the far end of the patio.

Maurice Berenger, a tall, elderly man, charismatic, with a full beard and a mane of flowing grey hair brushed back from his forehead, and his wife, Lisl, were seated at a wrought iron table, sipping wine, when Gerry appeared on the scene.

At once, Maurice gallantly rose to his feet and hurried towards her, smiling, words of welcome on his lips, at which point, overcome by emotion, Gerry burst into tears.

"My dear! What is it? What's wrong?" he asked concernedly, whereupon Gerry's flow increased, her face crumpled and, try as she might, she couldn't find her handkerchief.

Then suddenly Lisl was beside her, leading her towards the table, uttering soft words of comfort, handing her a packet of Kleenex tissues from the evening bag dangling from the arm of her chair, and Maurice appeared from the drawing room with a glass of brandy.

"Here, m'dear," he said kindly, "drink this. It will do you good."

Gerry drank obediently, spluttered, blew her nose, and dried her eyes. Lisl and Maurice exchanged worried glances. When she could speak properly, Gerry told them about the body in the garden shed.

"Good God," Maurice muttered, deeply shaken, "how appalling. May one ask – whose body?"

"My gardener, Liam McEvoy's. There was an empty whisky bottle and a half empty bottle of painkillers beside him."

"Good grief! McEvoy? That jaunty young Irishman? The last person on earth to commit suicide, I'd have thought."

"I don't think he did," Gerry said. "I think he was – murdered."

His crime writer's curiosity aroused, "What makes you say that?" Maurice asked intently.

"Because the lid of the tablet bottle was in place when it shouldn't have been," Gerry explained. "Not if Liam had decided to kill himself. Whisky alone wouldn't have done the trick, and he would have known that. It had to be the painkillers!"

"I see what you mean," Maurice said eagerly. "Hardly likely that a man sinking into oblivion would bother to put the lid back on a bottle. What did the police say?"

"That the bottle may not have been opened in the first place. But that doesn't make sense."

"You're right, it doesn't! What do you think, Lisl?"

"I think that we should change the subject." She smiled charmingly. "Gerry must be famished. I know *I* am. Let's have supper, shall we?"

"Sorry, darling. Yes, of course. No use letting good food go to waste." He knew exactly what she meant. Gerry had had enough drama for one day. A clever, sensitive woman, his wife.

Gerry's spirits lifted somewhat at the thought of food, and she hadn't realised how hungry she was until Lisl reminded her. Oh, what the hell, she thought, piling a plate with cold roast beef, potato salad and mushroom vol-au-vents, she'd start dieting tomorrow – or the day after.

Spreading a baguette lavishly with butter, "Anna Gordino mentioned that you are off on holiday tomorrow," Gerry said, wishing she had not worn her corselette, which was giving her gyp. "Where to? America? The Bahamas? The Riviera?"

Maurice chuckled. "No way! Been there, done that, as the saying goes. The fact is, we've found ourselves a hideaway, a kind of bolt-hole much nearer to home, haven't we, Lisl?"

"That we have, in a tiny fishing village in Yorkshire, of all places. We'd grown so tired of the 'rat-race', you see? Cruise liners, the Sphinx, the Pyramids – those interminable delays at Heathrow or wherever . . ."

"Then, two years ago," Maurice interrupted excitedly, "we invested in a caravanette with a view to touring the north of England, visiting out of the way places we'd missed out on before: Northumberland, for instance. Staying overnight at quaint village pubs and so on until, on our homeward journey, we chanced upon Robin Hood's Bay, and Black Gull House."

Lisl took up the theme. "Not that we were all that taken with it at first sight, the state it was in. But we had planned to stay a week or so in the area, and Black Gull was the only holiday home available at that time of year. So, in a sense, we were stuck with it, until . . ."

"Until we realised its potential," Maurice broke in, "as not just a holiday home but something more permanent. Its situation for one thing, the breathtaking view of the coastline and the sea from its upper windows. I'll never forget Lisl's face when she first saw the view from the attic window, in particular . . ."

"I knew at once that the attic would make a perfect studio for Maurice and me," Lisl continued mistily, "where I could paint to my heart's content, and he could write, if he felt like it, in such an idyllic setting, if only we could persuade the owner to sell us the house."

"That's when we came up against Miss Phoebe Carslake," Maurice continued. "The old lady didn't want to sell, and we had one hell of a job persuading her to change her mind. Remember, Lisl?"

"Remember? How could I possibly forget?" Lisl shuddered, and laughed somewhat nervously, Gerry thought, biting into a prawn and mayonnaise sandwich, which seemed odd in the face of Lisl's usual savoir-faire, her cool sophistication which made Gerry feel, at times, like a cart-horse stabled next door to a Derby winner.

Comparisons were odious, and never more so than now, Gerry realised. Here she was, sweltering in her red trouser suit, stuffing her face with food, and there was Lisl, a woman old enough to be her mother, reed-slender and lovely, as cool as a cucumber in an Indian cotton skirt, tank-top and open-toe sandals, smelling divinely of her special brand of perfume. So why the involuntary shudder? The nervous laugh?

Maurice answered the question unbidden. "It really was quite dreadful, darling, wasn't it?" he said. "Like something out of a Gothic horror movie. That darkened room, and the old girl, Phoebe Carslake, sitting in that high-backed chair, dressed all in black, with that yashmak thingummy covering the lower half of her face, wanting to know the reason why she should part with Black Gull House at the behest of a couple of strangers?"

"Thank goodness her sister, Miss Millie, had had a word with her beforehand," Lisl interposed. "But then, Millie was on our side all along in wanting rid of the property. After all, it was a considerable drain on her sister's resources, with so much repair work necessary to update the building. Phoebe should have welcomed us with open arms!"

"Well, that's all in the past now," Maurice said soothingly, pouring more wine. "The thing is, Gerry, when your book is finished to that end of September deadline, how would you feel about spending October with Lisl and me in Robin Hood's Bay?"

20

Gerry stared at him, open-mouthed. "Oh, but I – what I mean is, I wouldn't want to intrude on your privacy."

"Nonsense," Lisl said firmly, "we'd love to have you. There's room and to spare, and you'll adore Robin Hood's Bay. It's so charming and picturesque. Quiet, too, out of season, and there's lashings of hot water now the plumbing's been updated. Do say you'll come."

"I'd love to, and thanks for asking me." The Berengers' kindness towards her never ceased to amaze Gerry. "It's just that Anna Gordino might jib at being left on her own for a month, in view of the present circumstances. She's acting very strangely at the moment. This morning, for instance, when the police had gone, I found her in the kitchen armed with a bread knife, muttering something about being murdered in her bed if she didn't watch out. Now she's locked herself in her room, and I wouldn't mind betting she's taken the bread knife with her!"

Maurice stroked his beard, trying hard not to smile. Lisl said briskly, "Mrs Gordino is more than welcome to stay here with Mrs Temple whilst you're away. They seem to get on quite well together."

Did they really? Gerry pondered briefly. She'd never been aware of a blossoming relationship between the two women, but then, why should she? After all, she had not even known about Liam McEvoy's common-law wife, Zoe Smith.

She said, "Well, if you really want me, I can think of nothing nicer than spending a month with you and Maurice, and all that hot water!"

Maurice burst out laughing. "In which case, when we know the date of your arrival, the time and so forth, I'll be there to meet you, to help with your luggage. You'll need to park your car on the clifftop and walk from there to Black Gull House. The main street of Robin Hood's Bay is far too steep and narrow to admit traffic, thanks be to God. And just remember to pack your oldest clothes. Relaxation is the name of the game in Robin Hood's Bay."

Old clothes? Relaxation? She could manage the former with no trouble whatsover, Gerry thought, drawing in a deep breath of relief. It was dressing up that bothered her. Dressing down was a doddle . . .

Walking her home, her hand tucked into the crook of his elbow, Maurice said quietly, "Look, Gerry, about this Liam McEvoy affair, try not to worry about it unduly. Leave it to the police to sort out. They will, you know, in the long run."

"I guess you're right," Gerry conceded, "but I can't help feeling responsible."

"Responsible? In what way?"

"If I'd known something was bothering him, I might have prevented it from happening."

"Assuming that he did commit suicide?"

"I don't honestly know what to think any more. I feel so guilty that I didn't even know about his common-law wife."

"You mustn't blame yourself," Maurice said gently. "Try looking at it from a different angle – Liam's angle."

"I'm not sure what you mean."

"Simply this, m'dear. The threads of Liam's life had been woven long before you came on the scene. His fondness for alchohol, for instance. The likelihood is that he was also up to his ears in debt. What I'm saying is, no way can you be held responsible for the death of a man, however tragic, whose destiny was decided by circumstances beyond your control, long before he came to work for you."

"Thanks, Maurice. But what if Liam *was* murdered? What if he had no intention of committing suicide? What you've just said wouldn't make sense, would it?"

"Not on the face of it, certainly," Maurice said thoughtfully, "all the more reason why you should leave the matter for the police to deal with. After all, Gerry love, we – you and I – are writers, not detectives, and experience has taught me that the Police Force takes a dim view of crime writers on the whole."

They were standing on the top step of Gerry's house, she searching frantically in her shoulder-bag for her front door key.

When it was found at last in the pocket of her trouser-suit jacket, "Allow me," Maurice said gallantly, fitting it into the lock and opening the door for her. "Now, take my advice, go straight to bed and get a good night's sleep. Promise?"

"I'll try. Well, goodnight, Maurice, and thanks. Thanks for everything."

Bending down, he brushed her cheek with his lips. "See you in October?" he said lightheartedly on his way to the gate. And then he was gone, melting into the shadows of a warm, dusky August night.

Anna's light was on when Gerry went upstairs, and there were sounds of movement. She called out, "Anna, are you all right? What are you doing in there?"

The key turned, the door opened a crack. Anna's eyes resembled those of a bush-baby, wide and staring in her pale, frightened face.

"I pack. I go 'ome," she said breathlessly. "My mind she ees made up!"

"What on earth are you on about? Look, Anna, it's late. I'm tired, so are you. I don't understand what's got into you. Now go to bed and get some sleep. We'll talk about this in the morning!"

"I tell you I am notta 'ere in ze morning! I know what I see! I am notta liking what I see!"

"*What* did you see, for heaven's sake! Come on, Anna,

the truth now! Surely I have the right to know what all this is about?"

Anna said dramatically, "Thursday evening, I zee, witha my own two eyes, ze paddly-lock in place on ze door of ze shed!"

"*What*? Good grief! Then why didn't you tell the police?" Gerry stared at her housekeeper bemusedly, trying to make sense of this vital piece of information.

"I tell zem nozzing," Anna muttered hoarsely. "Bad theengs 'appen 'ere! I go 'ome where I am safe!"

So saying, she stepped back into the room and relocked the door.

Later, tossing and turning, unable to sleep, Gerry reflected that if what Anna said was true, if indeed the door of the garden shed had been padlocked on the Thursday, then bang went the theory that Liam had committed suicide there on the Wednesday.

On the other hand, he must have failed to return home on the Wednesday night. Why else would his common-law wife have rung the police station on the Thursday morning to report him as a missing person?

So where had he been, what had happened to him between Wednesday night and Friday morning – this morning – when she had, almost literally, stumbled across his corpse in a broken down hut at the bottom of her garden?

Darned if she knew for certain. Of one thing she was now entirely certain, that Liam McEvoy had not committed suicide – he'd been murdered!

Three

G erry had slept badly, and woke up with a headache combined with the feeling of something hanging over her, the same way she had woken, as a schoolgirl, on maths mornings.

The time was eight o'clock, late for her. No wonder she had a thick head. Getting up, she opened the fire-escape door and stood on the landing in her pyjamas to get a breath of air. Another hot morning, sticky and enervating.

From where she was standing, she could see the Berengers' terrace across the barrier of fencing, flowering shrubs, trees and privet which divided the two properties. Not that she noticed the terrace particularly – she had too many other things on her mind at the time – until, about to turn away, she heard someone calling her name. Then, looking down, she saw, dwarfed by distance, Lisl waving up to her, smiling, and remembered that the Berengers were going on holiday today. By the look of it, they were making an early start.

Feeling awkward and lumpish in her pyjamas, Gerry returned Lisl's greeting, smiled, waved back to her, and blew her a kiss.

At that moment, the Berengers' housekeeper, Mrs Temple, appeared on the terrace and stared up at her at which point Gerry returned indoors to dress before hurrying down to the kitchen to confront Anna Gordino, wanting to get to the truth of the matter regarding the padlock she claimed to have seen in place on the door of the garden shed the day before yesterday.

Mrs Gordino had a vivid imagination to say the least, and Gerry had learned to swallow her stories with a sizeable pinch of salt. To hear her talk, she had been a cabaret artiste, an artist's model, an actress and a ballet dancer, all in the heyday of her life.

Moreover, the man she had married, one Luigi Gordino, to whom she had glowingly referred as a restaurateur had been, in reality, the landlord of a run-down trattoria in Piedmont, overly fond of food, wine and other women; this Gerry had discovered when Anna, in less fanciful mood, had told the truth for a change.

Not that Gerry blamed the woman for spicing the truth with a few lies now and then to add lustre to life. Writers did it all the time, and got paid for it.

She would talk to Anna quietly and sensibly, Gerry decided on her way downstairs, expecting to find her house-keeper preparing breakfast. But the kitchen was empty. It was then Gerry realised, with a sinking feeling in the pit of her stomach, that she was alone in the house. The silence was absolute apart from her own breathing, and the soft, slopping sound of her espadrilles on the tiled floor as she crossed to the table to pick up the note Anna had left her.

She read: "I am gone, like I say. I know you think I lie. This is the truth I tell now. I am afraid to stay in this place. I return to Paris *a toute vitesse*. Forgive please. Anna".

Sick at heart at Anna's defection, Gerry wondered what had happened to frighten her so much. Unlikely now that she would ever find out. But she must do something to ease her mind.

It was then that she remembered Zoe Smith, Liam's common-law wife, who might well be able to provide vital information regarding his state of mind preceding his death.

Quickly making up her mind to pay the woman a visit as soon as possible, Gerry made up Liam's wage packet far in excess of the usual amount due to him, as a valid excuse for her visit.

Clambering into her red Mini, she gave the reporters and photographers gathered near her front gate what she hopefully imagined to be the V for Victory sign, a la Winston Churchill, the saviour of the nation during the last war, which she couldn't remember. Or was this the 'up yours' signal she was giving them? Oh, what the hell! She had more important things to worry about, right now, than a couple of upraised fingers revealing the back, not the front of her hand.

She had Liam's address, 10 Sesame Grove, firmly implanted in her mind. But could she find it? Could she heck as like! She'd been cruising the outskirts of Hampstead for what seemed an eternity, growing hotter by the minute until, idling the engine, she asked a passer-by the way.

The passer-by proved to be a cross-looking gentleman exercising his dog. When, winding down the window, she asked him the way to Sesame Grove, he said sourly, "You've just passed it," adding, "High time something was done about it, in my opinion, with all those squatters and drug-addicts bringing the neighbourhood into disrepute! And if you are one of those bloody do-gooders from the social services, you're wasting your time! What's needed there is a couple of bulldozers to clear the area entirely!"

"Well, thank you so much," Gerry said brightly, "but I'm a pest-control officer, not a social worker. And there's a lot of them about. Pests, that is! By the way, have you a 'poop-scoop' handy? In case you hadn't noticed, your dog has just left his visiting card on the pavement."

When the man had gone, looking startled and carrying a turd in a brown paper bag, Gerry locked the car and walked back to Sesame Grove.

Unfortunately, what the man said was true. The once gracious Victorian houses lining the street, now in varying stages of decay, bore the hallmarks of its drop-out population of unemployed youngsters who had never worked in their lives, and probably never would. A no-win situation which troubled Gerry deeply.

Liam, at least, had looked for work and found it, she thought, pushing open the gate of Number Ten and walking up a weed-embellished path to the front-door steps.

Pressing the bell-push marked McEvoy, awaiting a response to her summons, Gerry noticed that the ground floor bay window had been boarded up, and the steps leading down to the basement area were littered with empty beer cans, takeaway food cartons, and the detritus of last year's autumn leaves blown there from the pallid row of poplar trees lining the garden wall – or what remained of it.

The front door opened, a girl stood there. Gerry's heart went out to her. She smiled. "Are you Zoe Smith?"

"Yeah. Who wants to know?"

"My name is Frayling. Liam was my gardener. Can I come in?"

"No you bloody well can't! You can get lost, that's what you can do! All this is your fault! Liam an' me was doin' fine till he started workin' for you! So shove off an' leave me alone!"

She couldn't be more than seventeen, Gerry decided, a scrap of a girl with lank fair hair, as thin as a skinned rabbit, wearing faded jeans and a cotton T-shirt, eyes swollen with weeping.

Startled by Zoe's hostility, "All *my* fault?" Gerry said. "I did my best to help Liam, so in what way is it my fault?"

"As if you didn't know."

"I don't know, that's why I'm asking." Trying another tack, she said, "All I want is ten minutes of your time. To talk to you. Please, it's very important!"

"Oh all right, then. You'd best come upstairs." Zoe led the way to the top floor. "It ain't all that tidy, mind you. I ain't done much tidying up since . . ." Her voice trailed away.

Panting, Gerry followed her up to the flat, the sitting room of which looked as if a bomb had struck it. Zoe wasn't kidding when she said she hadn't done much tidying up. The sagging armchairs near the fireplace were strewn with newspapers and magazines, the low table in front of the hearth littered with the remains of a Chinese takeaway, stained coffee mugs and overflowing ashtrays.

Doors opening off from the main room revealed a similar state of confusion in the bedroom, kitchen and bathroom. The kitchen sink was piled high with unwashed pots, the bathroom floor was strewn with damp towels. The unmade bed, glimpsed through another open door, bore silent witness to the anguished hours Zoe had spent there alone, following the death of her lover.

And yet the flat was not dirty, merely untidy. The curtains at the dormer window had been recently washed and ironed, and the girl had placed a vase of pink dahlias on the sill.

"Well, now you're here, you'd best tell me what you've come for," Zoe said harshly, looping her hair behind her ears.

"For one thing, I came to give you this," Gerry said, handing Zoe the envelope containing Liam's wages. "I thought the bit extra might come in handy right now."

Opening the envelope, then throwing it aside, "I don't want your bloody charity," Zoe said fiercely. "Like I said, everything was fine till he started working for you. Then he started acting strange, bragging to his pals down at the pub that we'd soon be out of this dump! Standing them drinks he couldn't afford. Making things worse, not better!"

Sweeping aside a clutter of newspapers, the girl sank down in a chair and buried her face in her hands. Between sobs, she gasped, "He said that something big had happened to him, an' I thought you were it! He had quite a way with woman, had Liam. Or perhaps I don't have to tell you that?"

"Ye gods! So that's it? Well, thanks for the compliment, I don't think! I may be well built, but I'm not stupid! I'm a working woman, for Pete's sake, not a bloody femme-fatale! If you've got it into your head that Liam and I were having it away in a garden shed three times a week, you need your brain testing! Liam was no more interested in me than the Man in the Moon, nor I in him, at least not in the way you think! We were friends, that's all! I liked him enormously, and I'm sorry he's dead!"

Smarting at this latest blow to her pride, heading for the door, "I'd best be leaving now," Gerry muttered. "I'll see myself out!"

Rising quickly from her chair, "No, don't go," Zoe cried out unexpectedly. "I'm sorry if I got things wrong about you and Liam. The truth is, I'm in such a muddle right now I don't know what to think any more! You said you wanted to talk to me. What is it you want to know? Oh, please don't be mad with me! The police made me identify Liam's body, you see, an' I couldn't bear it – seeing him dead, I mean! I really couldn't!"

Crossing swiftly to the girl's side, placing a comforting arm about her shoulders, "I'm not in the least bit mad with you," Gerry said compassionately, "I'm your friend, believe me. All I want is to get to the bottom of this, this mess, the reason why Liam did what he did. You said he'd been acting strangely of late. But *why*? Think, Zoe, think! This really is very important!"

"I honestly don't know," Zoe confessed weepily. "He never confided in me, you see? He just told me to trust him, and I *did*! I *had* to! He was all I had, all I wanted. Now he's gone, an' I don't know which way to turn!"

"Try not to cry any more," Gerry said kindly. "Tell me

about the night he went missing. Have you any idea where he went to, that evening?"

"Just down to the pub," Zoe frowned, "to have a drink with his mates. That weren't nothing unusual. He said he'd be home about eleven when the pub closed, an' I'd best have summat nice ready for his supper. So I went to the Chinese takeaway for his favourites – sesame rolls, pork in sweet an' sour sauce, them crispy noodles he liked. Oh, what the hell does it matter now? He never came home to eat any of it.

"I was that worried when he hadn't showed up at midnight, I went round the pub to look for him, but it was closed. Then I went round the houses askin' if anyone had seen him. They looked at me as if I was soft in the head, so I came home an' waited. I didn't know what to think. When he hadn't come back all night, I rang the police station first thing next mornin'."

"Forgive me for asking," Gerry insisted gently, "but was Liam involved in drug-dealing?"

"No, he wasn't," Zoe said heatedly. "Liam wouldn't touch drugs. It was drink he liked, the pub atmosphere, what he called softening the rough edges of life, an' the more he drank the better he talked. He was a good talker was Liam, bein' Irish."

Staring into the past, she continued with feeling, "He could've been a writer if he'd put his thoughts on paper instead of spouting them aloud to anyone who'd listen. An' they *did* listen. Everyone liked Liam. That's why I can't understand why he did what he did. He wasn't depressed or anything, so why top himself?"

"Try to keep calm, love. Tell me about Mr Constantine. How did Liam come to work for him?"

"Oh, *that*. He delivered some wood one day an' they got talking. I'd just got to know Liam about that time. He said the old man wasn't exactly barmy, but gettin'

31

on that way. What Liam called eccentric, an' no wonder, livin' all alone in that mucky old house with no-one to take care of him.

"He said old Constantine took quite a shine to him, invited him in for a drink. That's when Liam offered to tidy the place up a bit. There was lots of empty bottles an' old newspapers lyin' about, so Liam took 'em to the recycling bins to get rid of 'em. That's how it all started. Then the old man asked him if he'd tidy the garden, an' Liam said yes. Not that he knew a damn thing about gardenin', but I 'spect you found out about that when he asked for his old job back?"

"The thought did occur," Gerry said wryly. "But that's not important. Tell me more about Mr Constantine."

"There ain't much more to tell, except that Liam really liked him; liked talkin' to him an' listenin' to the tales he had to tell about – you know – diggin' things up. Archie summat or other."

"Archaeology," Gerry supplied.

"Yeah, that's it! He said the old man had some real interestin' bits an' pieces lyin' around. Not that they sounded very interestin' to me. Just a load of junk, like that damn statue on the sideboard over yonder, the old man gave him. Chuffed to bits with it, Liam was. We had a bust-up about it, if you must know. I said an ugly thing like that belonged in the dustbin, an' that's where it's goin' next time I empty the rubbish!"

Glancing fearfully at the sideboard, she continued, "I told Liam it would bring us bad luck, but he wouldn't listen. He just laughed an' called me superstitious. But I was right all along. It *did* bring us bad luck!"

Gerry felt inclined to agree with her. The object in question was certainly ugly, almost repulsive; that of a naked female, full-breasted and bellied, crowned with an enormous head with the carved features of a jackal. An artefact probably unearthed by Mr Constantine in the heyday of his archaeological career, she surmised, which would, in her estimation, have best been left undiscovered.

Drawing in a deep breath, deeply shaken by the the sight of the statue, "What happened to Mr Constantine?" Gerry asked, discreetly wiping the perspiration from her forehead with the back of her hand, beginning to wish she had never come here in the first place.

"Oh, *that*?" Zoe said unconcernedly, "He had a stroke or some such, and went into a nursing home. Liam went to visit him a coupla times. So what?"

Zoe was growing impatient with the questioning, Gerry realised. Adroitly changing the subject, she said, "What will you do now? Just a thought, but you are welcome to stay with me for a while, if you want to."

Zoe said quickly, "Thanks, but Liam's twin brother Mick will be here soon to take care of things – the funeral arrangements an' so on."

"You will let me know if you need help?"

"Like I said, I'll be fine when Mick gets here. He'll know what to do." Zoe turned away to look out of the window.

"I'll see myself out," Gerry said. She might as well have spoken to the wind. Zoe wasn't listening.

On her way to the car, Gerry thought about the artefact Mr Constantine had given Liam. Could it possibly be valuable? If so, had this any bearing on Liam's optimism before his death?

Darned if she knew, and in any case she had pressing problems of her own to cope with right now. Shopping and cooking, for instance, now that Anna had disappeared into the wild blue yonder; a book to finish to a deadline; the media camped on her doorstep.

Possibly there was no such thing as bad publicity, but Bill Bentine wouldn't be best pleased with his star performer if photographs of her appeared on the front pages of tomorrow's newspapers giving the up yours, not the Winston Churchill V-sign.

Parking the Mini in the forecourt of a local supermarket, Gerry stocked a trolley with food enough to feed an army – all the fattening things she knew were bad for her – frozen pizzas, oven chips, sausages, steak and kidney pies, loaves of bread, lots of butter, packets of soup-mix, tins of salmon, ice-cream, a Black Forest gateau. Good for her soul if not her figure.

The phone was ringing when she reached home. Thankfully, the media had departed from her front garden.

Dumping her shopping bags, picking up the receiver, "Yes?" she said breathlessly. Then, less than enthusiastically, "Oh, it's you, Inspector Clooney! *Now* what?"

"I've been trying to reach you all morning."

"I've been out."

"I'm ringing about your housekeeper, Mrs Gordino."

"Anna? She isn't here! She left me a note saying she was going to Paris."

"A note?"

"Yes. I found it propped up near the cafétière when I came down this morning to find her missing."

"You still have that note, I take it?"

"Well, yes. Why? Is it important?"

"I shall want to see that note, Miss Frayling."

"What on earth for?" Gerry wrinkled her forehead. "What's all this about, Inspector?"

Clooney paused momentarily, then said matter-of-factly, "The body of a woman, believed to be that of Mrs Gordino, was discovered at eight o'clock this morning in a women's lavatory at Hampstead Tube Station."

"*What?*" Trembling violently, Gerry sank down on the bottom step of the staircase. "But that's not possible!"

Clooney continued imperturbably, "We shall of course

34

need positive identification before we can proceed further. I take it that you will be prepared to help in this respect? A police car will pick you up in a quarter of an hour."

"You mean you want me to . . . ?" For the second time that morning, Gerry might as well have spoken to the wind. Clooney had hung up.

Shocked to the core, Clooney had got it all wrong, Gerry thought wildly. Anna could not possibly be dead! Not *Anna*! It must be some other woman's body that had been discovered, some unfortunate woman who had suffered a massive stroke or had met with an accident, whom they – whoever 'they' were – had mistaken for Anna Gordino! It was all a dreadful mistake. It *must* be!

But it wasn't. The body she was later called upon to identify was that of Anna Gordino. And she hadn't suffered a stroke or met with an accident. She'd been strangled.

Four

"S it down, Miss Frayling."
Clooney noted that the woman appeared to be deeply shaken by her housekeeper's death, and the ordeal of identifying the body. But there were questions to be asked, and it was his duty to ask them.

The young WPC seated next to Clooney in the interview room looked at Gerry sympathetically across the desk, hoping the crusty old devil would go easy on her. Some fat chance of that, she thought, knowing him to be a man devoid of compassion so far as the opposite sex, in particular, was concerned. Rumour had it that his wife had left him yet again, for good and all this time, and no wonder. Being married to Clooney, she imagined, would be akin to being married to a brass-rubbing.

Clooney said, "The note you mentioned earlier, Miss Frayling. Have you brought it with you? If so, I want to see it."

"Yes, it's here somewhere." Unhitching her shoulder-bag, Gerry searched feverishly through the contents, to no avail. Finally, in desperation, she tipped the contents of the bag on to the desk.

There were notebooks and biros, bank books, cheque books, a bunch of keys, a bulging wallet, a bulky purse, a bar of Cadbury's nut milk chocolate, a bundle of bank statements, a pack of Menthol cigarettes, a throwaway lighter, and a tube of Smarties.

36

At last the note in question was discovered in the pages of a bank book, which she handed across the desk to her inquisitor.

When he had read the note, steepling his fingers, Clooney said coldly, "So you knew beforehand that Mrs Gordino intended leaving your employ and her reasons for doing so? This note states clearly that she feared for her safety beneath your roof because of a lie she had told you. What was the nature of that lie? I put it to you now, Miss Frayling, that you had quarrelled violently with your housekeeper on the night preceding her death."

"No, it wasn't like that at all," Gerry protested vehemently. "I had spent the evening with friends. When I came home around midnight, I found Anna in her room, packing her things, acting strangely. When I asked her what was wrong, she told me she had noticed the door of the garden shed was padlocked on the Thursday, which meant that Liam McEvoy's body could not possibly have been there on the Wednesday."

"I see," Clooney said scathingly, "and you have deliberately witheld this vital information from the police until now? May I ask why? Your clear duty lay in informing me right away of this important development."

"What? At one o'clock in the morning?" Gerry thrust back at him. "Talk sense, Inspector! In any case, I wasn't sure that Anna was telling the truth; that was the reason why I told her to go to bed and that we'd talk about it in the morning."

"Tell me, Miss Frayling, was Mrs Gordino in the habit of telling lies?" Clooney insisted.

"Not lies as such," Gerry said dejectedly, not wanting to put poor Anna in the wrong. "She just handled the truth carelessly, at times, to shore up her self-respect. Lots of women do, you know, and Anna was no exception. I'd simply learned to take everything she said with a pinch of salt.

"I knew, for instance, that her husband, Luigi Gordino, had not been the famous restaurateur of her imagination, but the owner of a run-down trattoria in Piedmont, with an overt interest in other women. The reason why she left him, I imagine."

"And you believed that story?" Clooney insisted.

"Yes, because I knew she was telling the truth that time, she was so upset!"

"Why, then, did you assume she was lying when she told you about the door of the garden shed she claimed to have seen locked last Thursday?" Clooney persisted relentlessly.

"I *didn't*! Not really! I just wanted to make absolutely sure, to talk to her calmly in the light of day. But I left it too late! Now she's dead. But if you think I had anything to do with her death, you're barking up the wrong tree! I liked Anna enormously. What more can I say? She was a great character. She had – style. Besides which, she was an excellent cook.

"Frankly, Inspector, I felt shattered when I found that note, when I realised she had left me. It came as a shock. I mean, sleeping on the top floor, at the back of the house, I hadn't even heard the taxi . . ."

"Taxi? What taxi?" Clooney interrupted.

"How should I know? But there must have been one. No way could Anna have lumped two heavy cases, a couple of hat-boxes and several carrier bags to the station under her own steam."

"So despite your claim not to have seen or heard a taxi, you knew precisely the amount of luggage Mrs Gordino had with her? How could you have known, unless you had witnessed her departure?"

"I'd have thought that was obvious. It stands to reason that, leaving home, Anna would have taken with her the same amount of luggage she'd brought with her. Maybe more?"

Oh, great, the WPC thought ecstatically, Geraldine was giving old Clooney a run for this money, and he didn't like it one bit. Now she was pointing out that the taxi firm involved must have a record of the journey.

But Clooney wasn't through with her yet. Now he had begun pumping her about her exact movements subsequent to Anna's defection.

"When you discovered the note, and realised that your housekeeper had quit the premises, what then?" he demanded. "Did you follow her to the station?"

"No, of course not. I just wandered about the house for a while, wondering what to do next. Then I decided to call on Liam McEvoy's girlfriend, Zoe Smith, to give her his wages."

"At what time, precisely?"

"I'm not quite sure. Around ten o'clock, I guess."

"Did anyone see you leave the house?"

"Well yes, as a matter of fact. About half the newspaper reporters and photographers in the London area, seeing they were camped on my doorstep at the time."

"I see. And then you called on McEvoy's – partner?"

"Yes. I've just said so, haven't I?"

"How long did you stay with her?"

"A quarter of an hour or so. Twenty minutes at the most," Gerry said wearily, sick at heart over the death of Anna Gordino, the trauma of identifying her housekeeper's body, that impersonal figure lying stiff and cold in the mortuary annexe – as if she had never lived, breathed, or even existed. As if she had already been dead for all eternity. Gerry shivered.

"Then what did you do?" Clooney persisted.

The WPC spoke up, risking a reprimand. "Sir," she said abruptly, "may I suggest a short break for refreshment, on Miss Frayling's behalf? A cup of tea or coffee, perhaps?"

Gerry smiled gratefully at the girl. "Thanks," she said,

"but I'd rather get this interview over and done with as soon as possible. I'm sure Inspector Clooney would, too. Now, where were we? Oh yes, after my visit to Miss Smith, I went shopping, in Hampstead High Street, for groceries, paying by Switch card, so there's bound to be a record of the transaction."

Clooney then switched abruptly to Anna Gordino's husband. Had she, Gerry, Luigi Gordino's address? And had they divorced or simply separated?

Gerry had no idea, and said so. All she knew, for certain, was that the marriage was over and done with, so far as Anna was concerned. She had never wanted to set eyes on the man ever again.

"Had Mrs Gordino friends and relations in Paris?" Clooney pursued relentlessly.

"Almost certainly, I imagine, since she had lived there all her life until she married Luigi," Gerry acknowledged heavily, sick and tired of the questioning. "But why ask me? Or is this some kind of guessing game we're into now? You're the detective, for God's sake, so it's up to you to find out about Anna's past life, isn't it?"

Oh, Hallelujah, the WPC thought. Geraldine had got the DI reeling against the ropes now, and serve him damn well right, the sour, pedantic old sod. More importantly, he knew it!

Glancing at his watch, Clooney said stiffly, "Very well, Miss Frayling, you are free to leave now. Interview terminated at sixteen thirty hours precisely."

The tape-recorder switched off, he added coldly, "If you would care to wait a while in Reception, Miss Frayling, I'll order a police car to take you home."

"Don't bother, Inspector! I'll walk!" Gerry said scathingly.

At home, she put away the groceries as a matter of

40

expedience, before the frozen food defrosted itself completely. That done, she went upstairs, stripped off, then
showered and washed her hair – a kind of ritual cleansing
– as if soap and water would somehow rid her of the misery
of the past few hours, the shocked horror of Anna's death,
the merciless questioning she'd undergone by the loathsome
Inspector Clooney.

What ailed the man, for God's sake? Did he really
suspect her of murdering poor Anna? It certainly looked
that way. No wonder she felt sullied, unclean, as a result of
the interview. Being made to feel like a criminal, knowing
he hadn't believed a word she'd said, having got it into
his thick head that she had quarrelled violently with Anna,
threatened her in some way, then followed her to the station,
lured her into a women's lavatory, and there had strangled
her to death.

Worst of all, how could she possibly prove her inno-
cence?

Clad in her writing gear, seated at her typewriter, elbows
on the desk, hair wet, staring out of her attic room
window, albeit unseeingly, Gerry wrestled mentally with
the problems confronting her, attempting to bring logic
to bear on the present situation, wanting to get the facts
straight in her mind.

Fact number one: Anna had stated categorically that she
had seen the padlock in place on the garden shed on the
Thursday. Thereafter, she had taken fright to the extent of
leaving the house in the early hours of this – Saturday
– morning, presumably to catch a tube train to Waterloo
where she would purchase a ticket to Paris. It had to be
Waterloo. No other venue was possible.

Fact number two: Anna must have told someone else,
apart from herself, that she intended to leave England this
morning. But who?

At that moment, Gerry's powers of deduction deserted her completely. Visions arose of a police cell, a hard bunk and a thin blanket. A full-scale murder trial at the Old Bailey, being sentenced to life imprisonment for a crime she had not committed, simply because she had no alibi for the crucial hour of eight o'clock this morning when Anna had met her . . . Waterloo.

It was then she remembered, with a heaven-sent feeling of relief, standing on the fire-escape landing, in her pyjamas, at a few minutes past eight: turning to wave goodbye to Lisl Berenger on the terrace of the house next door. Moreover, Mrs Temple, the Berengers' housekeeper, had witnessed that brief leave-taking. Oh, thanks be to God!

Clattering quickly downstairs to the hall telephone, Gerry hurriedly prodded the number of the local Police Station. "I want to speak to Inspector Clooney at once," she said buoyantly. "It's very important!"

She might have known that the pedantic old sod wouldn't do hand-springs at her ecstatic phonecall. All he said was, "The necessary enquiries will be pursued as soon as possible. I shall, of course, require Mrs Berenger's present address."

When darkness came, alone in the house, missing Anna terribly, wondering how she would possibly manage to cope without her, Gerry went up to her attic room, having locked securely every door and window beforehand, with one thought in mind. If there was a killer out there in the darkness, chances were she'd be the next victim. Even locked doors and windows would prove no deterrent to a madman who had already killed twice. First Liam McEvoy, then Anna Gordino.

At midnight, with a frisson of fear, she heard footsteps on the fire-escape.

Bearing in mind her supersleuth, Virginia Vale, she got up from her bed, switching on the outside light. Right, Gerry thought, she'd rush the bugger! Send him backward down the fire-escape heard over heels.

Flinging open the door, she came face to face with a young police constable, wide-eyed with fright, who said placatingly, "Please, Miss, I was told to keep an eye on the premises, to make sure you was all right, by order of Detective Inspector Clooney."

He added nervously, "My mate's in the garden, having a look-see, if you don't believe me."

"I do believe you," Gerry said fervently. "Do please come in! Ask your colleague to come in too. Have a cup of coffee, a sandwich, a glass of orange juice, a slug of whisky – a roast beef dinner!"

"Well, thanks, Miss, but no thanks, if you don't mind. We're on duty, you see. Another time, perhaps?"

"Any time. Any time at all," Gerry assured him warmly. She added, "You did say, didn't you, that Detective Inpector Clooney had asked you to keep an eye on me? Well, wonders will never cease! I thought he had me earmarked as the chief suspect. Apparently I was wrong!"

"I don't know owt about that, Miss," the constable said, backing down the fire-escape, thanking his lucky stars that he hadn't landed arse over tip on the patio below. "Just as long as you are OK."

"Yes, I am, for the time being. But I'd be ever so grateful if you would continue to keep an eye on me. The truth is, I'm scared stiff!"

She wasn't the only one, the constable thought, descending the iron staircase, blanching at the memory of a very large lady towering above him on the fire-escape landing; that shock of surprise when their eyes met, as if he were the villain of the piece, she some kind of Judo-freak about to seize him by the short and curlies.

Meeting up with his mate in the garden, "Let's get out of here," he muttered, "the sooner the better."

It was then that the killer, watching and waiting, realised that the time for action concerning Geraldine Frayling must wait a little while longer. Too dangerous, at the moment, with the police on the prowl, and the fire-escape light on, to attempt a third murder.

Now for the garden shed. Thank God for the thickly crowded trees, the deep shadows beneath the overhanging branches.

Five

August had edged into September, but the weather was still unbearably humid, the coroner's courtroom as stuffy as a haybox.

Bill Bentine, lean, lithe and dishy, had elected to act as Gerry's escort, fearing that, left to her own devices, she might well give the Press another unfortunate V-sign.

One could never tell with his most lucrative client, and what she might say on the witness stand caused beads of perspiration to stand out on his forehead. "Don't say more than you have to," he advised her, entering the courtroom. "Save your ingenuity for the last chapter of *The Blasted Heath*. How's it coming along, by the way?"

"Put it like this, I haven't quite decided whodunnit yet, but not to worry, I'll think of something. You know me!"

"Yeah, that's just it! The reason *why* I worry!"

"Look, Bill, I'll have to answer the coroner's questions, you know that as well as I do."

"Yes, but don't add any fancy embroidery. Just answer the man's questions and leave it at that. Remember this enquiry is to establish the cause of Liam's death based on the known facts; whether or not he committed suicide . . ."

"But I know he didn't! *I* know he was murdered!"

"There you go again," Bill said impatiently. "That's for the coroner, not you, to decide!" He added bemusedly, "*Now* what's the matter? What is it? What's wrong?"

"That man over there," she said shakily, "the one with

45

Zoe Smith. I thought for one awful moment that Liam . . . Zoe told me that Liam and his brother were twins. She didn't tell me they were identical twins!"

She really had thought, for one ghastly moment, that she was seeing Liam himself, miraculously restored to life. The resemblance was uncanny – the same colour hair and eyes, the same build, the same devil-may-care expression on the face of – not Liam – but Michael McEvoy.

Having heard the available evidence, the coroner reached the conclusion that the death of Liam McEvoy warranted further investigation. Despite forensic evidence that the deceased had died from a lethal combination of alcohol and painkilling tablets, there were certain flaws in the original belief that he had committed suicide.

According to the testimony of Miss Zoe Smith, McEvoy's common-law wife, the deceased had not been depressed prior to his death. Indeed, he had seemed more than usually optimistic about the future. Also, according to the testimony of his employer, Miss Geraldine Frayling, who had discovered the body in her garden shed, the lid of the half empty bottle of painkilling tablets had been in place. On the other hand, the whisky bottle near the body had been uncapped.

No suicide note had been found; there were no finger-prints on either the whisky or the tablet bottles in question. There was, however, forensic evidence to suggest that the lethal dose of alcohol and painkilling tablets had been forcibly administered to the deceased prior to his death.

According to the expert testimony of the police patholo-gist, Mr Wilfrid Benfield, cuts and bruises in the wrist areas of the deceased suggested that he had been for-cibly detained, against his will, and made to swallow the lethal cocktail of drugs which had caused his death. In this event, he, the coroner, was duty bound to adjourn the inquest to allow the police time to pursue further enquiries.

The hearing over, grabbing Gerry's elbow, Bill hustled her into the fresh air of the carpark. "Well, what can I possibly say now, except I'm sorry?" he asked. "But did you really have to go into the smell inside the shed, and the bluebottles?"

"I thought you'd be pleased with my performance," Gerry said mildly. "Honestly, there's no suiting some people." She added, ascerbically, "Hey, why all the rush? What *is* this? The hundred metre dash in the next Olympics?"

"In case you hadn't noticed, here comes the Press gang," Bill said resignedly. "I might have known they'd be here! Just promise me you'll keep your hands in your pockets!"

Gerry grinned wickedly. "Why? Are you afraid I'll give 'em the Hitler salute? As if I *would!*"

He wouldn't put it past her, Bill thought as they headed towards his car, a roomy Golf hatchback. On their way to the eyrie, Gerry asked if he'd care to come in for a drink, not really thinking he would – a busy agent with an office to run.

To her surprise, he accepted the invitation. "Yes, why not?" he said, "I've always wanted to see how the other half lives."

"I bet you don't do too badly yourself," she quipped on the way up the garden path.

"Hmmm, interesting," he mused, glancing up at the Victorian façade, "very 'Gaslight'!"

Unlocking the door, she teased, "Wait till you see inside. I daresay you'll find it a bit overpowering compared with that bachelor pad of yours you're always on about. I just figured that modern furniture wouldn't be right here, though I had the kitchen stripped and modernised. No way could I have lived with a stone sink and wooden draining boards."

"Blimey!" Bill exclaimed, stepping into the hall, "That's some staircase you have there. Turkey carpet and brass stair-rods, no less. Very impressive! How many rooms have you? Or have you lost count?"

"There were twelve at the last recce," Gerry told him, leading the way to the drawing room.

"Quite a lot of space for just one person," he said teasingly. "Have you thought of taking in lodgers? Oh, I'm sorry, that was in poor taste. Forgive me?"

"If you mean am I scared of being alone in the house now Anna's gone, well yes, I suppose I am a bit nervous," Gerry confessed, crossing to the sideboard to pour him a drink from her latest acquisition, a three-decanter tantalus handsomely mounted in mahogany with the requisite brass facings, lock and key. "Silly of me, I know, but I have the feeling that someone out there is watching me. And I don't mean the police."

She shivered slightly despite the warmth of the day. "Well, you know me and my imagination? Why would anyone want me out of the way? Come to think of it, why would anyone have wanted Anna out of the way, unless . . ." She stopped speaking abruptly.

"Unless – *what*?" Bill asked urgently.

"Unless she had seen something apart from that padlock. Some*one*, perhaps? A person she recognised? Oh, I don't know what to think any more!" She smiled lopsidedly. "What will you have to drink, by the way?"

"Thanks, but I'll skip the drink for the time being," Bill said. "Look, Gerry love, this is important! If what you say is true – and assuming that it *is* true, who, apart from yourself, could possibly have known that Anna intended leaving home the next day? It stands to reason that someone else must have done! Her killer, apparently!"

"I know, Bill! I've been over it a hundred times in my mind, but it still doesn't make sense! Hardly likely, is it, that she phoned the killer beforehand, virtually signing her own death warrant?"

"True enough," Bill said thoughtfully, "but she may well have phoned someone else when you were out of the house, having supper with the Berengers . . ."

"I wish I'd stayed home now," Gerry interrupted hoarsely. "I knew Anna was upset that night. I thought she was just being hysterical over the death of Liam McEvoy when she locked herself in her room to begin packing, otherwise I wouldn't have left her alone in the house. I'd have got to the bottom of things then and there!"

"I know, but you mustn't blame yourself. How were you to know? But what if, when you had gone to the Berengers, Anna telephoned someone: told that someone she was frightened, and why?"

"Well, yes, that's possible, I suppose," Gerry conceded, "except that Anna hadn't any close friends in the neighbourhood that I know of. Frankly, Anna was something of a loner, besides which, the language-barrier was a bit of a problem. She didn't speak English particularly well. I had difficulty communicating with her myself, more often than not."

"Even so, my bet is that Anna telephoned someone that night," Bill persisted. "Of course! Got it!" he said, with the air of a latter day St Paul on the road to Damascus, "British Telecom will have the answer! They'll have, on record, the precise details of outgoing calls on your number: the number called, the time and the duration."

"Yes, of course," Gerry said breathlessly. "Why didn't I think of that? Thanks, Bill!"

Glancing at his watch, he said, "Well, I'd best be on my way. Sure you'll be all right on your own?"

"Of course I shall. Don't talk so daft. I have work to do, a book to finish to a deadline, remember?"

Walking down the path to his car, turning to wave

49

her goodbye, driving to his office in Red Lion Square, Bill thought that, despite her girth and larger-than-life personality, Gerry Mudd was not nearly as tough as she pretended to be. Like a hard-boiled sweet with a soft chewy centre. A bit of a humbug at rock bottom.

She had worked hard all afternoon. When twilight came, feeling suddenly lonely, vulnerable and hungry, Gerry went downstairs to cook herself a meal. She would have dearly liked to eat her supper on the patio, by lamplight, but that would be asking for trouble if the killer was lurking in the shadows, awaiting a heaven-sent opportunity to throttle her with his bare hands.

Nervously, she swished the curtains across the sliding plate-glass door leading to the patio, making certain they were securely locked before reconstituting a packet of her favourite cauliflower and broccoli soup, aware of the silence of the house, missing Anna terribly, wondering what would happen about her funeral, if Luigi would be sent for to make the necessary arrangements?

If only she knew what was happening. She'd gladly make the arrangements herself, give poor Anna the finest funeral possible. But where? Common sense told her that Anna would wish to be buried in her native country – la belle France – not laid to rest in foreign soil. Certainly not in Italy.

Suddenly the doorbell rang. The cauliflower and broccoli soup boiled over the rim of the pan, and there she was, looking a wreck in her bath-sheet and espadrilles, her hair scragged back from her face with a rubber band, not knowing which to do first, rescue the soup or answer the bell.

Oh, sod the soup, she thought, rushing through to the hall to demand the identity of the bell-ringer through the letter-box.

"It's me, Gerry, your so-far friendly agent, Bill Bentine, remember?"

"Bill!" Gerry opened the door. "What the hell are you doing here?"

He handed her a bottle of wine, then lumped indoors an overnight bag. "I decided you needed a watchdog," he said cheerfully. "Any old corner will do, a Bonio and a bowl of water!"

"Watchdog? Sure you don't mean – guardian angel?" Gerry had never been so pleased to see anyone in her life before.

"Whichever. I say, that's a fetching outfit you have on! Very a la posh!"

"I've been working! I wasn't expecting company!" she blurted, feeling utterly ridiculous in her déshabillé, "I'll just pop upstairs and put some clothes on!"

"Slip into something more uncomfortable, you mean?" Bill said teasingly.

"You know darn well what I mean! Go through to the kitchen, I'll be down in a minute. I was just starting to cook supper."

"Hmmm, yes, I caught wind of it when I came in," Bill laughed. "What are we having, char-grilled cauliflower?"

When Gerry came downstairs ten minutes later, wearing her dirndl skirt and sloppy sweater, Bill had ditched the soup, cleaned the top of the cooker, opened the wine, and slipped a couple of lamb chops under the grill.

"Hope you don't mind my making myself useful," he said, handing her a glass of Sauvignon. "There, get that down you whilst I make the salad. Or would you prefer oven chips?"

Watching him closely, "Oh, salad," she said, lying through her teeth. "I didn't realise you were so domesticated."

"I'm not really, but everyone has to eat, and salad's far easier to prepare than a three-course dinner when I arrive home tired out after a hard day at the salt-mine. How's the wine, by the way?"

"Fine. Just fine!"

"Okay, you win," he said lightly. "Where are the oven chips?"

"In the freezer." Gerry sighed happily, grateful for the presence of her guardian angel, at the same time wondering why Bill had never married. Perhaps he was gay, or asexual? One never really knew about men nowadays. One thing for certain, she felt entirely at ease in his company – a laid back, intelligent, considerate human being with a fine sense of humour. A friend worth having. And handsome, to boot. Too good-looking, perhaps, for a plain girl such as herself?

The chops, which he had grilled with a sprinkling of herbs, were tender and delicious. Her sense of ease sprang from the deep down certainty that no attractive man, in his right senses, would wish to make a pass at a vast female such as herself. Perhaps she should join Weight Watchers? Avoirdupois was a hard burden to bear at times such as this, she considered wistfully, tucking into a hefty portion of oven chips.

After supper, when the kitchen table had been cleared and the washing-up done, she and Bill went through to the drawing room to talk and relax a while before bedtime.

He said, from the depths of a Victorian armchair near the fireplace, "You're a surprising person, you know, Gerry."

"Oh? Why?" she asked, handing him a glass of whisky from the tantalus on the sideboard.

"Well, take this house for example. No offence, but I thought you'd have plumped for a modern bungalow, or a flat."

"No way," Gerry said in her forthright fashion. "After my upbringing in a council house in Clapham, I wanted something different, more romantic, a home with character, an old house with lots of space: a kind of stronghold."

"Or a – hideaway?" Bill suggested quietly.

"Well yes, if you like! And why not? I'm not exactly Virginia Vale, am I? A size ten, all lithe and lovely, with rich parents and a public school education?"

"That's where you're wrong," Bill reminded her. "You *are* Virginia Vale, her creator, therefore her alter ego. She could not possibly have been born without you! Do you understand what I'm saying, Gerry? Whatever the size difference between you and Virginia doesn't really matter a damn!"

"It does to me," Gerry confessed, close to tears. "Honestly, Bill, I *hate* the way I look! All this – blubber!"

"Then do something about it!"

"Right then, I will! No need to get shirty with me!"

"I'm not."

"Yes you are!"

"You're tired," Bill said. "Come to think of it, so am I. Shall I kip down on the sofa?"

"Certainly not! You'll sleep in a proper bed. I switched on the electric blanket before supper, so it should be well aired by now. And I'm sorry I snapped," she added contritely. "I really do appreciate your being here, you know?"

He laughed. "Yes? Well, what are friends for?" The thing I like about you, Gerry, is your honesty, your lack of pretence – rare attributes in this day and age, believe me, and I should know. Your mind would boggle if you knew how many writers, nowhere near as successful and talented as you are, think the world owes them a living. Well, it doesn't! For what it's worth, you are one of the few really nice women I've respected and admired in my life so far. Now, you'd best show me to my room before I fall asleep on my feet!"

"Well, this is it," she said, opening the door, and switching on the bedside lamp. "The furniture may be a bit old-fashioned, but not the mattress and bedding. I do hope you'll be comfortable." She added shyly, "You're my first ever houseguest, as a matter of fact. And the bathroom's just along the landing."

"Thanks, Gerry love. It's fine! Just great! Where's your room, by the way?"

"Oh, I sleep upstairs in my so-called studio." She added, "Just in case I feel the urge to get up and start writing in the middle of the night."

"I see. Well, night, Gerry. Sleep well, and God bless!"

Getting into bed, Gerry sighed deeply and lay thinking about Bill's appearance on her doorstep, the nice things he'd said to her, the way he had taken care of her. His handsome, lived-in face, eyes crinkling at the corners when he laughed.

Was it remotely possible that he did find her fanciable after all? No, of course not, she told herself severely. She should be so lucky. Wide awake, she heard comforting sounds from the floor below; running bathwater, the tune he was whistling, 'These Foolish Things', and she caught a whiff of pungent male bath soap.

When Bill had stopped whistling and the house fell silent, Gerry switched off her bedside light and drifted off to sleep to dream of a dark shape, a footstep beside her bed, a male presence in her room, leaning over to kiss her . . .

"Oh, Bill," she murmured drowsily, in the hinterland between sleep and wakefulness, dreams and reality. Then, suddenly, she was fighting for breath. Wide awake, she realised she was not being kissed but in the process of

54

being smothered to death with a pillow held over her face, that the man kneeling beside her on the bed was not Bill but the murderer of Liam McEvoy and Anna Gordino.

Never before had she been so thankful for her weight, the strength of her arms, legs and lungs. Kicking and threshing, she fought her attacker with every ounce of strength she possessed.

Scratching and clawing like a wild animal, lungs almost at bursting point from lack of air, gripping the man's wrists, she forced back the pillow, determined not to give in to him, her breath coming in short gasps until finally, making full use of her well developed right leg, she drove her kneecap, with full force, into his crotch.

Now her assailant was on the floor, grunting with pain at the contact of her knee with a vulnerable part of his anatomy, and she was yelling, at the top of her voice, "Bill! Where the hell are you?"

"Coming," he called back to her bemusedly. "Oh, where the hell's the bloody light switch?"

The fire-escape door was wide open when Bill appeared on the scene. The killer had disappeared into the darkness.

Shakily, Gerry switched on her bedside light. Breathing heavily, "He went that way," she gasped.

Lunging towards the fire-escape, Bill went after him, to no avail. The murderer had melted into the shadows.

"Some fine watchdog I turned out to be," Bill said despondently, returning to Gerry's room running his fingers through his thatch of fair hair. "No sign of him, I'm afraid. What happened exactly?"

"He tried to smother me," Gerry said weakly, "and he damn near succeeded. He would have done if I hadn't woken up in time to fight him off!"

"Oh, you poor kid! How awful for you," Bill murmured

sympathetically, sitting on the bed beside her, placing a comforting arm about her shoulders.

"Oh, stuff all that mush," Gerry said tartly. "If you want to make yourself useful, go downstairs and ring the police!"

She added ascerbically, "You might at least have brought a sodding torch with you!"

Turning on the threshold, feeling deeply ashamed of himself, "You are quite certain that your assailant was a man, then?" Bill asked.

"Well yes, pretty sure," Gerry threw back at him, "unless women have dangly bits between their legs, which I very much doubt! In other words, I kneed the bastard, and I'd do the same again, given the chance! In fact I can think of nothing I'd like better!"

Six

"**B**e sensible, Gerry," Bill said seriously, "no way can you stay here alone after what happened last night."

They were having breakfast in the kitchen. Bill, showered and shaved, had come down early to make coffee and toast before going to the office. "I'll come again tonight and the night after that, but I have to go to Wiltshire to see a client, at the weekend."

"Thanks, Bill, but I can't just pack up and leave with a book to finish to a deadline. I'm into the final chapter, but I haven't got it quite right yet. I really need to concentrate at the moment, and the only place I can concentrate is here."

"So what are you going to do?" Bill said tautly. "Sit at that dormer window of yours asking for a bullet through the brain?"

"It won't come to that," Gerry said matter-of-factly. "The tree surgeons are coming this morning to start work on the garden. Besides, I have the feeling the killer is a night-hawk who wouldn't risk taking a pot-shot at me in broad daylight."

"Fair enought," Bill conceded, "but when darkness falls, what then? Especially when I'm away next weekend?"

He added hopefully, "Why not ask your mother and her husband to stay with you?"

Gerry looked at him aghast. "Who? Marilyn and Poncy? You must be joking! They'd be as much use as a chocolate fireguard! Besides, no way would Ma come here to stay!

She'd as soon spend a weekend in the Victoria and Albert Museum!"

"Sorry! Just an idea!" Bill said quickly, swallowing his last mouthful of coffee.

Turning at the front door, "See you tonight around half-seven," he said lightly, "and I'll remember to bring a 'sodding' torch with me this time!"

When he had gone, Gerry went into the drawing room to draw back the curtains, remembering her mother's reaction to the house the first time she had crossed the threshold. Demeaning, to put it mildly. Picking and poking and finding fault with everything she saw, for instance . . .

"What the 'ell's this?" she'd demanded, inspecting the tantalus. "Locking up the booze now, are you? Afraid someone will nick it when you're not looking? Oh, I get it, that rummy housekeeper of yours, so called? Fond of a drop, is she?"

Anna had been alive at the time, so had Liam.

"Shut up, Ma, she'll hear you!"

"Serve her damn well right if she did! You might at least have hired a respectable English woman instead of a bloody foreigner! The trouble with you, my girl, money's gone to your head! You must have spent a fortune on all this – junk! I mean to say, what's the use of it?"

Gerry had realised then the impossibility of explaining to her mother her joy in possessing items of Victorian bric-a-brac she had merely dreamt of owning, as a schoolgirl, when, on her way to the library, she had stopped to steam up antique shop windows with her eager expellations of breath.

Soon, the tree surgeons would be here to begin hacking their way through her jungle of a garden.

Frankly, she wouldn't be sorry if they left it looking like

a World War One battlefield – all stumps, no trees, no overhanging branches, no shadows. She might even decide to have the whole damn area floodlit. One thing for certain, she would ask the workmen to demolish the garden shed as quickly as possible.

When they arrived, a team of five men and their overseer – a Mr Philip Antrobus – all lean, lithe and handsome, clad in overalls, helmets and Glo-bright tunics. They brought with them a variety of tools, a generator and a donkey-engine by the back entrance of her property, where Gerry discussed, with Mr Antrobus, whose lank fair hair dangled shoulder-length beneath his headgear, the possibility of clearing the area entirely of trees, at which suggestion he appeared deeply shocked.

"We are tree *surgeons*, not *vandals*," he said prissily, straightening his helmet, "and you have some very fine trees here, I might add, without which, I venture to say, your garden would lack variety and charm, not to mention a certain degree of privacy."

He was right, of course, Gerry decided. She said meekly, "OK, you win! Just one thing, I'd like you to demolish my garden shed as a matter of priority. It's pretty old and rotten anyway, so it shouldn't take much shifting."

"Demolition work is not, strictly speaking, within our remit," Antrobus said coldly.

"Oh, that's settled then," Gerry replied airily. "I expect your men would be pleased with a nice little bonus when the job is done? I'll lead the way, shall I?"

Her breeziness was akin to whistling in the dark. The very sight of the shed made her feel physically ill. She wanted rid of it and its unpleasant memories as quickly as possible. Then, "Oh lord," she said hoarsely, "I don't believe this!"

She had stopped walking to stare in horror at the shed; the broken padlock, the sagging door swinging loosely on its rusted hinges.

Antrobus looked startled, with some justification, as Clooney, accompanied by a uniformed police sergeant and a WPC, hove into view on a steep path leading from the back gate.

"Someone's been here!" Gerry cried dramatically. "Look, Inspector, the shed's been broken into!"

"Have you touched anything?" Clooney demanded.

"No, we've only just got here. I was showing Mr Antrobus the shed with a view to having it knocked down!"

"Let me look!" Clooney stepped forward, treading warily, like a cat on a hot tin roof, Gerry thought, following in his wake, leaning sideways to see round him, wanting to take a look for herself. It was, after all, *her* shed.

"Hmm, someone's certainly been here," Clooney remarked, "the place has been vandalised."

He wasn't kidding. Shelves had been toppled, bags of compost torn open, plant pots smashed to smithereens, seed trays upturned, holes dug in the floor, spiders' webs disarrayed, empty paint tins kicked into touch.

"He must have been a tall vandal," Gerry croaked, "to have got his head taffled up in those spiders' webs!"

The WPC stifled a giggle. Giving her a look that could kill, Clooney felt for his mobile phone. Gerry and the WPC exchanged glances, Antrobus tossed his head and angled his shoulders, the sergeant, standing rock solid, pretended not to notice. The Scene of Crime team would be here soon, he surmised, to take photographs and check for fingerprints, in accordance with Clooney's phonecall to headquarters.

"What shall I do now?" Antrobus enquired petulantly of his employer. "My men need seeing to!" The men in question were standing at a safe distance, awaiting instruction.

Assuming control of the situation, "I'll speak to you later," Clooney said dismissively to the tree surgeon. You, sergeant, wait here, the SOC team's on its way. You, WPC

Graham, will accompany myself and Miss Frayling to the house."

Light dawned. "So you've come about last night?" Gerry said ingenuously. "Of course, the attempt on my life? And there was I thinking you'd come about the shed!"

Clooney sighed deeply. His day had begun badly with a letter, from his wife's solicitor, stating that she was about to initiate divorce proceedings on the grounds of neglect and mental cruelty. Now *this*!

For the life of him, Clooney could not decide whether or not Geraldine Frayling was the innocent fool she appeared, or a very clever lady indeed who had either committed or engineered two murders so far, who had vandalised her own garden shed, and who dreamed up the attempt on her own life, last night, to cover her tracks. Even so, albeit reluctantly, he knew that he was barking up the wrong tree.

Faced with Clooney, Gerry experienced once more the feeling that her brain was rattling about in her head like a rotten walnut in its shell. His close questioning concerning the events of last night, what he referred to as her 'attempted murder, so called', proved the straw that broke the camel's back.

"You don't believe a word I'm saying, do you?" she demanded angrily, rising to her feet to confront him. "So what's *your* theory, Inspector? That I held a pillow over my own face? That I vandalised my own shed? If so, you must be a croissant short of a continental breakfast!

"You listen to me, Inspector Clooney. When the killer tried to murder me last night, I was not alone in the house. My agent, Bill Bentine, was sleeping on the floor below. When I called out to him for help, he came up to my room to find the fire-escape door wide open, the intruder well away by that time. Well, ask Bill if you don't believe me!"

"Calm down, Miss Frayling," Clooney said coolly. "No

need to be abusive. I came here to investigate the incident at your request, as I recall; to ascertain the facts of the matter. If you have a problem with that, it it not of my making, I assure you. It is my duty to ask questions, to establish the truth, to differentiate between facts and fiction."

"In other words, between truth and lies?" Gerry thrust back at him. "So why have I the feeling you take everything I say with a pinch of salt? Oh, I get it! It's because I write books for a living, isn't it? Well, okay, so I tell lies for money, but that doesn't mean I can't tell the difference between fact and fiction. And your remark regarding my 'attempted murder, so called', got right up my nose, in view of the fact that someone – a man – really did try to put paid to me last night, and you'd better damn well believe it!"

Ignoring her outburst, Clooney said levelly, consulting his notebook, "If you have quite finished, Miss Frayling, I feel it my duty to inform you that your alibi for the morning of the death of your housekeeper, Anna Gordino, has been confirmed by Mrs Lisl Berenger and her housekeeper, Mrs Anita Temple, who saw you on your fire-escape landing at eight o'clock on the morning in question.

"Also, Mrs Temple has admitted to receiving a phonecall from Anna Gordino on the night preceding her death, saying how reluctant she was to leave you in the lurch, at the same time stating her intention to leave for Paris early next morning – due to circumstances beyond her control.

"Unfortunately, the nature of those circumstances were not made clear to her at the time. Apparently, Mrs Gordino hung up the phone abruptly, leaving the conversation in mid-air."

"I see. Well, thanks for telling me, Inspector," Gerry said thoughtfully. "But Mrs Temple would know you'd find out about that phonecall sooner or later, wouldn't she? All you had to do was ring BT."

*   *   *

Bill Bentine arrived on Gerry's doorstep at precisely seven thirty that evening, a bottle of wine in one hand, a torch in the other. Sniffing the air, "So what's on the menu tonight?" he enquired.

"I haven't even thought. The fact is, I've had one hell of a day!"

"Tell me about it."

So Gerry told him about Mr Antrobus, the garden shed, the arrival of Inspector Clooney and his team, losing her temper during the interview. "Making a damn fool of myself, as usual," she said dejectedly. "But at least there was some good news on the agenda. Clooney told me that my alibi for the time of Anna's murder had been confirmed, that Mrs Temple admitted to having received a phonecall from Anna the night before her death."

Bill listened intently, at the same time making preparations for supper – tuna salad and jacket potatoes, mushroom and cheese omelettes.

For the first time, Gerry seemed uninterested in food. All this was really getting to her, he thought. He said sympathetically, "Would it help to tell me the whole story from beginning to end? There's a lot I don't know."

"Where shall I begin?" she asked forlornly. "It's all such a muddle."

"Talking about it might help," he said encouragingly. "How did you come by this house, for instance?"

"I wanted a place of my own," Gerry said wistfully, "and it was going for a song, the state it was in. Mr Constantine was something of a recluse, you see, who hadn't taken care of the property . . ."

"Mr Constantine? You mean that archaeologist johnny who . . . ?"

"Yes," Gerry said eagerly, "that's the one! Fancy you knowing about him!"

"Well, he was pretty famous in his time," Bill mused,

peeling mushrooms. "So you bought his house for a song, then what happened?"

Once she got going, there was no stopping her. Whisking eggs, washing lettuce, scrubbing potatoes, Bill listened, enthralled, to Liam's involvement with Mr Constantine, Gerry's visit to McEvoy's common-law wife, Zoe Smith, the strange artefact Liam had brought home with him, now destined for Zoe's dustbin.

"But that statue thingy could be worth a small fortune," Bill broke in excitedly, slamming the door of the microwave oven on the jacket potatoes. "She should at least have it valued by a reputable antiques dealer!"

"Oh, Bill, do you really think so?"

"Well, it's worth a shot, isn't it? What has Zoe got to lose – apart from the statue, which she wants rid of anyway?"

Perking up, Gerry said, "I'll visit Zoe the first thing tomorrow morning. Anything else you can think of?"

Opening a tin of tuna, he continued, "You did say, didn't you, that Mr Constantine was in some nursing home or other? You don't happen to know which one?"

"No, I don't, but Lance Bellingham might know," Gerry responded eagerly.

"Lance Bellingham? Who the hell's he when he's at home?" Bill asked, popping a knob of butter into the omelette pan.

"The estate agent who sold me the house," Gerry supplied, beginning to take an interest in the food department. "What *are* we having for supper, by the way?"

When he told her, "Oh," she said flatly, "that sounds – nice."

Talking things over with Bill had done wonders for Gerry's muddled thought processes. Filling him in on details of her various skirmishes with Clooney, she recalled what she termed her 'grilling' at the local nick the day of Anna's murder, and her overwhelming feeling of relief when she recalled having waved to Lisl from her fire-escape landing at the crucial time of the murder, an incident she had completely forgotten about until it came to the matter of an alibi.

"It was just one of those summat and nothing things," she explained to Bill, over supper. "I was feeling a bit rough at the time. I'd just stepped out on the fire-escape to get a breath of air. Thank God Lisl saw me, or I might have been banged up by now!"

"Thank heaven for small mercies," Bill said fervently.

"Mind you," Gerry continued, adding a sizeable knob of butter to her jacket potato, "I can see Clooney's viewpoint to some extent, first Liam, then Anna ending up the way they did; it must have seemed a bit fishy, more than a little coincidental, since they had both been in my employ." She shivered slightly. "It doesn't bear thinking about, being the prime suspect in a murder case . . ."

The idea struck Bill as ludicrous. "The man may be a bit on the thick side, but not that pudding-headed surely? What gets my goat is his damned insensitivity in putting you through the trauma of an in-depth interview so soon after . . ."

"Identifying Anna's body, you mean?" Gerry said softly, recalling the horror of it. "Well, yes, it wasn't a very pleasant experience. I – I'd scarcely got over the shock of finding Liam's body in the shed. Oh, let's talk about something else, shall we?"

"Of course, love. I'm sorry," Bill said contritely, wishing he'd kept his mouth shut. Getting up to clear away the first course dishes, he gently asked, "So what would you like for dessert?"

"There's some Black Forest gateau and ice-cream in the fridge," Gerry reminded him.

*   *   *

Later, in the drawing room, "Look, Gerry," Bill said, trying not to sound too intense, "I meant what I said, this morning, about your not being alone here over the weekend. I'd feel a hell of a lot better if you booked in at a hotel while I'm away. I'll not have a moment's peace of mind otherwise."

"But what about the book?"

"Sod the book!"

"That's all very well to say," Gerry said primly, "but you won't be so cocky if it's not on your desk by the end of September. Besides, I want it finished and out of my hair before I shuffle off to Robin Hood's Bay to spend October with the Berengers. So there!"

"All right, Gerry, have it your way," Bill conceded, "but for God's sake, be careful!"

"Don't worry, I shall," she said blithely.

"There are times when I could murder you myself, with my bare hands," Bill shot back at her, tongue-in-cheek.

"Then why don't you? Let me guess! Because you like the cut of my jib, perhaps? Because you have a penchant for overweight damsels in distress? More likely because you, Bill Bentine, are the nicest, kindest person I've met in my life, so far. So now you know!"

"Wanna bet?" he threw after her as she headed towards the door on her way to bed. "Hasn't it occurred to you that I might just have my own best interests at heart? After all's said and done, what possible use would I have for an unfinished manuscript by a defunct author?"

"You could take a stab at finishing it yourself, I suppose," Gerry suggested, halfway up the stairs, pausing to look over the banister at Bill's upturned face in the hall below. "But not to worry, I'll finish the book myself, come hell or high water!"

She added breathlessly, "Well, goodnight, Bill, and sleep well."

"You too, Gerry," he replied quietly, thinking what a nice lass she was.

Seven

The night had passed uneventfully.

Perhaps the killer, Bill thought, going down to the kitchen to make coffee and toast, had felt unfit for action given his sore masculine appendages, which must still hurt like the devil, and serve him damn well right, the murderous son-of-a-bitch.

Opening the glass doors leading to the patio, the air was much fresher this morning, he realised, stepping outside to sniff the scent of moist earth. Rain had fallen during the night. Gentle rain, hence the clearer, less humid atmosphere.

He turned, smiling, when Gerry entered the room in her dirndl skirt and sloppy sweater. "Did you sleep well?" he asked, coming indoors to pour the coffee.

"No, scarcely at all, as a matter of fact. I felt far too excited, turning things over in my mind."

"Things? What things?"

"Well, visiting Zoe Smith to find out about that statue; calling on Lance Bellingham to ask him the whereabouts of Mr Constantine; figuring out the ending of *The Blasted Heath*! What's more, I've done it! It came to me around three o'clock! I know now who dunnit, and why, despite all the red herrings I'd planted along the way, which had me flummoxed at one point, I must admit. Then, in the early hours of this morning, everything started to slot together like the pieces of a jigsaw puzzle."

Smiling happily, "Boy, that coffee smells good," she sighed contentedly, sitting herself down at the table to smother a slice of toast with butter and Cooper's thick-cut marmalade. "You really know how to spoil a girl, don't you?"

"So I've been told, from time to time," Bill admitted modestly, "though the women in my life, so far, didn't need spoiling. They were already well and truly spoilt!"

"I see," Gerry responded tartly, "and I'll bet any money they were all skinny blondes with shoulder-length hair who looked great in bikinis – which just goes to show you can't judge a sausage by its skin!"

"Well yes, something like that," Bill conceded teasingly, "though they weren't all blondes." He paused. "How did sausages creep into the conversation, by the way?"

"Because that's what we're having for supper tonight! And I don't mean chipolatas!"

Bill grinned like the Cheshire Cat. "Have it your way. You're the boss! I'll pick up a couple of pounds of jumbos from Waitrose on my way from the office."

Men, Gerry thought savagely, when he had gone, wishing that she had long blonde hair and looked great in a bikini.

Retracing her steps to Number Ten Sesame Grove and ringing the doorbell, awaiting an answer to her summons, she thought at least her visit to Lance Bellingham earlier that morning, had borne fruit. He had told her, albeit unwillingly, that Mr Constantine was now being cared for in The Anchorage – a nursing home set in an acre or so of privately-owned land on the far side of Hampstead Heath. At the same time he warned her that the old man did not take kindly to visitors with whom he could not possibly communicate, since his stroke had rendered him speechless. Gerry pondered, wondering about Bellingham's caginess on the subject – as if he had something to hide. A pair of sore testicles, perhaps?

When eventually the front door opened and Zoe Smith appeared in the vestibule, not wasting time, "I've come about that statue Liam brought home with him, remember?" Gerry said. "It could be worth a great deal of money! Please may I come in? I really need to talk to you!"

"Yeah, I know," Zoe said dismissively. "Mick – Liam's brother – sold it to a market trader for fifty quid! Well, I told you, didn't I, that Mick would take good care of me, and he has! Now, if you don't mind, you'd best be off, 'cos I'm busy! Mick will be back soon, wantin' his dinner, an' I've a meat pie in the oven!"

So saying, she closed the front door firmly in Gerry's face.

Turning away, deep in thought, not looking where she was going, Gerry bumped into Mick McEvoy at the garden gate.

Heart lurching at the sudden, unexpected encounter, and despite the twin brothers' uncanny physical resemblance to one another, Gerry knew instinctively that there was a world of difference between her happy, bemused alcoholic gardener, Liam McEvoy, and his worldly-wise, sharp as a tack, sober brother Michael.

Laying on the charm, "Oh, 'tis sorry I am, to be sure, bumping into you the way I did, not looking where I was going," Mick McEvoy said courteously, tongue-in-cheek, stepping aside to let her pass.

Immediately, Gerry's mind went into overdrive. In a matter of seconds, she had weighed up the possibility that Mick McEvoy might well have been responsible for the vandalisation of her garden shed and been the one who had held a pillow over her face the other night. Why not, if Zoe had let slip some item of information, however innocently, which had led Mick to believe that his brother had hidden something of value in the shed?

But no, that didn't make sense, Gerry realised. The

vandalisation of her garden shed, yes, most certainly. Attempted murder? No, and yet . . . Taking a calculated risk, "No need to apologise, I assure you," Gerry said lightheartedly. "By the way, are you feeling better now? Is the pain beginning to wear off a little?"

His veneer of charm forgotten, "And just what the hell is that supposed to mean?" Mick McEvoy uttered hoarsely. "Just who are you anyway? Oh yes, it all comes back to me now." He chuckled nastily, "You were Liam's bit on the side, weren't you? The one who discovered his body in that broken-down garden shed of yours?"

Edging past him at the garden gate, "The question I asked you related simply to the pain of losing your brother, what else?" Gerry said mildly.

"What are you doing here anyway?" he asked suspiciously. "Been pestering Zoe again, have you? She told me you'd been round, nosey-parkering, asking questions, making a damn nuisance of yourself."

"No, nothing of the sort," Gerry replied airily, "I just came to tell her that statue she wanted rid of could be worth a lot of money, but it's gone now, so why worry? They say what you've never had, you'll never miss. Well, good-day, Mr McEvoy. Enjoy your meat pie!"

"Here, just you hang on a minute! You mentioned money. How much money?"

Gerry puckered her forehead. Enjoying herself enormously, she said, "Hmm, well, difficult to be precise. Around fifteen grand, I imagine, to a bona fide collector. Maybe more!"

So saying, she nipped smartly to her car, leaving McEvoy in a state of shock, hands gripping the gate for support. And serve him right, she thought, at the same time wondering if Mick had taken his brother's place in Zoe's bed yet. She wouldn't put it past him. He was that kind of man. Rotten to the core.

*　　　*　　　*

Now for The Anchorage, and Mr Constantine.

This was a spacious building filled with light and air, fresh flowers, framed hygiene certificates on the wall behind the reception desk in the foyer. It was a bit like a high class hotel until one spied, in an adjoining lobby, a clutter of zimmer-frames, walking sticks and wheelchairs, and caught a whiff of antiseptics, cooking and old age which no amount of air-freshener could dispel, Gerry thought, approaching the willowy young receptionist behind the desk.

"Yers," the girl said loftily, taking in at a glance Gerry's dirndl skirt, sloppy sweater, espadrilles and horn-rimmed glasses, "How may I help you?"

"I'd like to see Mr Constantine," Gerry explained, wishing she had worn her red trouser suit.

"Oh? Well, jerst a second," the girl said icily, "I shall have to consult Matron Smithson." Picking up the phone, she prodded four numbers with the forefinger of her right hand. A pause, then, "Ah, Matron," she said genteely, "Gilly here. A person wishes to see Mr Constantine." Another pause, then, "Yers, of course, I'll arsk her to take a seat."

"Where to?" Gerry asked brightly. "The seat, I mean."

"I beg your pardon?"

"Granted, I'm sure," Gerry riposted, in one of her devil-may-care moods. "No need to feel embarrassed. Everyone does it once in a while. A quick squirt of air freshener should do the trick."

"Well, *really*!" The receptionist glared at her, deeply affronted.

Gerry continued mischievously, "Know what, love? The last time I copped a load of fingernails your length was in a Tibetan monastery in Outer Mongolia. Summat to do with the monks' religion, you know? They weren't allowed to grow their hair so they grew their fingernails instead. Fortunately, they didn't have computers. Just as well, perhaps, otherwise they'd have got nowhere fast!"

Jumped up kids who put on airs and graces and looked down on those who weren't smartly dressed, acted as a red rag to a bull so far as Gerry was concerned.

Matron Smithson appeared from her office at that moment, a thin, middle-aged woman with a face that might come in handy for chopping wood, wearing a starched white bib and tucker decorated with mini-medals, despite which, she seemed decidedly ill at ease.

"Good morning," Gerry said cheerfully, "my name is Frayling. Geraldine Frayling! I expect you've heard of me? I'm the celebrated crime novelist, you know?"

Matron flinched slightly. "You'd better come through to my office," she croaked, as if she had a frog in her throat, and glancing quickly from left to right, as though expecting a side-on attack from a zimmer-frame.

"No calls for the time being," she told the gobsmacked receptionist. "This way please, Miss Frayling."

Brushing past Gilly, Gerry murmured, sotto voce, "OK love, you can close your mouth now. Your tonsils are showing!"

Matron's office, painted a brilliant white, resembled an igloo. The window was curtainless, covered with a modern version of a venetian blind. The desk, plain and functional, resembled the control centre of a prison warden's inner sanctum with its phalanx of computers, phones and folders.

Glancing about her at the grey metal filing cabinets beneath a further display of framed health and hygiene certificates, Gerry reached the conclusion that running a nursing home, at this level, had little to do with mercy, all to do with money – a means of extorting high rates of payment from the well-heeled, rather than a haven of peace for the poor and poorly.

She knew instinctively that patients unable to afford further room and board at The Anchorage would be hustled elsewhere when their cash ran out.

Disliking the set up intensely, "I came to visit Mr Constantine," Gerry said coldly, "so why have you brought me to your office?"

The matron said huskily, "For the simple reason that Mr Constantine is no longer with us."

"Why? Had his money run out?" Gerry asked scathingly, prepared to do battle on the old man's behalf. "My God, what kind of a place is this anyway?"

"No, I assure you, money didn't enter into it! The fact is that Mr Constantine died in the early hours of this morning: that is the reason why I brought you to my office, to break the news to you as gently as possible."

"Oh, I see. I'm so sorry," Gerry murmured, deeply ashamed of her outburst. "He suffered a further stroke, I imagine?"

Matron Smithson said hoarsely, speaking as through a Vox-a-phone, "I'm afraid not. The fact is that he, poor Mr Constantine, was – murdered! Smothered to death with a pillow!"

The ensuing silence could have been cut with a knife, then Gerry said disbelievingly, "But *why*? Why was he murdered? How could such a thing possibly have happened here, of all places? Surely there must have been nurses on duty to keep watch over him?"

"Of course there were," Matron Smithson admitted, deeply distressed. She added bitterly, "Oh, I know what you're thinking, that I own this nursing home, that all this is my fault. But I *don't*, and it *isn't*: I am simply the administrator, the 'patsy' if you prefer!"

"Then who does own it?"

"A consortium of local businessmen, but I'm the one who'll be held responsible for Mr Constantine's death, and the police will be here at any moment to start asking questions. Questions I can't possibly answer. I mean to say, I haven't a clue what happened. It just beggars belief that anyone could be wicked enough to murder a helpless, harmless old man like Mr Constantine."

The police, Gerry thought wildly, imagining the expression on Clooney's face if he found her at the scene of yet another murder. Ye gods, he'd have her in the dock at the Old Bailey before she could say Jack Robinson.

She said nervously, edging towards the door, "I'm truly sorry about what's happened. Now, if you'll excuse me, I feel in need of some fresh air."

Quitting The Anchorage at a rate of knots, hastening to her Mini, switching on the ignition, she headed towards the gates with a spurting of gravel beneath the wheels, as if she was driving a getaway car for a gang of bank robbers.

Missing a gate post by inches, heart pounding in her chest, dreading coming bonnet to bumper with a police car, she did not slacken speed until she was well clear of the nursing home when, in an empty lay-by, she switched off the engine, and sat there, trembling like a leaf, deeply shaken by the murder of Mr Constantine in a place of comparative safety, by a merciless, presumably mad, serial killer.

She, thank God, had possessed the strength and will-power to fight off his attack. Poor Mr Constantine, on the other hand, would not have stood an earthly chance of survival when a pillow was placed over *his* face; a man in his condition, a stroke victim, unable to even cry out for help.

But why had he been so brutally murdered? There must be some common denominator connecting the deaths of Liam McEvoy, Anna Gordino, Mr Constantine, and her own attempted murder. But *what*? Revenge? Gain? A desire or urgency to silence those who knew too much? But too much about *what*, for God's sake?

The more she thought about it, the more strongly emerged the idea that the 'common denominator' was somehow linked to the house she had mentally dubbed 'The Eyrie', with its former owner, and that ugly statuette he had given to Liam McEvoy.

The likelihood was that the strange artefact *was* worth a great deal of money after all; that the reclusive Mr Constantine had been sitting on a small fortune of similar objects among his personal possessions. So what had happened to his personal effects prior to his admittance to The Anchorage?

Only one way to find out. Not that Gerry relished the thought of a second visit to Lance Bellingham's office in one morning, but presumably he would know what had happened to Mr Constantine's belongings when the house had been cleared . . .

Lance Bellingham, a fair-haired, stockily built man in his early thirties, a junior partner in the agency founded by his father, Rupert Bellingham and his colleague, Sidney Charters, after the war, sighed deeply and rose unwillingly to his feet when Gerry entered his sanctum, wondering what the hell she wanted this time. A little of Miss Frayling went a long way, in his opinion.

"I've been to The Anchorage," she said, without preamble.

He waited expectantly, wondering what was coming next.

"Mr Constantine's dead," she announced dramatically. "Do you mind if I sit down? I've had a bit of a shock!"

"Please do. Can I get you anything? A cup of tea? Coffee?" More used to clubbing than coping, he added bluffly, "One knew, of course, that the old gentleman hadn't long to live."

"That's as may be. The thing is, he might have lived a bit longer if someone hadn't pushed a pillow over his face!"

"You mean that Mr Constantine was *murdered*?" Bellingham sat down heavily in the swivel chair behind his desk. "But *why*?"

"That's what I'd like to know, and you may be able to help," Gerry said eagerly.

"Help? In what way? I don't see how," he protested, beginning to wish he had never become involved in matters pertaining to the sale of the old man's property to its new owner; a fraught scenario from the word go – a weird eccentric on one hand, a pushy, overweight crime novelist on the other.

"It's quite simple, really," Gerry explained breathlessly, "I take it that Mr Constantine's furniture and effects were put into store before the house was sold?"

"Well, yes," Bellingham conceded, "so what? No other alternative was possible at the time, with the old man still alive, and no one knowing for certain what he wanted done with his belongings. I made the necessary arrangements myself, as a matter of fact, to have his household effects stored, pro tem, until the matter resolved itself one way or the other, which it has now, apparently."

He paused, frowning, "What I fail to understand is your interest in the matter of Mr Constantine's repository of broken-down sticks of furniture and so on. A quite disgusting hoard, I assure you!"

Tightly crossing her fingers, Gerry said, "But there may be a clue to his murder and – oh well, to be honest, I'm researching a new book at the moment."

"The answer is no," Bellingham said stiffly.

"But there may be papers," Gerry suggested eagerly.

"Hardly likely. Mr Constantine's private documents are in the hands of his solicitor, Basil Edgerton, for safekeeping.

There is nothing in the repository of interest to anyone except a second-hand dealer."

"In which case, what harm in my taking a look?" Gerry said persuasively. "You do have the key, don't you?"

"That is beside the point." Bellingham was fast losing patience, beginning to bluster. "The key is for emergency use only."

"Oh, and what constitutes an emergency, in your opinion? Or perhaps you have your reasons for not wanting me to look inside the repository?"

"Now look here, Miss Frayling . . ."

"No, *you* look, Mr Bellingham. I've made a perfectly straightforward request. As a crime novelist, I do have a nose for clues. There has been a series of particularly nasty murders linked to Mr Constantine's property – which I bought from you in good faith, remember?"

Remember? Would he ever forget? Knowing when he was beaten, "All right, you win," Bellingham said resignedly. Geraldine Frayling was fast becoming a nuisance. Might as well give in, otherwise, perish the thought, she'd never give him a minute's peace.

Gerry had never been inside a repository before, and she didn't much like it. It was all so soulless, dim and dusty – reminiscent of the crypts in Highgate Cemetery – sad, lonely and forgotten, with pyramids of unwanted furniture stacked in portacabins – the modern day equivalent of those crypts in Victorian graveyards.

In one such cabin reposed Mr Constantine's earthly possessions, a medley of brass bedsteads, flock mattresses, massive Victorian wardrobes, chests of drawers, tables and chairs, plus tea chests containing items of cracked household china, discoloured pots and pans, and books, literally hundreds of books; hefty, leatherbound tomes, bespeaking their former owner's literary turn of mind, his intellectual capacity in his heyday as a world renowned archaeologist.

"What will happen to all this stuff now?" Gerry asked wistfully, thinking how sad it was that these forlorn belongings comprised the sum total of a man's earthly existence.

Bellingham shrugged his shoulders dismissively, "It will be auctioned off eventually, I daresay. Not that it will bring much. People don't want this kind of rubbish nowadays."

"It isn't all rubbish," Gerry reminded him, spotting a Victorian whatnot cluttered with nineteenth century bric-a-brac – a pair of Staffordshire dogs; Goss china ornaments; an epergne; an egg-holder in the form of a hen sitting atop a china nest; a Sunderland lustre jug; treasures she would love to possess.

But Bellingham wasn't listening. His mobile phone had bleeped suddenly, and he had turned his back on her to answer the call.

Fingering the lustre jug, Gerry discovered a scrap of paper tucked inside, which she quickly transferred to her shoulder-bag.

"Tell me," she said, crossing the carpark, "was Mr Constantine really alone in the world? Had he no friends, no relatives?"

"None that I know of," Bellingham replied impatiently, glancing at his wristwatch – a Rolex, which figured.

"Had he ever been married?"

"Once, a long time ago, I believe." Heading quickly towards his silver-grey Mercedes, "Now, if you don't mind, I'm already late for a luncheon appointment."

"Oh, what a pity," Gerry said pleasantly, "just as I was about to put a little further business your way. But first things first. Where are you lunching, by the way? Claridges, the Savoy Grill? Personally, I prefer Barney's Hamburger Joint in the Old Kent Road. Nowt posh, of course, but his clients are *real* people, not cardboard cutouts!"

Bellingham hesitated, and was lost. "A little further business?" he enquired, half in and half out of his car. "Possibly you could give me an inkling?"

"Oh, it's nothing much really," Gerry supplied modestly, "I was simply thinking in terms of a cottage in Cumbria, a pied-à-terre in Piedmont, a bungalow in the Bahamas, all three as a matter of fact. But not to worry. After all, there are other estate agents in the Yellow Pages!"

Getting into her Mini, switching on the ignition, lowering the window, "Well, goodbye, Mr Bellingham, enjoy your lunch," she called out to him, relishing the heartwarming feeling that the pompous bastard had received his come-uppance, that she had effectively ruined his appetite for the time being, since he had swallowed all the stuff and nonsense she'd fed him about Cumbria, Piedmont and the Bahamas, as greedily as a trout swallows a fly.

Money, plus greed, was the name of the game for the likes of the Lance Bellinghams of this world, she realised, bowling out of the carpark, and she'd bet any amount of the former that he was kicking himself right now.

A pity, really. Given half a chance, she'd have saved him the trouble.

Eight

"Well, what kind of a day have you had?" Bill asked when he arrived on the doorstep that evening.

"Fraught," Gerry said tautly. "I've started supper, by the way; made the salad and beaten the eggs."

"I thought we were having bangers," he said warily.

"We're not now! A girl can change her mind, can't she?"

Holding up his hands in a gesture of compliance akin to that of a suspected bank robber wishing to prove himself unarmed, "That she can," he agreed heartily. "Just give me time to adjust, is all I ask. I've had a pretty fraught day myself, as it happens."

"Sorry, Bill. I didn't mean to bite your head off." Tears flooded her eyes and rolled down her cheeks.

"My dear girl, whatever's the matter?" He had never seen Gerry cry before.

"I went to the nursing home to see Mr Constantine, and, oh Bill. I was too late! He'd been – murdered. Someone had smothered him to death with a pillow!"

"Oh dear God, how dreadful! The poor old man! I'm so sorry." Gently he drew the weeping Gerry into his arms, providing a shoulder for her to cry on, beginning to wonder if there was some kind of jinx on her. Feeling in his pocket, he handed her a clean handkerchief to mop up her tears.

Withdrawing from his arms, ignoring the proffered hanky, using a torn-off strip of kitchen roll instead and thinking she

81

mustn't become too attached to Bill's shoulder to cry on – she wasn't the clinging vine type – she said, "Thanks, Bill, I'm fine now," drying her eyes and blowing her nose. "Sorry I made such a fool of myself. I'd had a bit of a shock, that's all."

"With good reason, I'd say," Bill murmured sympathetically, returning his hanky to his trouser pocket.

Consigning the shredded and damp strip of kitchen roll to the pedal bin near the sink, "Has it struck you," Gerry asked, washing her hands, "how close to home all this is? This house, I mean."

"The thought had occurred," Bill confessed, "the reason why I want you out of here while I'm away. Please, Gerry, be sensible. I'm off to Wiltshire tomorrow morning, first thing. I'd cancel the trip except that she, my client, will probably have a nervous breakdown if I don't put in an appearance. Me too, come to think of it," he added wryly. "Can you imagine, a three-book contract and writer's block into the bargain?"

"Tell me about it!" Gerry went back to her egg-whisking. "Or let me guess! This emotionally-challenged client of yours wouldn't be a slender, blue-eyed blonde with a penchant for Italian swimwear, by any chance?"

"Yeah, as a matter of fact," Bill conceded, tongue-in-cheek. "She also has a bald-headed husband, three teenage children, two gallumping great labradors, and a cat with a penchant for sharpening its claws on my trousers."

Gerry sniffed haughtily. "No wonder she has writer's block!"

"Here, let me see to those eggs before you knock the bottom out of the bowl," Bill suggested. "Meanwhile, I want you to consult the Yellow Pages; find yourself a nice comfy hotel somewhere – the Outer Hebrides for preference – book in for the weekend, otherwise I'll never have a minute's peace of mind."

"All right then, if you insist," Gerry said meekly, touched by his concern for her welfare, and going through to the hall to consult the directory.

Returning to the kitchen, minutes later, "Well, that's taken care of," she said briskly.

"Great," Bill enthused, adding a knob of butter to the scrambled eggs, "so where are you staying? The Ritz, Claridges, The Savoy?"

"Huh? You must be joking! What? Pay out those fancy prices? No way! I'm staying at Barney's Hamburger Joint in the Old Kent Road!"

After what Gerry thought of as a lightweight supper of scrambled eggs, salad, paté, French bread and vanilla ice-cream, she told Bill about her visit to the repository and the scrap of paper she had found tucked inside the Sunderland jug.

"There I was thinking I'd discovered an important clue to the murder," she said, "but as far as I can make out, it's just a shopping list dating back to the sixteenth of February. Here, take a look."

Searching in her shoulder-bag, which she regarded as a portable office, finding the scrap of paper, she handed it to Bill to peruse.

"Hm," Bill said, "an odd kind of shopping list. Two bottles of the hard stuff, and the word 'Eggs', underlined. Perhaps he had a penchant for egg flips and baked custard? And what's this scrawled underneath? 'Ask L.M.' Could that refer to Liam McEvoy, I wonder?"

"Yes, of course. Why didn't I think of that? Liam would have been working for him about that time," Gerry supplied eagerly. "I expect Mr Constantine meant to ask Liam to nip down to the shops for him the next time he saw him?"

"Possibly, but I don't think so, somehow," he said,

pondering the strange message. "I should hang onto this, if I were you," Bill suggested. "It may be important."

Returning the scrap of paper to her shoulder-bag, thinking that her visit to the repository had been a waste of time, she added, "Mr Constantine's important papers are in the hands of his solicitor – a Mr Basil Edgerton, according to Lance Bellingham." Brightening a little, "I wonder if it would be worthwhile paying him a visit? What do you think?"

"He wouldn't tell you anything," Bill said. "Solicitors are notoriously cagey individuals, in my experience. They have to be, it goes with the job; client confidentiality and all that jazz."

"But if I asked him something comparatively simple and uncompromising?" Gerry insisted.

"Like what, for instance?"

"Well, the name of his wife, for starters. Lance Bellingham told me that Mr Constantine had been married, in the dim and distant past, and she may well be alive and kicking for all we know, living in genteel poverty somewhere or other, baking little mutton pies to earn an honest crust."

Bill burst out laughing. "Honestly, Gerry, you and your imagination! So where are you really going to spend the weekend?"

"I've already told you! Barney's Hamburger Joint! Barney Bowler and his wife Maggie are good friends of mine, I'll have you know. Barney was a heavyweight boxer until his retirement from the ring ten years ago, Maggie a was lady mud-wrestler. Now Barney runs the hamburger joint and Maggie takes in lodgers in the flat over the caff."

"Really? I thought you were kidding."

"Whatever gave you that idea? Oh, I get it! Now I'm rich and famous, I'm supposed to have rich, upperclass friends, is that it? Well, hard cheese! Maggie and Barney Bowler are the salt of the earth, and they'll take care of me just fine!"

A brief silence ensued, during which she poured Bill a

stiff whisky from the tantalus and a glass of sherry for herself. Then, regretting her spirited reply to Bill's innocent remark, she said gaily, "Let's drink a toast, shall we? Here's to ex-boxers, bald-headed husbands, lady mud-wrestlers, labradors, and writers' blocks! Down the hatch!"

"By the way," Bill asked later, on a more serious note, "any news of Anna Gordino? Have the police come up with anything yet?"

"Not that I know of." Gerry shivered slightly. "I imagine they're trying to contact her husband for questioning. One thing's for sure, Inspector Clooney's bound to have found out that I was at The Anchorage this morning. Then I'll be in more trouble! Talk about a living nightmare!"

"I know, love," Bill said sympathetically, "but don't let it get you down. Even that wooden-top Clooney must realise you're simply a victim of circumstances beyond your control?"

"Thanks, Bill, but from Clooney's viewpoint, given a motive, I could have bumped off Liam, Anna and Mr Constantine, and I could have been lying that night when I told you that someone had tried to kill me! All I did was point to the open fire-escape door and say, 'He went that way', and you believed me!"

"My dear girl," Bill said, getting up from his chair, ready for bed, "I'd believe you if you told me that black was white and that mist is caused by the sun striking an iceberg!"

"What time are you leaving, in the morning?" she asked wistfully, at the foot of the stairs.

"Around half-seven," he told her, "to miss the traffic before doddling down to Devizes, stopping for coffee en route, and taking a walk on the Wiltshire Downs to breathe in a bit of fresh air before turning up at my hostess's cottage in time for lunch."

He sighed deeply. "Knowing Clarinda, she'll have been up since the crack of dawn, setting the dining table, preparing the grub, and so on."

"You mean Clarinda Clarkson, the romantic novelist?" Gerry said scornfully. "The author of all those historical 'bodice rippers'?"

"The self and same," Bill admitted cheerfully. "Why? Are you a fan of hers?"

"No I am *not*," Gerry said prissily. "All those intimate details of the male anatomy she goes into so thoroughly. How come she knows all that stuff anyway?"

"Well, she *is* a married lady," Bill reminded her, "so presumably she knows what's what in that department: the 'dangly bits' between the legs, and so on. Even unmarried ladies appear to know all about those, so what's the problem?"

"Knowing about them is one thing; writing about them in detail's another matter entirely," Gerry said loftily. "Just remember to padlock your pyjamas, that's all!"

Lying sleepless in their separate bedrooms, Bill wondered uneasily if Gerry was falling in love with him. Surely not? At least he hoped not, for her sake.

In the room above, Gerry wondered if she was falling in love with Bill Bentine? She hoped not, for her own sake. Despite their depth of understanding and their present easygoing relationship with one another, her common sense warned her that Bill, with his penchant for slender blondes, was unlikely to fall for a heavyweight author with mouse-brown hair scragged back from her face and fastened with a rubber band.

Ah, well, in the words of Bette Davis in that old black and white Hollywood film, *Now, Voyager*, 'Why ask for the moon? We have the stars.'

Up early next morning, Gerry was in the kitchen, before

Tantalus

Bill appeared on the scene, being determinedly jolly, as befitted a fat lady about to boil eggs and butter the toast.

"It's a lovely morning for your journey," she said cheerfully. "Did you sleep well? I did, and I'm really looking forward to my weekend with Maggie and Barney."

"Wish I could say the same about my weekend in Wiltshire," Bill said glumly. "Clarinda Clarkson in her down and out moods is a pain in the neck, to put it mildly. I'll have to sit and talk to her for hours on end to convince her that her legion of fans are awaiting her next novel with bated breath – not to mention her publishers, who will likely cancel her three-book contract forthwith if she doesn't finish the first to her end of December deadline."

"Four minutes or five?" Gerry asked conversationally, hovering over the egg pan. "What I mean is, do you like the yolks hard boiled or runny?"

"Runny," Bill said dourly, wondering how come Gerry seemed so happy and carefree all of a sudden, just when *he* felt in need of a shoulder to cry on.

On the point of departure, Bill scribbled his mobile phone number on the back of an envelope – just in case.

"Ring me if you need me," he said. "What time are you leaving, by the way?"

"As soon as I've packed a few duds," she told him, starting the washing up.

"And when will you be back?"

"First thing Monday morning, to see to 'Eric Bloodaxe' and his lop-happy gang. Tell you what, I'll have masses of wood for the winter. Log fires in every room, come Christmas – if I live that long!"

She locked the front door behind her with a sweet feeling of relief at the prospect of a weekend break ahead of her.

Today, Saturday, she had planned a shopping spree in the

87

West End, a visit to a hair stylist and lunch in Fortnum and Masons before booking in at Barneys later in the day.

Checking the contents of her shoulder-bag beforehand, she had ditched most of its contents, including Mr Constantine's shopping list, on the kitchen table. She badly needed a new bag in any case. This one was beginning to resemble a drayman's belly, all sag, wag and drag, and no wonder, considering the amount of rubbish she had stuffed into it.

Hefting her overnight valise, portable typewriter and several folders into the boot of the Mini, she drove away from The Eyrie in high spirits until, struck by a sudden thought, she stopped the car abruptly and backed the way she had come – a matter of a few yards.

Hastening to the Berengers' front door, she rang the bell and waited until the housekeeper answered the summons.

"Sorry to bother you, Mrs Temple," she said brightly, "I just thought you should know that I'm going away for the weekend. I hope you won't feel too lonely, and I thought you might worry if you saw no sign of life."

"Thank you, Miss Frayling, but Mr Berenger's nephew, Tim Bowen, has been here these past few days, and he'll be staying till the start of the new term. He teaches at public school, if you recall, hence the longer vacation period."

"Oh yes, of course." Gerry paused, remembering Bowen's owl-face and thick-lensed glasses. Then, "By the way, I understand that my housekeeper rang you the night before her – murder? What prompted her to do that, I wonder?"

"I haven't the faintest idea," the woman said frostily. "Obviously she was deeply disturbed. Indeed, I gained the impression she'd been drinking, since what she said amounted to nothing more than gibberish."

"Really? That's odd. Anna didn't drink, and she couldn't have been gibbering entirely, could she, when she told you she was leaving for Paris early next morning?"

Mrs Temple seemed nonplussed momentarily, then, gaining control, "I have told the police all I know about that unpleasant incident," she said acidly. "Now, if you'll excuse me, I have work to do." So saying, she closed the door firmly in Gerry's face.

Having front doors closed in her face was fast becoming a feature of her life, Gerry thought wryly, harbouring the strong feeling that Mrs Temple had not told the police the whole truth and nothing but the truth, and smelling a rat in the shape of Tim Bowen, who might well have crept up her fire-escape the other night to stuff her face full of pillow. He'd been in the right place at the right time, Gerry considered carefully, and he might not be quite as daft as he appeared. At least she hoped not, for his sake.

Oh, what the hell? She was sick and tired of all the worrying and wondering, and in the frame of mind to enjoy herself for a change, to splash out on some new clothes, a new hairstyle, to treat herself to a few luxuries – money no object.

Maggie and Barney Bowler welcomed her with open arms.

"Hey, you're looking good," Maggie commented when the initial embraces were over. "What have you done to your hair, by the way? No, don't tell me, let me guess. You've had it highlighted and blow-dried? Right?"

"Got it in one," Gerry confessed, feeling giddy and lighthearted all of a sudden. "Do you approve?"

"I'll say I do," Maggie assured her. "And that outfit you're wearing's a knock-out! I mean, ankle-length skirts, cashmere sweaters and lots of dangling gold chains are all the rage nowadays, aren't they?"

"You don't think I've gone OTT, then?" Gerry enquired anxiously.

"No way! After all, you're a famous, bestselling authoress nowadays, so why not live up to it?"

Maggie paused momentarily, then, "What beats me an' Barney is, why *us*? Why choose to spend the weekend here when you could be living it up at the Savoy?"

Gerry said simply, "It's a long story. Let's just say that I needed to be with friends I knew I could trust to take care of me for the time being. And I'd trust you and Barney to the ends of the earth and back." Tears filled her eyes. "You see, I think someone's trying to kill me right now and, frankly, I'm scared stiff of being alone."

"Fair enough," Maggie muttered. "Now you come upstairs with me, darling! You'll be as safe as the Bank of England here. I've got a nice room all ready for you, an' no bugger'll get past me an' Barney, I promise you! I'd like to see 'em try, that's all!"

The room Maggie had given her was small but well-furnished. There was a single bed with a pink duvet and pillows, a bedside table with a pink shaded lamp, a long white painted dressing table in front of a dormer window overlooking the street below, and a small adjoining bathroom, all spotlessly clean, on the top floor of the house.

"Now don't you worry none," Maggie said firmly, "you can have your meals sent up to you, if you like. There's a radio, a TV and a telephone, as you can see, an' my room an' Barney's is just across the landing, should you need help during the night."

"Thanks, Maggie," Gerry said gratefully. "I'm beginning to feel better already."

"Hmm, I see you've been shopping," Maggie remarked, eyeing the carrier bags Gerry had brought with her. "Owt special?"

"Why not help me unpack and find out?" Gerry suggested, knowing that Maggie was itching to take a look at her purchases. "It's underwear mainly, knickers, nightgowns and so on, a couple of Wonderlift bras, stockings and a dressing gown. Oh, and I treated myself to a new shoulder-bag, lots of makeup, another long skirt, several more sweaters, two pairs of shoes, and a – bath-sheet."

Suitably impressed, "Quite a collection," Maggie commented drily. "He must be quite a guy . . ."

"Who must?" Gerry frowned.

Maggie chuckled, "The guy you're in love with, of course. Why else all the fancy lingerie an' that outsize bottle of perfume, the new hairdo an' all them gold chains?"

Gerry sighed deeply. "Chance would be a fine thing," she said wistfully. "He doesn't even see me as a – woman. He's into skinny blondes with emotional problems. Mind you, he hasn't seen me in anything so far apart from a bath-sheet and espadrilles, a dirndl skirt, a sloppy sweater and a pair of clapped-out pyjamas."

"Pyjamas, eh?" Maggie cocked an eyebrow. "Well at least that seems like a step in the right direction."

"No, it wasn't like that at all!" Gerry said, then shivered slightly. "I'd rather not talk about that right now, if you don't mind."

A sensitive being, despite her weight and her arm muscles, which resembled those of an American 'Ice-tong' man's, Maggie changed the subject adroitly. "How are your Ma and Da getting on nowadays?" she asked. "We don't see much of them hereabouts since they split up with one another. Well, that's the way of the world, folk never knowing when they're well off . . .

"They must be proud of you, though, makin' such a name for yourself. Who'd have thought it, Gerry? Remember when they first brought you here, wantin' hamburgers an' chips after a visit to the pictures: too shy to say boo to a goose!"

Gerry smiled wistfully. "Yes, Maggie. I remember."

"Well, I'd best be off now," Maggie said reluctantly. "Saturday nights are our busiest nights of all in the caff. But you must be starving hungry by now, so what would you like sent up to you? A couple of hamburgers an' chips?"

Her mouth watering at the thought, but turning away from temptation, "No," Gerry said firmly, "I'll just have a tuna salad, a jacket potato and a couple of Ryvitas."

"I have to hand it to you, girl," Maggie said admiringly, on the threshold of the room, "you've certainly got guts. Rather yours than mine, thank the Lord! I mean, Ryvitas, for gawd's sake!"

She added, "So when are you going to tell me the whole story? Why are you so scared of being alone?"

"It's a long, complicated story, I'm afraid," Gerry said. "We'll talk later, shall we?"

"It could be quite late," Maggie warned her, "after the caff closes for the night."

"I don't care how late," Gerry said simply. "You see, I really do need to talk to someone I know I can trust implicitly, and *you* are that person, believe me."

Maggie nodded understandingly. "I'll have a tray sent up to you," she said briskly, and then she was gone, clattering down the stairs to lend her husband a helping hand in the caff.

Nine

A girl came up later with Gerry's meal on a tray, to which had been added a cafétière of coffee, a jug of cream and a slice of chocolate cake.

"Mrs Bowler said to ring down if you want summat more substantial later. Just dial zero. Nine if you want an outside number," the waitress said.

"Thanks, love."

The trouble with salads was, they were so cold and boring, Gerry thought, but she'd had quite a shock in that West End store when she'd caught sight of herself in the fitting-room mirrors. It was then that she'd decided that enough was enough, too much more than plenty. If she ignored her stomach for a while, refused to cater to its whims, hopefully it would go somewhere else when it realised it wasn't getting enough to eat, taking her bust and thighs with it. There must be someone out there who'd be glad of her cast-off avoirdupois – Zoe Smith, for instance, or one of Bill Bentine's skinny-ribbed girlfriends.

She hadn't meant to think about Bill, but now she wondered what he was doing this evening. Mollycoddling Clarinda Clarkson, most likely, with her cat, hopefully, using his trouser leg as a scratching post. Miaow.

Perhaps she should get a cat, Gerry thought wistfully – a nice little kitten in need of a good home, who would claw its way up her drawing room curtains and knock her ornaments for six. Better still, a guard dog – a bull-terrier, a Rottweiler, an Alsation or a bad-tempered Jack Russell.

Resisting the temptation to dial zero and order a hamburger and chips, pushing aside the tray and the remainder of her salad and pouring a third cup of coffee, she looked out of the window at the street below, wondering if she dare risk a phonecall to Bill.

But no, better not. She'd best have a shower, wrap herself in her new bath-sheet and slip into bed to listen to the radio or watch television; simply relax for a change, except that she wasn't used to relaxing. Perhaps the shower would help her to unwind?

Entering the bathroom, she realised she hadn't brought a cap to protect her expensive new hairstyle. But necessity was the mother of invention. Refusing to be beaten, she entered the shower wearing a Harrods' plastic bag on her head.

She felt really good now. Snuggling beneath the duvet, she heard, as a lullaby, the sound of traffic streaming unceasingly along the Old Kent Road; saw, drowsily, the fast fading light of a September sky beyond the window, and fell asleep thinking of ankle-length skirts, cashmere sweaters, gold jewellery and lace-trimmed underwear. So who cared if her stomach was rumbling like a percolating coffee-pot?

She awoke to the sound of knocking; Maggie's voice on the landing asking if she was all right.

Lumbering out of bed, she unlocked the door. "Sorry," she said, "I must have fallen asleep. What time is it?"

"Just after midnight," Maggie told her. "Sorry to disturb you, but you had me worried."

"I haven't been sleeping all that well lately," Gerry explained, getting back into bed.

"Wanna talk about it?" Maggie asked, plumping down on the edge of the bed.

"It all began last April, when I bought a house in Hampstead," Gerry said reminiscently, telling Maggie the story from beginning to end, filling in the details as she went along. She relived the horror of the police questioning, her own attempted murder at the hands of an unknown assailant, the feeling she had that the killer was out there somewhere, patiently awaiting his chance to strike again in the fullness of time.

"My God," Maggie murmured hoarsely when the tale was told. "Now I can see why you came here, you poor kid! But surely what you need is a full-time bodyguard? And that damn fool Clooney should make certain you have one!"

Her dander rising, "Let's go over the names again," Maggie said firmly. "Could Michael McEvoy have murdered his brother? Suppose Liam had told him he was into something big, an' Michael wanted a piece of the action?"

"But Michael was in Ireland at the time."

"Huh, so *he* says, but supposing he wasn't? What if he'd nipped over from Ireland on the quiet, bumped Liam off, an' made it look like suicide? Then, having got Liam out of the way, what if he followed Anna Gordino to the Hampstead tube station, strangled her for whatever reason, then had a go at you?"

"But how could he have known that Anna was leaving for Paris that morning? It was a spur of the moment decision on her part. The only person who knew, apart from myself, was the Berengers' housekeeper, Mrs Temple."

"Then *she* must have done it," Maggie concluded triumphantly.

"She couldn't have," Gerry reminded her. "I saw the woman on the terrace next door at the time of the murder. No way could she have been in two places at once."

"No, but she could have told someone else that Anna was skipping the country! Suppose she rang that someone after Anna had rung her? Suppose she had an 'accomplish'?"

95

"That's possible," Gerry conceded, "but hardly likely. Mrs Temple is scarcely the hardened criminal type. In any case, why would she have wanted poor Anna out of the way?"

"Huh, that's as clear as the nose on your face," Maggie riposted sharply. "Because Anna knew the identity of the murderer of Liam McEvoy, and she had to be silenced! My guess is that Anna blurted the news to Mrs Temple on the telephone the night prior to her murder, an' Mrs Temple got in touch with the killer right away to warn him that the game was up unless he put paid to Mrs Gordino as quickly as possible."

"You may well be right," Gerry admitted warily, "but that doesn't explain why the killer wanted me out of the way, too, or why he felt it necessary to murder poor Mr Constantine. Frankly, Maggie, I haven't a clue why any of this happened in the first place. All I did was buy a house, in good faith, then suddenly – there I was up to my neck in not *one*, but *three* murders! Plus one attempted murder – my own!"

"So what about this Tim Bowen character?" Maggie persisted. "Could *he* be the murderer? You said you felt that someone was watching your every move, and he was handy enough. Could he have been 'bird watching' all along from the house next door?"

"But he wasn't there the night I had supper with the Berengers," Gerry reminded her.

"So what? He could have caught a train to London after Mrs Temple's phone call and lain in wait for Mrs Gordino early next morning. An' what was to stop him nipping round to that there nursing home to see Mr Constantinople out of harm's way? All he'd have to do was put on a white coat an' hang a 'periscope' round his neck, an' no-one would have given him a second look. Well, you know what they say, the best place to hide a banana is in a fruit dish."

Maggie warmed to her theme. "I think we're into a drug-smuggling gang here! I think that gardener chap cottoned on, an' that's why he was bumped off!" Maggie had a penchant for black and white American gangster films on late-night television.

"But Zoe Smith told me that Liam wasn't into drugs, and I believed her," Gerry demurred.

"Mebbe not, but he might have been into a spot of blackmail," Maggie said darkly, "in need of money. Mebbe that's why he was so optimistic about the future, cos he saw a way of earning a bob or two without having to work for it."

A brilliant thought occurred. "P'raps that 'statuesque' old Mr 'Constantinople' gave him was stuffed full of heroin or 'ecstatic'!" Maggie said eagerly.

"In which case, why resort to blackmail?" Gerry queried. "If the statue was stuffed full of drugs, why leave it on the sideboard? No, Maggie, it won't wash. If there were drugs inside that carving, and Liam knew it, he'd have been laughing all the way to the bank. All he had to do was find a dealer – not too difficult nowadays, I imagine – pocket the proceeds, and he and Zoe would've been away from Sesame Grove in ten seconds flat!"

"Well, I'm sure I can't make head or tail of it," Maggie confessed, getting up from the bed. Then, "Gawd's truth, is that the time? Barney'll be in bed by now, fast asleep, I shouldn't wonder. I shouldn't have kept you gassing all this time. But you can sleep late in the morning; stay in bed all day if you've a mind to."

"Thanks, Maggie, but I'm an early bird as a rule. No offence, but I might just take myself off somewhere. I'm not used to being cooped up in one place. In any case, it's darkness, not daylight, that I'm afraid of." When Maggie had gone, shedding her bath-sheet, Gerry slipped into one of her new nightgowns, washed her face and combed her hair, scarcely daring to look at herself in the bathroom mirror, fearful that she'd made a dreadful mistake in having her hair highlighted. She wondered what Bill would think when he copped an eyeful of her new coiffure and caught a whiff of Channel No. 5; that she'd lost her marbles, most likely, in trying to make a silk purse from a sow's ear.

Funny, she thought, getting back into bed, she'd never cottoned onto the new-fangled adage that 'Big is Beautiful': coined, most probably, by a fifteen stone American chat show hostess with a penchant for peanut butter sandwiches for breakfast.

One thing for certain, she'd felt a damn sight better emerging from that West End store wearing a long black skirt, uplift bra, cashmere sweater and lots of gold chains, bracelets and earrings, than she had ever done in her dirndl skirt or tomato red trouser suit, which she now intended getting rid of, along with her clapped-out pyjamas, ancient dressing gown, and various other worn-out items, the very minute she reached home on Monday morning.

Wide awake, Gerry thought longingly of home: her attic room beneath the stars, her collection of Victorian *objets d'art*, the tantalus on the drawing room sideboard, the what-not she had bought for a song in the Portobello Road last May, along with a boxful of Goss china ornaments, several Victorian figurines, two crystal-lustred oil-lamps, several items of Victorian silverware, and a violet embellished dressing table set comprising a ring-tree, powder-bowl, tray and twin candlesticks.

Less happily, she envisaged her present situation as the prime suspect in three murder cases which had nothing to do with her, which she could not even begin to fathom.

In the hinterland between wakefulness and sleep, she imagined Mrs Temple, not as the acme of respectability she pretended to be, but a consummate liar with the appearance of an elderly maiden aunt, with eyes of steel behind her gold-framed spectacles. Tim Bowen, an ineffectual young man who sweated profusely and pushed back his forelock of dark hair with the back of his hand whenever called upon to string more than two words together, as a serial killer . . . a banana in a fruit bowl, wearing a white coat, with a 'periscope' about his neck; striding the deck of a submarine, sinking without trace into the deep fathoms of sleep . . . Blessed, forgetful sleep, born of a clear consience and the overwhelming need of sleep to 'knit up the ravelled sleeve of care', according to William Shakespeare, the Bard of Avon, who, curiously, in Gerry's fleeting dreams, somewhat resembled Bill Bentine, in doublet and hose, arriving on her doorstep to hand her a bottle of wine with one hand, a flaming torch with the other . . .

Wide awake in the early hours of next morning, Gerry knew that, despite her typewriter and the folders of notes she'd brought with her with a view to finishing the final chapter of *The Blasted Heath*, no way could she settle down to write in an alien atmosphere, this neat, impersonal apartment in which, despite its aura of safety, she felt as trapped as a butterfly in a lepidopterist's net.

Dialling zero, she ordered breakfast in her room.

"Whaddayou want?" the waitress asked. "The full mazuma? Eggs, bacon, sausages, tomatoes, fried bread and mushrooms?"

Gerry swallowed hard. "No thanks," she croaked, "just toast, coffee and a boiled egg."

"Suit yerself," the girl said.

"Is Mrs Bowler there?" Gerry asked. "If so, I'd like a word with her."

"Naw. She an' Barney don't come down till nine on Sundays. Me an' Linda come in early to set up shop for the regulars till har-past nine."

"Oh, I see. Well, I'll leave Mrs Bowler a note on my way out."

"Rightio. I'll bring your breakfast up as soon as it's ready."

The day was sunny and bright. Leaving a note for Maggie at the counter; after breakfast, Gerry drove to Portobello Road street market where the stallholders were setting out their wares, feeling more confident than she had done for ages in her new gear, with her brand new bag slung over her right shoulder and a couple of Sunday papers tucked under her left arm. She was intent upon enjoyment, a few blissful hours spent rummaging for bargains of bric-a-brac, bargaining happily with the stallholders, hopefully spotting a piece of Linthorpe or Leeds pottery or a Mizpah brooch.

Already the market was thronged with people crowding about the stalls: tourists with cine-cameras, professional buyers in search of stock, parents with young children, keeping a wary eye on their off-spring as they played hide-and-seek among the stalls – people drawn, as if by a magnet, to the heartbeat of the city of London on a jewel-bright, warm September morning.

Unburdening herself to Maggie the night before had been a mixed blessing, Gerry thought, the reaping up of unpleasant memories a mental exercise she could have well done without. Not that Maggie's curiosity had worried her unduly, since she was using the caff as a temporary bolt-hole, and Maggie had the right to know why. She had simply wanted to forget about the murders for the time being, to relish a change of scenery, and to forget her troubles for a while.

Some fat chance of that, apparently! Standing near one of the stalls, fingering a hand-painted fan with ivory sticks and wafting the outspread rice-paper in the manner of a

Victorian lady flirting outrageously with a member of the opposite sex across a crowded ball-room, her eyebrows shot up to her hairline when she spied, not twenty feet away from her, the last people on earth she had expected to see – Christian Sommer and Tim Bowen's sister, Cassie.

Ignoring the stallholder's patter and look of surprise when her potential customer put down the fan and disappeared as if the devil was after her, Gerry headed for the nearest café, heart pounding, hoping to heaven they hadn't seen her, unable to shake off the feeling that their presence in the street market, however seemingly innocent, was far from coincidental.

The café was crowded. Choosing an about-to-be vacated table at the back of the room, feeling like a fugitive from justice, Gerry ordered coffee and a salad sandwich from the waitress who came to clear the table, and sought refuge behind one of the newspapers she had bought earlier that morning, her hands shaking like leaves as she spread out the pages.

"Mind if we join you?"

"Huh? No, of course not." Lowering the paper, Gerry smiled up foolishly at Christian Sommer and Cassie, certainly sure now that they had been following her. Far from sure why.

"Ah, Miss Frayling, what a delightful surprise," Sommer said urbanely. "What are you doing here?"

"I could ask you the same question."

"Bargain hunting. I happen to deal in antiques, if you recall? Cassie and I often come here on Sundays, don't we, darling?"

"Yes," Cassie said off-handedly, "quite often." She was inspecting her impeccably manicured fingernails, and the square-cut emerald ring on the third finger of her left hand.

Both were casually dressed in slacks and lightweight

cashmere sweaters, looking as self-confident and relaxed as only people who know they are beautiful can look.

"And have you found any? Bargains, that is," Gerry said, as the waitress came to the table with her salad sandwich and coffee. "I haven't. Not yet, anyway."

Sommer smiled faintly, with a dismissive shrug of his shoulders, "The fault of the *Antiques Roadshow* programmes on TV, I'm afraid. Now, mistakenly, every member of the public harbours the belief that they know as much about antiques as the experts."

"I know," Gerry said artlessly, "I'm one of 'em!"

Cassie snickered, showing her gums. Sommer snapped his fingers at the waitress, a gesture which evinced no immediate response for the good and sufficient reason that the poor girl was fairly rushed off her feet.

Giving his snapping fingers a rest, picking up the conversation where it had left off, "Really? I had no idea that you were an antiques buff," Christian continued charmingly.

"Oh yeah. In fact, I came across quite a nice little collection, the other day, in a furniture repository, of all places."

"Really? How fascinating. May one enquire . . ."

Weighing him up, recalling his snapping fingers at the waitress, the look of displeasure on his face when the girl had, justifiably, ignored that demeaning gesture on his part, Gerry wondered what she had ever seen in him, apart from his looks.

". . . why a repository, of all places?" He was trying hard not to sound too interested, but Gerry knew that he *was*. Very interested indeed.

She said, again artlessly, throwing a pebble into the pond and watching the ripples spread, "I shouldn't have been there at all, of course, but there were extenuating circumstances. You see, I had just discovered that the previous occupant of my house, the archaeologist, Mr Constantine, had been murdered, and well, being a crime-writer, I hoped to find a clue to his murderer."

"And – did you?" Sommer asked tautly.

"No," Gerry said wistfully, thinking she had, perhaps, missed her true vocation as an actress. "All I found was an old shopping-list inside a Sunderland lustre jug, but I did cop an eyeful of Goss china ornaments, a pair of Staffordshire dogs and a Victorian egg-holder, which I'd give my eye-teeth to possess when they come up for auction."

"How enterprising of you," Sommer said thinly, "and how dreadful . . . so famous a figure as Mr Constantine with a long and distinguished career as a world-renowned seeker of . . ."

"Buried treasure?" Gerry suggested winsomely. "Yeah, I know. It does seem a shame, doesn't it, that the poor old man was probably robbed blind of half his possessions before his death? Artefacts worth a small fortune, for instance?"

Sommer's eyelids flickered momentarily, as if he had received a nip on the ankle from a seemingly friendly poodle. "Have you evidence to support that theory?" he asked.

"Not as such, but I'll bet any money I'm not far wrong." Taking a calculated risk, she continued, "I'd lay a hundred pounds to a hayseed that my gardener, Liam McEvoy, who worked for Mr Constantine before the poor man suffered a stroke, knew he was being systematically burgled, and by whom and tried a spot of blackmail, and that's why he, Liam, was murdered."

Sommer smiled silkily. "You have quite an imagination," he said. "No wonder your books are so successful. But how does all this tie in with the murder of your housekeeper? I take it the deaths were connected in some way?"

"Oh, that's fairly straightforward," Gerry said, making

things up as she went along – a writing habit of hers – "Liam told Anna the name of his blackmail victim, so she too had to be silenced."

"All very cloak and dagger," Sommer said dismissively. "Ah, here's the waitress. About time too. What shall we have, Cassie? Coffee and sandwiches, or would you prefer something on toast?"

"Coffee," Cassie said sulkily. "I'm not hungry."

"How about you, Gerry? Would you care for another cup?" Sommer enquired charmingly.

"No, ta very much. I'd best be on my way. I'm staying with friends."

"Of course. We heard you were away for the weekend," Sommer said smoothly.

"You did? How come?"

"Mrs Temple told me," Cassie supplied, looking bored.

"I see." Gathering together her belongings, Gerry wondered what else Mrs Temple had told her?

Sommer said quickly, "Just a thought. Since we're here, and you are obviously into antiques, perhaps you'd care to take a look at my shop? I might add, in all modesty, that I happen to own the finest collection of Victoriana in London. Do say you'll come. You can call your friends on my mobile, if you like."

Virginia Vale would have been proud of her. "Thanks," Gerry said brightly, "I have the number here somewhere, scribbled on the back of an envelope."

The palms of her hands moist with perspiration, having found the envelope in her shoulder-bag, Gerry made the call. When Bill answered, "Oh, hello, Bill darling," she said breathlessly, "it's me, Geraldine."

"Huh?" Now he'd be thinking she'd really lost her marbles. "What's up?" he asked.

"Just to let you know I may be a bit late for lunch, but you and Virginia go ahead without me."

"What the hell are you on about?"

"Thanks, darling, I knew you'd understand. The fact is, I've been invited to a private viewing at Christian Sommer's galleries in Chelsea, and you know how mad I am about antiques? My apologies to Virginia. Tell her not to worry, I'll warm up my lunch in the microwave, if that's OK. Shouldn't be more than an hour or two at the most, so don't send out a search party just yet, all right? 'Bye, *darling!*"

Ten

It was an impressive set up, with vast plate glass windows, and discreetly wrought security shutters behind which could be glimpsed Louis Quinze furniture, velvet drapes and jardinières of Madonna lilies. The massive main entrance beneath an arched colonnade, hung with baskets of flowers, bore the lettering 'Antiques and Fine Art Galleries'.

Not what one might describe as a 'penny arcade', Gerry thought, beginning to wish she hadn't come, but at least Bill knew where she was if she happened to do a disappearing act.

"We'll park in the goods yard, go in through the side entrance," Sommer told Gerry, at the driving wheel of her Mini. Abandon Hope All Ye Who Enter Here, she thought nervously, imagining tomorrow's headlines: 'Mysterious Disappearance of Well-Known Crime Writer'. Perhaps they'd assume she'd done an Agatha Christie?

Sommer strode forward to switch off the security alarm, Gerry following in his wake, Cassie bringing up the rear. Lumme, what a place, she thought – a bit like that Hampstead repository, as quiet as a tomb, this being Sunday, lacking the comforting presence of the workforce. No typists, sales persons, furniture handlers, cleaners and packers: no one. How she wished it was Monday. There were far too many long corridors and empty rooms for her liking, and the lift, when they came to it, was one of those noiseless, strip-lit affairs with folding doors, imparting no sense of movement, emitting a strange purring sound reminiscent of an overfed feline.

The dreadful thought occurred that she might well be in the clutches of a couple of cold-blooded killers who had lured her here for the sheer pleasure of doing away with her, but there she went again, letting her imagination run riot. Even so, Gerry retained the strong impression that today's meeting had been planned for a specific purpose. But how could Sommer and Cassie have known her whereabouts unless they'd had her under surveillance since she left Hampstead? Was it remotely possible they, or one of them – Cassie, for instance – had been in the house next door when she'd called on Mrs Temple, and followed her every move until she had landed at Barney's? If so, she could be in dire trouble.

Thank God for that phonecall to Bill. Sommer must have felt pretty certain she'd refuse the offer of his mobile, and must have cursed himself as a fool when she'd accepted the offer and told Bill where she was going to this afternoon.

What would Virginia Vale do in a spot like this? Gerry wondered. Play it cool, came the answer; difficult under the circumstances, with heat running up under her uplift bra and new Gossard girdle, beads of perspiration dewing her forehead, and her glasses beginning to steam up and slide down her nose in this sticky situation.

When the lift stopped and the doors opened, "Are you feeling unwell, Gerry?" Sommer asked. "You seem somewhat hot and bothered, if you'll forgive my saying so."

"No, I'm fine," she lied bravely. "I just have a thing about lifts: confined spaces, you know? My psychiatrist told me not to worry about it unduly. Such a clever man. He advised me to try standing in the cupboard under the stairs for a quarter of an hour each day, with my eyes closed, and" – mopping her brow with the back of her hand – "I do believe it's beginning to work!"

"I see," Sommer said smoothly, "in which case, possibly you'd prefer to give my Victorian collection a miss for the time being? Come upstairs to my penthouse apartment for a bite to eat? A glass of champagne?"

"No, honestly, I'd far rather see your collection, if you don't mind," Gerry smiled, with the air of a simple-minded schoolgirl resisting the advances of the Head Prefect behind the bike-sheds in the playground, wondering where Cassie had got to all of a sudden. She'd been behind her one minute, gone the next. "After all, that's why I came here in the first place, isn't it? To admire your Victoriana?"

"But of course, and I can promise that you won't be disappointed, if you'll just follow me."

So saying, Sommer led the way along a corridor to a room, on the threshold of which Gerry drew in a breath of sheer delight. The items on display were grouped in spotlit showcases of varying sizes, reminiscent of the Brontë museum at Haworth. There were Victorian dresses and accessories, men's apparel as well as women's in a towering glass edifice lining the far wall. Other cases contained a bewildering variety of nineteenth century toys, household appliances, china and glass, silverware, texts and samplers, hand-painted fans and Valentine cards, Dorothy-bags, vinaigrettes, dance programmes, invitation cards to long-forgotten soirées, jewellery of every description, including jet mourning rings, lockets and necklaces.

"Oh, this is marvellous," Gerry breathed ecstatically, forgetful of her suspicions concerning Christian and Cassie for the time being, feeling that she had been transported into a world far removed from the twentieth century's hustle and bustle, until Sommer said, "Of course, my collection is far from complete as it stands at the moment."

"Really? I'd have thought it was pretty well comprehensive on the whole. What's missing?" She was looking at a china egg-holder as she spoke, of the kind she'd seen in the Hampstead repository.

"Certain papers and personal effects of famous people," he explained lightly, almost dismissively, as though keeping a curb-rein on some inner excitement bubbling away beneath his ice-cool exterior.

"Oh? Who, for instance?" Gerry asked innocently.

"Queen Victoria for one," he said, with a shrug of the shoulders. "A near impossibility, I'm afraid, for obvious reasons. Lord Carnarvon for another, relevant to his discovery of the Tomb of Tutankhamun. Such an exciting subject, archaeology, don't you agree?"

"Yeah, I guess so, though I'm not much interested in the subject myself," Gerry replied, alert once more to the danger of her present situation, knowing that her life probably depended on acting the fool right now, as it had done when she'd concocted the cock-and-bull story of her non-existent psychiatrist's advice to stand in a cupboard. "Take that nasty wood carving Mr Constantine gave to my gardener Liam McEvoy, for example, before the poor old man went into The Anchorage nursing home."

Glancing at her watch, edging towards the door, "Oh lumme," she wittered, "is that the time? I really must be going now, otherwise my friends will never invite me to eat with them again! Such a lovely couple. You've probably heard of them? Virginia and Bill Clarkson-Clooney? Ginny's an investigative reporter on the *Sun* and Bill's with MI5."

"Really? How interesting," Sommer said sourly, leading the way to the lift, harbouring the feeling that Gerry was lying through her teeth, but unwilling to find out for certain. "So, tell me, what happened to that wood carving you mentioned?"

"Oh, *that!*" Gerry shuddered slightly, entering the lift, "Liam's brother, Michael, sold it for fifty quid to a man in a pub. Frankly, I wouldn't have paid fifty pence for it, it was so darned ugly!"

And all the time the lift was descending, along with Gerry's stomach, to the ground floor. At least she hoped that's where they were heading, not to the basement, where nasty things might happen.

She could have cried with relief when the lift doors opened and she was on her way to her Mini, faced with the realisation that she was darned lucky to still be alive and kicking, and recalling the precise moment when she had known, beyond a shadow of doubt, that Christian Sommer's taradiddle about adding the effects of the famous to his collection had been uttered for a specific purpose.

Driving back to the Old Kent Road, Gerry felt herself deeply shaken by her sojourn within the confines of Sommer's 'Antiques and Fine Art Galleries', convinced that she had been lucky to leave those premises in one piece, and not stabbed to death, strangled, poisoned or dismembered, her lifeless body chucked into the Thames. She thanked God for the many books she had read, apart from crime novels, during her schooldays at Clapham Comprehensive, mainly as a matter of interest, so as to enlarge her vocabulary and add to her store of knowledge. Books concerning Robert and Elizabeth Browning, for instance, or Queen Victoria and her beloved consort, Prince Albert; Oscar Wilde; Lawrence of Arabia and Rasputin and Lord Carnarvon, the discoverer of the Tomb of Tutankhamun – not during the reign of Queen Victoria, but that of George the Fifth!

Sommer must have known that? If not, he should be running a pie factory, not an antiques gallery. His mistake had lain in underrating her intelligence. Not that she blamed him in that respect, having done her best to convince him that she was a pork pie short of a picnic. One fact emerged clear and strong: he desperately wanted to lay his hands on

Mr Constantine's, not Lord Carnarvon's, artefacts. Enough to kill for them?

"My God, where the hell have you been?" Maggie demanded when Gerry entered the caff. "I was just about to ring the police. Damn it, you've been gone since half-eight this morning and it's coming up to four now!"

"I know, Maggie. I'm sorry, but please don't go on at me, I've had one helluva day."

"You're not the only one! Why didn't you hang a placard round your neck? 'Come and get me, two shots a penny!' You could've ended up in an alley with your throat cut!"

"Maggie's right," Barney interposed gruffly. "We've been worried sick about you. Now you'd best sit down and get summat to eat inside you."

"Thanks, Barney, I'm not hungry, but I could murder a cup of coffee."

"So where've you been all this time?" Maggie insisted, seating herself opposite Gerry at a formica-topped table.

"It's a long story, and I'm too tired to tell it right now, but I think I know who the killer is."

Suddenly the door flew open and a dishevelled-looking man strode into the caff.

"Bill! Where have you sprung from?" Gerry asked, open-mouthed with surprise. "How did you find me?"

"With considerable difficulty," Bill said crossly. "And where do you suppose I've sprung from? Wiltshire, that's where! Clarinda Clarkson will probably never speak to me again. There she was, about to dish up the duck when the phone rang, whereupon I leapt to my feet like a lunatic, rushed upstairs to collect my gear, dashed down again, said, 'Sorry, gotta go', and went, peas flying in every direction. Since when I've broken every traffic rule in the book, spent the past hour braying on the door of an arty-farty antique shop in Chelsea and trying to find a parking space in the

Old Kent Road. Now here you are, drinking coffee, looking as if butter wouldn't melt in your mouth!"

"Wanna cup?" Gerry asked mildly.

Bill grinned. "I thought you'd never ask."

Dumping his overnight bag on the floor, smiling warmly at Maggie, "You must be Mrs Bowler," he said. "Gerry's told me so much about you and your husband. I'm Bill Bentine, Gerry's agent." Sliding on to the bench next to Gerry, he added, "I'd be eternally grateful to you if you could put me up for the night, that way I could escort my – client – home in the morning, make certain there are no nasty surprises in store for her."

"Yes, sure, I just happen to have a single room vacant on the second floor," Maggie said, anxious to give romance a nudge in the right direction, wondering what the hell was going on between the pair of them, why Bill had driven all the way from Wiltshire in such a devil of a hurry. Darned if she knew, but she was bound to find out sooner or later.

When Gerry dialled zero from her room an hour later, Maggie was up there like a bullet from a gun.

"So what's been going on?" she demanded. "Darned if I can make head or tail of it."

When Gerry told her, "You must have been barmy going to that Christian Sommer's antique shop on a Sunday," Maggie said severely. "You might've been as dead as mutton by now if you hadn't had the savvy to ring Bill from the Portobello Road!"

"I know, but the last thing I envisaged was that he would drop everything the way he did, leaving Clarinda Clarkson in the lurch."

"Must be love," Maggie suggested mistily.

"Oh, *fudge!*" Gerry replied sharply. "Bill's no more interested in me than the man in the moon. I'm just not his cup of tea, that's all!"

"Aye, but there's many a slip 'twixt cup and lip, think on," Maggie reminded her on her way to the door, "and at least you've got that fakey antique feller out of your hair, which can't be bad. Him an' his girlfriend Casserole, or whatever the devil her name is. It makes my blood run cold thinking of her upstairs, putting poison in the smoked salmon sandwiches, whilst you were busy inspecting his antiquities!"

On the threshold of the room, "By the way, are you and Bill doing anything special tonight?" Maggie asked off-handedly.

"No, of course not. Whatever gave you that idea?" Gerry sighed deeply. "Knowing Bill, he'll probably stay in his room fiddling about with that laptop computer of his." Frowning suspiciously, "Why do you ask?"

"Oh, no reason," Maggie said airily. "And what will *you* do?"

"The same as usual, I guess. Take a shower, get into bed, watch television or listen to the radio. Who cares?"

The phone rang a little later and Bill invited her to dine with him that evening.

"Thanks, Bill, but I've seen enough of the outside world for the time being," Gerry replied.

"So have I, come to think of it," he said persuasively, "which is why I've ordered a table for two downstairs, in the dining room behind the caff. Please say you'll come?"

Maggie had really gone to town on the decor, Gerry thought, with a bit of a lump in her throat. The table for two was set with a pristine white cloth, red paper napkins and a centrepiece of red dahlias. A two-bar electric fire was all aglow in the fireplace beneath a mantelpiece crowded with shining brass ornaments, and she had placed a red-shaded lamp on the fumed-oak sideboard to add a touch of glamour to the occasion.

Bill looked pretty good, too, Gerry thought, in a black polo-neck sweater, his hair still faintly damp from the shower, and smelling of his favourite cedarwood soap.

When they were seated, narrowing his eyes, his head held a little to one side, he said, "There's something different about you tonight, 'but I can't for the life of me figure out what it is."

Oh great, she thought, wondering why she hadn't simply worn her dirndl skirt, sloppy sweater, and had her head shaved into the bargain.

Then he said, holding out a hand to her across the table, "Sorry, love, your new hairstyle's a knock-out, and so is that perfume you're wearing. Did you really believe I hadn't noticed?"

"Well, yes, knowing you," Gerry said warily. "So what's this dinner party really in aid of? And what are we having to eat, anyway?"

"Duck and peas," Bill said mischievously, "in memory of Clarinda Clarkson. I fixed the menu with Maggie beforehand, but not to worry, we're having asparagus for starters and Black Forest gateau for dessert, plus lots of mashed potatoes and gravy with the main course, if that's OK with you?"

"Really?" All this, and heaven too, Gerry thought blissfully.

Her state of euphoria was destined not to last long, however, when Bill wanted to know what she had been doing at Sommer's galleries.

"Oh, don't you start," she said. "I've already been hauled over the coals by Maggie."

"I'm not surprised. Really, Gerry, you should have known better than to put yourself in such a dangerous situation."

"But I knew that Sommer was up to something, and I wanted to find out what it was. It was too much of a coincidence when he and Cassie showed up in the Portobello Road and followed me into that café, so I led him on deliberately, feeding him information about my visit to the repository, saying I'd been there hoping to find a clue to Mr Constantine's murder. Then I mentioned the artefacts and said I reckoned the old man had been systematically burgled before his stroke, that Liam knew by whom, had tried a spot of blackmail, and that's why he'd been murdered."

Bill groaned. "Ye gods, no wonder Sommer lured you into visiting his blasted emporium. I shudder to think what might have happened if you hadn't made that phonecall."

"I couldn't have, if Sommer hadn't invited me to use his mobile. That was a big mistake on his part," Gerry explained eagerly. "He did it to lull me into a sense of security, I suppose. He got the shock of his life when I called you 'darling' and ranted on about being late for lunch and warming up my grub in the microwave."

"He wasn't the only one," Bill reminded her. "I flipped completely when you said not to send out a search party just yet."

Gerry giggled. "Wish I'd been a fly on the wall!"

"This is no laughing matter, young lady! Had you no idea what you were letting yourself in for? I'm deadly serious! You knew you'd been followed deliberately. So what did you do? Marched in headlong where angels might fear to tread, fairly asking for trouble."

"I know, but it was a risk I had to take! Don't you see, Bill, I *had* to find out why Sommer was so desperate to show me his Victorian collection, and I *did* find out. It was a ploy to discover more about Mr Constantine's artefacts. A bit clumsy really, pretending it was Lord Carnarvon's artefacts he was after . . ."

"*Lord Carnarvon*?" Bill looked bewildered. "What the hell's he got to do with it?"

Maggie sailed through from the kitchen at that moment. "Ready for coffee?" she asked, whisking away the pudding plates.

"Oh yes please," Gerry replied gratefully, "and thanks for a wonderful meal. The duck was delicious, wasn't it, Bill?"

"We couldn't have fared better at the Savoy," Bill assured her.

Maggie glowed. "Right then, coffee for two coming up," she said. "Owt else?"

Bill grinned. "A stiff glass of brandy wouldn't go amiss," he said, wiping his forehead with the back of his hand.

"Why? Suffering from shock, are you?" Maggie riposted.

"Something like that," he admitted.

"Hey, what about me?" Gerry said plaintively. "I'm suffering from shock, too!"

"Gerry, love, you *are* the shock!" Bill said, tongue-in-cheek.

It had been a lovely evening. On the landing outside her room, "Goodnight," Bill said, kissing her cheek, "ready for home tomorrow?"

"Yeah, I guess so."

"You don't sound too sure."

"I'm a bit tired, that's all. It has been quite a weekend, all things considered."

"Then you'd best get a good night's sleep," Bill said gently, heading downstairs to his own room, pausing halfway down to smile up at her and blow her a kiss.

Gerry was in bed, still wide awake, when Maggie knocked at her door around midnight.

"Come in, it isn't locked," Gerry called out to her.

Next thing she knew, Maggie's arms were about her, holding her in a motherly embrace, the kind of embrace Gerry had often longed for and never received from her real mother.

"Look, Gerry love," Maggie said tenderly, "just remember that Rome wasn't built in a day, but everything will turn out fine in the end, you'll see! Now just you lie down, go to sleep, an' stop worrying, and just you remember it isn't your size, but what's inside you that counts, and any man worth his salt will realise that sooner or later."

Awake early next morning, Gerry packed her belongings and went downstairs to the caff to order coffee and a poached egg on toast rather than a bacon butty.

Minutes later she was joined by Bill looking as if he had scarcely slept at all. He was presumably anxious to get back to his office to order flowers for Clarinda Clarkson, just as she, Gerry Mudd, was anxious to return home to keep an eye on "Eric Bloodaxe" and his team of tree surgeons.

They went in convoy, Gerry in her Mini, Bill following in his hatchback.

"I'll go in first," he said on their arrival, opening the door for her and picking up a fan of letters on the vestibule carpet, one of which had been opened – the envelope bearing a North Yorkshire postmark.

"Someone must have been here," Gerry said bleakly, "tampering with the mail."

"You stay there," Bill said grimly. "I'll take a look round."

She watched him enter first the drawing room, then the kitchen. Seconds later, he returned. "The patio doors have been opened," he said, "but there's no sign of vandalism and nothing appears to be missing."

But something was missing. "It's gone," Gerry said

117

disbelievingly, staring at the items she had cleared out of her shoulder-bag on Saturday morning.

"What has?"

"Mr Constantine's – *shopping list!*"

Eleven

Inspector Clooney was not the happiest of men. He now had three murder enquiries on his hands, all of which were linked in some way to Geraldine Frayling.

Spreading out his case notes on his desk, he went over the facts once more. So far, in the case of Liam McEvoy, it had been established that he had died from a lethal concoction of alcohol and Co-Proxamol painkillers, forcibly administered, when his hands were tied behind his back.

The pathologist's report had revealed evidence of bruising about the lips and wrists of the deceased, of rope fibres embedded in various cuts in the wrist area, concurrent with the victim's attempts to struggle free of his bonds.

Death had occurred around midnight on the Wednesday preceding the discovery of the body two days later. In the analyst's opinion, the victim had been murdered elsewhere, and his body carried to the garden shed several hours after his demise. The empty whisky bottle and the half-consumed bottle of tablets had been left there to suggest that he had committed suicide.

The rope fibres indicated that the victim could have been killed in a warehouse or factory where rope was either manufactured or used for other purposes. And since there were no fingerprints on either the whisky or the tablet bottles, the killer must have worn gloves.

Mistake number two, Clooney thought grimly. Not only had the killer left the lid of the Co-Proxamol bottle in place, he had overlooked the fact that, if McEvoy *had* committed suicide, his fingerprints would have appeared on both bottles.

Therefore, the killer, presumably a man, was no professional assassin but a rank amateur. More than likely someone who, threatened by McEvoy, had needed to ensure his silence as quickly as possible, which tied in with Zoe Smith's testimony that Liam had bragged about a change of lifestyle to come, hinting that he was into something 'big'. A scenario which smacked of blackmail, in Clooney's experience. And so, as a matter of deduction, the killer must be a person of some substance financially, worth blackmailing. But who?

Further perusal of his case notes recalled to Clooney's mind, his recent visit to The Lamb and Flag – McEvoy's local 'watering hole' – where he had interviewed the landlord, the barmaids, and a cross-section of Liam's regular drinking companions of the bar-parlour, all of whom had stated categorically that he had left the premises that Wednesday evening just before closing time. He'd been 'tanked up', as usual in high spirits, saying that he had a little matter of business to attend to before returning home for a Chinese nosh-up, and his 'missis' would give him hell if he was late.

So presumably, Clooney concluded, the 'little matter of business' McEvoy had mentioned might well have taken place in some vehicle or other parked near The Lamb and Flag? And he must have been confident that the transaction wouldn't take long to complete, in view of that Chinese 'nosh-up' awaiting his return home.

But Liam hadn't returned home that night, for the good and sufficient reason that he had died around midnight, in a factory or warehouse of some kind, his hands tied behind his back, being force-fed whisky and painkilling tablets, the poor devil; and on the following morning, his distraught partner, Zoe Smith, had rung up the police station to report him missing.

Then, Clooney considered, head in hands, had come the murder of Anna Gordino to complicate his enquiries, which, he realised, must have had some strong connection with the murder of Liam McEvoy. Though for the life of him he couldn't see how, at this precise moment in time, unless Anna had either known or guessed the identity of the killer.

Referring to his notes, Clooney cursed inwardly the fact that he had so little to go on. The Berengers' housekeeper, for instance, had admitted to receiving a phonecall from Anna Gordino on the night preceding her murder which, according to Mrs Temple, had been little more than gibberish, ending with Mrs Gordino hanging up the phone abruptly – and no one could prove otherwise.

Moreover, Mrs Temple had an unshakeable alibi for the time of Anna Gordino's murder; so, come to think of it, had Geraldine Frayling – alibis substantiated by Lisl Berenger when his colleagues of the North Yorkshire police had interviewed her in Robin Hood's Bay.

Clooney felt that his choice of female suspects was somewhat limited; a highly respectable old biddy who looked as if butter wouldn't melt in her mouth on one hand and a smart-alec fiction writer on the other, forever turning up in the wrong place at the wrong time, making his life a misery, poking and prying into matters that didn't concern her.

What the hell had she been doing, for instance, at The Anchorage nursing home shortly after the murder of Mr Constantine, and poking round the repository where his goods and chattels were stored? And what about that so-called 'shopping list' she'd discovered in a Sunderland lustre jug, which had now mysteriously gone missing?

Clooney had had good and sufficient reasons for wanting to keep Geraldine under surveillance since the murder of

Anna Gordino. He'd been surprised, to put it mildly, when his team of plain-clothes officers had reported her weekend movements, beginning with her brief conversation with Mrs Temple on the Berengers' doorstep, including her shopping spree in the West End, her puzzling choice of accommodation – not at the Savoy or Claridges, as one might have expected – but at a hamburger caff in the Old Kent Road.

On the other hand, she had met up with a wealthy antiques dealer and his female companion in the Portobello Road the following morning, and had gone with them to an address in Chelsea, later returning to the Old Kent Road, from which address, namely 'Barney's Hamburger Joint', she had emerged, after breakfast, accompanied by a male companion, driving a Golf hatchback.

Food for thought, Clooney pondered silently, thinking ahead to his retirement, come December, wondering what he'd be given by way of a present commensurate with his twenty-five years' service with the Hampstead force; a barometer, most likely, or, with his luck, a dozen silver pastry-forks!

If only he could crack this case, he would at least retire from the force with a modicum of self-respect. How to set about cracking it, however, he hadn't the faintest idea. Nothing seemed to add up. There were literally too many dead ends.

Returning to his case notes, Michael McEvoy's papers were in order, Clooney considered carefully. He had arrived in England when he said he had, with a passport and flight ticket stub from Dublin to Heathrow, to prove his veracity. And, yeah, he had sold the artefact Mr Constantine had given to Liam, at Zoe Smith's request. So what? She'd considered the damn thing unlucky, so he'd sold it to a man in a pub for fifty quid. He'd never seen the man before or since, and he couldn't be sure which pub, being a stranger in this part of the world.

And no, he knew less than nothing about his brother's private affairs. They hadn't been close since Liam came to England to live three years ago. They weren't into letter-writing or phonecalls, though they'd exchanged Christmas cards, and Liam had always sent birthday greetings to their mother and sisters.

Had he and his brother been on good terms? Yeah, sure they had. And when the all-clear was given and Liam's body released for burial, he would accompany the body back to Ireland, at his mother's request. A devout Catholic, she wanted her son interred in the family plot, with a proper church service beforehand, attended by a full complement of aunts, uncles, cousins, in-laws, friends and neighbours, according to Irish tradition.

Clooney got the picture. Booze, food and lamentations; incense and laudation for a loser in life who'd had the misfortune to be murdered in the pursuance of some dodgy deal or other. Almost certainly blackmail. But how to prove that theory?

His interview with the estate agent, Lance Bellingham, had also done little to enhance Clooney's perspective. To all intents and purposes, here was an eminently respectable young business executive, expensively educated, with apparently nothing to hide. Yes, of course he had been instrumental in selling Mr Constantine's property to its present owner. What was wrong with that?

Granted, the property had been in a run-down condition at the time of the sale, but the building was structurally sound, in a sought after neighbourhood, with land attached. Nevertheless, Miss Frayling had insisted on a price reduction of ten thousand pounds in respect of the modernisation of the kitchen area in particular.

Had Mr Constantine objected to the lowering of the initial asking price?

"Well, naturally he grumbled a little at first, as old people

123

are inclined to do if they feel they are being exploited in any way."

"Had Mr Constantine grounds for feeling that he was being exploited?"

"No, not really, after I'd explained to him that he'd be wise to sell the property as quickly as possible rather than let it stand empty indefinitely."

"And he was happy with that?"

"Put it this way, Inspector, he signed the contract." Bellingham had added, somewhat patronisingly, "You must remember that Mr Constantine was a highly intelligent man who realised on which side his bread was buttered."

"I see. And this, despite his stroke?"

"I'm an estate agent, Inspector, not a doctor! All I can say, Mr Constantine appeared to be in full control of his faculties when he signed the contract."

"Yet on the morning of his murder, he was apparently too weak to call out, to summon help?"

"Presumably so. I can only surmise that his condition had worsened considerably prior to his – death."

"Surmise, Mr Bellingham? But surely, as a shareholder in The Anchorage, you must have been fully aware of Mr Constantine's state of health?" A slight pause, then, "You *are* on the board of directors, aren't you?"

"No, Inspector, not any more. I sold my shares to a friend and colleague of mine – a solicitor, Basil Edgerton, twelve months ago, due to pressure of work, when I realised that my apologies for absence far outweighed my attendances at the monthly board meetings."

"Fair enough. Now, tell me, Mr Bellingham, what prompted you to grant Miss Frayling access to Mr Constantine's repository within hours of his murder?"

"Huh?" Caught off-guard by the unexpected question, wondering how the hell the man confronting him had come by his information, Bellingham blustered, "Because she was making a damned nuisance of herself! The fact is, she'd been here to my office earlier that morning, wanting to know the name of Mr Constantine's nursing home. Returning later to tell me he'd been murdered, she demanded to he taken on a look round the repository in search of clues to his murder, knowing that I had a key to the place in my possession . . . And, well, frankly, Inspector, I just wanted rid of her!"

Clooney knew the feeling precisely. He said, "So you took her to the repository? Then what happened?"

"Nothing! She just stared about her, asked what would happen to the old man's belongings now he was dead. I told her they'd be auctioned off, most probably — though most of it was rubbish, in my opinion, which no-one in their right senses would bid for anyway!"

"Now, Mr Bellingham, I want you to be particularly clear and precise about this. Did you happen to notice a scrap of paper that Miss Frayling removed from a Sunderland lustre jug?"

Appearing totally gobsmacked, "I'm sorry, Inspector, I'm not with you," Bellingham demurred. "What scrap of paper? And I wouldn't know a Sunderland lustre jug if I saw one!"

"Thank you, Mr Bellingham," Clooney sighed deeply, "now, if you don't mind, I'd like the address of that solicitor colleague of yours."

"Oh, Basil Edgerton, you mean? Sure thing, I'll write it down for you! Just pray to heaven that Geraldine Frayling hasn't winkled out of him, already, the name of old Constantine's ex-wife, though I wouldn't put it past her. The woman's a menace!"

All things considered, Clooney felt inclined to agree with him. Quitting Bellingham's office, snapping out the address of Basil Edgerton to his driver, Clooney added the estate agent's name to his list of suspects, for the simple reason that he had disliked the man intensely and felt that he was holding something back. In any case, suspecting everyone, however remotely connected with a murder enquiry, came with the job, the often dull procedure of thorough investigation instilled into him throughout the past twenty-five years, that detailed sieving of information which would, given a lucky break or two, lead him eventually to the identity of the killer.

Basil Edgerton proved to be an elderly gentleman, immaculate in grey pinstriped trousers, black alpaca jacket, white silk shirt, Old School tie – Eton or Harrow, Clooney couldn't be sure which – wearing gold-framed spectacles, and what resembled a well-known shredded breakfast cereal on his egg-shaped head, which Clooney correctly assumed to be the remains of a once golden thatch now flattened and spread about as a reminder of the man's hirsute youth, when he had possibly resembled Bubbles or Little Lord Fauntleroy.

Obviously, Edgerton was edgy about Clooney's intrusion into his late client's affairs, but, as the Inspector pointed out to him, this was a murder enquiry, and questions relevant to the death of Mr Constantine must be asked, and answered.

Clooney's first question, "You are, I believe, on the board of directors of The Anchorage Nursing Home?" took Edgerton by surprise.

"Yes, but I fail to see what that has to do with the death of Charles Constantine!"

"Please bear with me, Mr Edgerton," Clooney said calmly, "you, of all people, should know police procedure like the back of your hand. Now, how long had you known Mr Constantine?"

Wetting his lips with his tongue, "Thirty-five years or so," Edgerton replied uneasily.

"What kind of man was he?" Clooney insisted.

"A very clever man. A famous man in his time. A well-known archaeologist. But surely that is a matter of record?"

"Was he a rich man?"

"Not by present day standards, but he came from a reasonably well-to-do family whose financial support enabled him to pursue his chosen career."

"How did you come to meet him?"

Edgerton sighed deeply, "I really don't see . . . Oh, very well then. We were members of the same Lodge. He, Mr Constantine, Charles, had returned to England after a long expedition to the Middle East, with a view to finding a suitable property in which to write his memoirs."

"I see. So am I correct in thinking that a relatively young man intended taking an early retirement? Didn't that strike you as odd?"

"Not at all! Retirement was the last thing he envisaged, I assure you. Indeed, after writing his memoirs, he travelled extensively in India, Russia and South America."

"And yet, as you have already stated, he was not a rich man?"

"I said not by present day standards," Edgerton riposted sharply. "He had money, of course, by way of a legacy following the death of his parents and the sale of the family home in Yorkshire, plus the sale of his memoirs to a well-established publisher, whose name escapes me at the moment."

"So it would be true to say that he was reasonably well-off?" Clooney persisted. "Rich enough, at any rate, to purchase a house in Hampstead and to finance his subsequent trips to India, Russia and South America?"

"Well yes, I suppose so," Edgerton conceded unwillingly.

"And am I right in supposing that, prior to his death, having sold the Hampstead house to its present owner, Miss Geraldine Frayling, for a considerable sum of money, Mr Constantine died a very rich man indeed?"

Edgerton remained silent. Clooney continued relentlessly,

"Now we come to the matter of Mr Constantine's will, the beneficiaries and so on. In other words, who stood to gain by his death? Yourself, perhaps?"

"Most certainly not!" Edgerton's face flushed the colour of boiled beetroot. "That is a monstrous suggestion, which I deeply resent, I might add! The bulk of my late client's estate has been willed to the British Museum, along with various virtually priceless artefacts discovered by him in the heyday of his fame as a world renowned archaeologist."

"All right, Mr Edgerton, no need to get upset, I am simply doing a job here," Clooney reminded him, "attempting to discover why a sick old man was so brutally murdered. There must be a deeply compelling reason why some person unknown wanted him dead! Well, I want to know the name of that person, to bring him to justice, to see him robbed of his freedom for the next thirty years or so!"

He continued less forcefully, "Mr Edgerton, what we have here is a cold-blooded killer responsible for three murders so far, plus an attempted murder! Now, I want from you every scrap of information relevant to the past life of Charles Constantine."

"Very well then, Inspector, I'll do my best to help you in any way possible," Basil Edgerton conceded, sinking into the swivel chair behind his desk. "The fact is, I'm rather tired of being questioned for the time being. There was that overbearing woman yesterday, for instance, wanting to know the name of Mr Constantine's ex-wife."

"And you told her?"

"I *had* to! I'd never have got rid of her otherwise! In any case, she already knew that Charles had been married once, a long time ago, and all she really wanted to know was the name of his wife."

Half closing his eyes, Edgerton murmured, "A woman called Phyllis something or other. I'm sorry, my memory is not what it was. It was, however, a liaison which I never fully understood. You see, to my way of thinking, Inspector, Charles was not the marrying kind."

"I take it, then, that the marriage was not a success?" Clooney persisted. "A seemingly pointless question, perhaps, since there had been a divorce. But I want to know about that marriage, and what caused the breakdown. I take it that you handled the divorce on your client's behalf?"

"Yes, but I'd rather not discuss it, to do so even now would seem a betrayal of Charles' trust in me, the poor old boy."

"I understand, and I respect your feelings, but the fact remains that I need to know the details. What I am trying to establish is the identity of anyone who may have held a grudge against the deceased. His ex-wife, perhaps, or a member of her family?"

"I hardly think so, Inspector. All this happened a long time ago. The chances are that Phyllis Constantine is also dead and gone now."

"You knew her quite well, I imagine?" Clooney probed.

"I met her several times, of course, though quite frankly, Inspector, I did not care for the woman at all. She had a strangely cold and unattractive personality. In my view . . ."

"Please, go on. You were about to say?"

"Simply that I felt she had married Charles not for love, but money, for the kudos attached to being the wife of a world-renowned public figure, and I was not far wrong in that belief. Nor was she content to allow her husband to rest on his laurels. Soon she had inveigled him into further expeditions for the sole purpose of . . . Oh dear, I really shouldn't be saying all this." Mr Edgerton mopped his perspiring brow with a white silk handkerchief.

"Please don't distress yourself. I get the picture," Clooney said grimly. "Mrs Constantine, I take it, was more interested in unearthed rather than buried treasure? Works of art, for instance, going for a song in remote corners of the world, to be shipped back to England and sold, on their return home, for tantamount to a small fortune? I'm right, aren't I?"

Edgerton nodded his head in agreement. "Yes, I'm afraid so. Poor Charles, such an honourable man. I can quite understand why he became reclusive after the divorce. He had been so deeply wounded by his wife's duplicity."

"Duplicity?" Clooney queried, gently for him.

"Oh yes, the dear chap," Edgerton said wistfully, staring into the past. "It came as a dreadful shock to him when Phyllis simply disappeared one day, leaving him a letter saying she no longer wished to live with him – that she had found someone else who cared far more for her than he ever could.

"All I can say is, thank God for that letter which gave Charles his freedom from that ill-fated marriage of his. Well, there you have it, Inspector. Now, if you don't mind, I really don't feel up to answering any more questions."

"Not to worry, Mr Edgerton, you have been most helpful," Clooney assured him, rising to his feet. "I'll see myself out."

Then, as an afterthought, on the threshold of the office, "Just one more thing. You mentioned Mr Constantine's family home in Yorkshire. Can you remember where it was situated?"

Edgerton wrinkled his forehead beneath its shredded wheat adornment. "I'm sorry," he murmured, "I can't remember exactly where. Close to Whitby, as I recall, but I can't be sure."

Clooney's driver almost passed out with astonishment when his boss invited him to a sandwiches and shandy lunch at a nearby pub – his treat! Wonders would never cease, he thought, and why look a gift horse in the mouth?

Twelve

On his way to The Anchorage after lunch, Clooney recalled his recent face-to-face with Geraldine Frayling, when he'd been summoned to the break-in, though nothing had apparently gone missing except a scrap of paper purloined from the Hampstead repository. "And what had she been doing in the repository?" Clooney asked coldly, beginning to wonder if the woman had a death wish.

The story had been told haltingly, with a great deal of backtracking and repetition, including Gerry's visit to the nursing home to see Mr Constantine.

"For what purpose?"

"To find out about the statuette he gave Liam McEvoy."

"What statuette?"

At least he hadn't dragged her down to the 'cop-shop', Gerry thought afterwards, although he had reprimanded her severely about the paper she'd removed from the lustre jug. "But it was only a bit of a shopping list," Gerry said desperately, "not one of the Dead Sea Scrolls."

"Yet someone thought it worthwhile breaking into your premises to remove that list?" he had uttered in a voice like broken glass. "Now, I want to know the precise wording of that list."

When she had told him, "And what about that letter I found opened this morning?" Gerry reminded him. "What kind of a burglar breaks into a house to steal a shopping list and read a letter addressed to me?"

"Who was the letter from?" Clooney insisted.

"From Lisl Berenger, reminding me that I'm due to spend October with her and Maurice in Robin Hood's Bay, when I've finished my book."

"Is that all?"

"Well, take a look for yourself, if you don't believe me," Gerry said, knowing he would anyway.

At The Anchorage, "I've told you all I know," the matron said shakily. "There's nothing I can possibly add to my previous statement. This isn't fair, Inspector! I have a difficult job to do here, now I'm beginning to feel like a criminal. Word gets around, you know. Soon, I imagine, the governing body will tell me that my services are no longer required. In plain language, I'll be fired!"

"No need to distress yourself unduly, Miss Smithson," Clooney said calmly. "It appears likely that Mr Constantine met his death at the hands of an intruder posing as a doctor, carrying a medical bag and wearing a false identification label in his lapel, in the early hours of the morning when, as you have already stated, the reception area is usually unmanned, and the night staff are occupied with their duties in other parts of the building.

"In any event, the intruder made his way to Mr Constantine's room unseen and unchallenged, and to the best of our knowledge and belief, he left the building by means of the second floor fire-escape."

"I see," the matron said sharply, "so what do you want from me?" They were seated in her igloo of an office, Miss Smithson on the edge of her chair, looking pale and strained, obviously on the defensive, worried sick about losing her job.

Taking his time, flicking open his notebook, Clooney said, "I understand that Mr Constantine was brought here following a stroke which had impaired his power of movement to a great extent, although he was mentally alert enough, at the time, to agree and to sign a contract relevant to the sale of his property to its present owner?"

"If you say so, Inspector, though I knew nothing whatever about his private affairs."

"Quite so, Miss Smithson. That is beside the point at the moment. What concerns me is the state of Mr Constantine's health at the time of his murder."

Up in arms, Miss Smithson said fiercely, "Oh, I get it! You're trying to point the finger at me, aren't you? Well, all I can say is, due to round the clock nursing, for which *I* was responsible, the old man was showing definite signs of improvement!"

"In what way?" Clooney asked.

The matron sniffed audibly, "Well, he'd started being awkward for one thing, complaining if the food was not to his liking, wanting things that were bad for him – eggs in particular."

"*Eggs*?" Clooney frowned, recalling the old man's shopping list which had mysteriously gone missing from Geraldine Frayling's kitchen table.

"Yes, *eggs*! Apparently he had a great fondness for them, which were certainly not on his diet sheet. Being so high in cholesterol, they were absolutely forbidden!"

Rising to her feet, "Now, if you'll excuse me, Inspector, I have important work to do in respect of the other patients in my care. Mr Constantine, God rest him, was not the only one, remember!"

"He was the only one to have been murdered," Clooney said grimly.

Sitting at her typewriter one morning a couple of weeks later Gerry thought that Philip Antrobus and his gang had done great things with her garden.

Once upon a time she hadn't been able to see the wood for the leaves, now she couldn't see the leaves for the wood.

133

Pollarded wasn't in it. At least a potential killer would not be tempted to lurk on property where the trees resembled paintbrushes, and cunningly placed spotlights illuminated the paths when darkness fell.

When the rickety garden shed had been fingerprinted and photographed from every angle both inside and out after the vandalism episode, she had given Antrobus the go-ahead to get rid of it once and for all, had a new shed erected in a less conspicuous part of the garden, and the old site grassed over.

Now she missed intensely those glo-jacketed workmen flitting among the trees, the buzzing of the chainsaws, the thumping of the donkey-engine, just as she missed the presence of Anna Gordino in the kitchen, doing her Edith Piaf impersonation.

Apparently, Anna's husband Luigi had taken some finding, having sold his trattoria and moved away from Piedmont to take up residence with a rich, elderly widow in Siena once Anna had quit his field of play. Clooney had, at least, had the courtesy to inform Gerry that Signor Gordino had agreed to undertake his late wife's funeral arrangements, thankfully in France, not Italy – arrangements sponsored, no doubt, by the rich widow.

"Thank you for telling me, Inspector," Gerry said slowly, appreciatively. "I'd like to send flowers . . ."

"The funeral took place last week," Clooney said briefly.

"I see." Close to tears, Gerry replaced the receiver. That afternoon, she had bought a huge bunch of red roses in memory of Anna, which she'd left in the porch of the Catholic church where Anna had worshipped her Maker, as regularly as clockwork, every Sunday morning between eight and nine a.m., before returning home to The Eyrie to begin breakfast: lots of fragrant coffee, fluffy omelettes, and hot buttered toast.

But life went on. Gerry was now into the final editing of

The Blasted Heath; yet her spirits were at a low ebb for some unknown reason.

Of course she was looking forward to her holiday in Robin Hood's Bay with the Berengers, she told herself severely. On the other hand, she'd hate being parted from Bill Bentine for a whole month, though he, more than likely, would be glad to relinquish his 'guard dog' duties for a while, and to arrange, once her back was turned, a candlelit dinner for two with one of his blonde, bimbo girlfriends, as a prelude to a night of passion beneath a duvet in that bachelor pad of his. She had never crossed the threshold of his bachelor pad, Goddammit, but he was bound to have a bed and a duvet, wasn't he?

She had really slogged her guts out to finish *The Blasted Heath* on time. When Bill arrived on her doorstep the last evening in September, hefting his usual overnight gear and a bottle of wine, Gerry said primly, "Well, here it is, the completed manuscript of *The Blasted Heath*, and I hope you're satisfied!"

"Satisfied? I'm mystified," Bill confessed, attempting to hold his overnight bag with one hand, the bottle of wine and the manuscript with the other. "Why are you so uptight all of a sudden? Have I done or said something to upset you – by remote control, perhaps?"

"I'm tired," she said defensively, "and I've a lot on my mind at the moment."

"Just as well you're off on holiday tomorrow, then," Bill said mildly, going through to the kitchen. "What time are you leaving, by the way?"

"As early as possible." He wants rid of me, she thought. He can't wait to see the back of me. And he hadn't even bothered to glance at her manuscript.

Women, Bill thought, glancing in dismay at the open, empty refrigerator, and the puddle beneath it. He'd never begin to understand them if he lived to be a hundred, so why waste time trying?

"I'm defrosting the fridge," Gerry said, stating the obvious. "Just one more mess for me to clear up before morning!"

"Not to worry, I'll help," Bill said cheerfully. "Er – what are we having for supper?"

"I couldn't care less! I'm not hungry!"

Oh Lord, Bill thought, it's the manuscript. She's mad because I haven't mentioned it. Not that she'd given him much of a chance, bunging it at him the way she had before he'd had time to close the front door behind him. So that was it? Of course.

He said engagingly, "I'm really looking forward to settling down with Virginia Vale at bedtime."

"I'll just bet you are," Gerry said scathingly, heading towards the stairs. "Now, if you'll excuse me, I'm going to take a long, hot bath, and have an early night!"

"Like hell you are," Bill said sharply, feeling like John Wayne. "You're going to sit down, have a glass of Chardonnay, relax, and tell me what the hell's got into you. In case you've forgotten, this is our last evening together for a whole month. I'd imagined a nice relaxed dinner for two, a word or two of civilised conversation, not you going off in a huff and me swabbing the kitchen floor in the early hours of the morning!"

Sitting down abruptly, she said tearfully, "The truth is, I don't really want to go away at all."

"Why ever not?" Bill asked, opening the wine. "I thought you were looking forward to it." He added tenderly, "Look, love, you'll feel much better when you're on your way – away from this house and its bad memories of the past few weeks. No wonder you're tired out after all you've been through recently, quite apart from working like the devil to get your book finished on time, which I knew you would – being the dedicated, professional writer that you are."

Blinking away her tears, Gerry gasped, "Oh, Bill, do you really mean that?"

"Of course I do. Now, I'm bloody hungry, even if you're not. So shall I pop down to the village for Chinese takeaway or a parcel of fish and chips?"

"No need. There's plenty of tinned stuff in the cupboards," she reminded him.

Bill said, "OK, leave me to see to the grub. Now you have your bath, powder your nose and comb your hair. Come down when you're ready. All right?"

When Gerry ventured downstairs an hour later, wearing a long skirt, black tank-top, lots of dangling gold jewellery, with her newly-washed hair framing her face, she could scarcely believe her eyes.

Bill had set the kitchen table with a checked red and white cloth, red paper napkins and a red candle in a silver holder. There was tinned salmon in a cut glass dish, accompanied with tinned new potatoes and a hard-boiled eggs and tomato salad. He had swabbed up the little pool of water near the fridge, and was standing near the table, about to light the candle, when she came into the room. "Looking like a French waiter in a Paris bistro," he remarked, pouring more wine when they were seated. "Feeling better now?"

"Much better. Thanks, Bill."

Later, in the drawing room, Bill asked, "Does the admirable Clooney know you're going on holiday?"

"Yes, I told him on the phone this morning, otherwise he'd have had Interpol on my trail, knowing him."

"Have you finished your packing?"

"There wasn't much to pack. I'll be dressing down, not up, according to Maurice's instructions."

"It's a long journey by road," Bill remarked. "Sure you'll be up to it in one fell swoop?"

"I think so. In any case I'll be stopping now and then for coffee and a bite to eat, and I'm not due in Robin Hood's Bay till around five in the afternoon. Maurice will be there in the carpark to meet me . . ." Her voice trailed away, and she shivered slightly.

Bill frowned, "What's wrong, Gerry? Is there something you're not telling me?" Taking the bull by the horns, he continued, "You've been acting a bit strangely all evening."

"I'm not sure. Oh don't get me wrong, I like Lisl and Maurice enormously, it's just that they seem connected somehow with what's happened here recently."

"Go on."

"Well, Cassie and Tim Bowen are Maurice's niece and nephew, Mrs Temple is their housekeeper, and it was they who introduced me to Christian Sommer in the first place. All a bit close to home, don't you think?"

"The thought had occurred," Bill admitted. "So why not cancel the visit? Just send them a telegram saying you've changed your mind at the last minute."

"No, I couldn't possibly do that."

"Why not?"

"Because they've been good to me, especially Maurice, taking me under their wing they way they did when I came here to live, introducing me to their circle of friends. Besides, it isn't my style to let people down at the last minute without a darned good reason, and, come November, we'll still be neighbours. Can you imagine how awkward it would be if we were no longer friends?"

"Yes, of course I can, and you are absolutely right," Bill said wholeheartedly. "So why not go away and enjoy yourself for a change? At least you won't be looking over your shoulder every minute, in fear for your life, listening for footsteps on the fire-escape. Moreover, if Clooney has his buttons sewn on correctly, he'll have the killer behind bars come Christmas!"

He added, tongue-in-cheek, "What shall we have for Christmas lunch, by the way? Roast duck and peas?"

Up at the crack of dawn next morning, Bill helped Gerry downstairs with her luggage, one small suitcase, an overnight bag, a pair of boots and an old anorak, which he stowed away in the boot of her car.

When she was safely settled in the driver's seat, with a road map on the passenger seat beside her, "Now, be sure to drive carefully," Bill advised her through the open window. "Be sure to keep in touch. Phone me if you need help. In other words, whistle and I'll come, my lass!"

"You mean like 'These Foolish Things'?"

"Huh? Well, whatever turns you on."

"You whistle it all the time, in the bathroom."

"Do I?"

"'Bye, Bill."

"'Bye, Gerry! Take good care of yourself."

"Not to worry, I'll be fine, just fine!"

Famous last words! Drawing away from the kerb, waving Bill goodbye, and heading the Mini north, in the general direction of a remote fishing village called Robin Hood's Bay, had Gerry realised that she was about to drive headlong into danger, she might well have cancelled the trip after all.

Thirteen

The day was fine and clear, crisp and sunny. The outskirts of London behind her, the M11 motorway ahead of her, Gerry began to relax, glad of a change of scenery, stopping now and then for coffee, spotting former titles of hers in the service stations' book racks, feeling grateful to Virginia Vale for the good things in life which she had made possible – a fine house, financial security, friendship.

It would be nice, she thought, to spend time with Maurice and Lisl, to breathe in salt air, feel sand beneath her shoes, dabble in rock-pools, explore the North Yorkshire country-side, a vast area of natural, unspoiled beauty according to the handbook tucked inside the glove compartment – rich in folklore, picturesque villages, smugglers' haunts, country pubs and with strong artistic and literary connections.

Bram Stoker, for instance, had based his classic thriller *Dracula* in the seaport of Whitby, and Leo Walmsley, author of *Turn of the Tide*, had once lived in Robin Hood's Bay, and there had been an artists' colony, including as a member Laura Knight, centred in the fishing village of Sleights, scarcely a stone's throw away from Robin Hood's Bay.

So why the hell had she felt so reluctant, initially, to embark on this journey, Gerry wondered. The answer came pat. Deep down, she possessed little or no confidence in herself as a person. Her only confidence lay in her writing, those blissful hours spent alone at her typewriter when she had no need to care a damn about her appearance, as long as her publishers continued to stump up five figure advances for her latest brainchild and the movie and TV moguls were prepared to stump up considerably more for the film and television rights to the latest exploits of her alter ego, Virginia Vale.

Bill Bentine, bless him, Gerry thought, had guided her every inch of the way so far, and she'd miss him like crazy during the month ahead. At which point, as the weather changed imperceptibly mid afternoon, the sky darkened and the first spots of rain hit the windscreen, she wondered what, if any difference at all, the influx of another huge amount of capital would make to her lifestyle? She didn't want more money. She wanted – love.

Crossing the moors towards her Robin Hood's Bay carpark destination, her pre-arranged meeting with Maurice at five o'clock that afternoon, the weather worsened. The sky became inky black, rain came down like stair-rods, thunder rumbled, and lightning, like pitchforks from hell, split the sky over the sea on the dimly discerned horizon, filling Gerry with a deep sense of foreboding, loneliness and vulnerability, as if the world had shrunk suddenly to the size of her little red car.

Signposts were hard to read, the wipers could scarcely cope with the downpour, the countryside was wild and rugged, somehow threatening and unfriendly with the sunlight gone and the moors rolling away to low, heather clad hills, sheep-dotted and edged in places with crumbling dry stone walls. Unfamiliar scenery at best, stygian at worst, extremely frightening and worrying in her present state of fatigue towards the end of a long journey.

Now her thoughts were centred on getting to the carpark on time for fear of Maurice having to wait longer than necessary in the swiftly falling rain. Then, to her relief, she came to a fork in the road and a signpost pointing the way to Robin Hood's Bay. Clusters of houses, some with lighted windows piercing the gloom, sped by. A long, steeply curving hill would down between tiny spaced out shops, farm gates, stone built cottages and red brick villas, at the bottom of which lay a flat area of more closely integrated villas interspersed with a scattering of shops, hotels and boarding-houses. And, glory be, the carpark! – devoid of vehicles – on which stood the forlorn figure of a man beneath a brightly coloured golf umbrella.

Stumbling from the car, so stiff she could scarcely stand upright for a moment, "Maurice," she called out to him. "I'm here! I made it!" She was expecting a warm hug and a kiss, his usual form of greeting, but the man beneath the umbrella bore little or no resemblance to the ebullient human being she had said goodnight to on her doorstep just over a month ago. This grey-faced man with sunken eyes seemed like a stranger to her now, apart from his beard and mane of greying hair, wet with rain.

With a clutch of fear at her heart, "What is it, Maurice?" Gerry asked. "Are you ill?"

Catching the urgency of her question, attempting a smile, "No, of course not," he said, brushing her cheek with his lips. "At least nothing to worry about, just a bit of a tummy bug, that's all. Now, the sooner we're home and dry, the better. Let me give you a hand with your luggage." He winced slightly with pain as he spoke. Then, "It isn't far. I'll lead the way, shall I?"

Steps and a narrow roadway plunged down between tiers of stone built cottages which appeared to have sprung, mushroom-like, from the ground beneath. Lighted windows shone through the rain, and there appeared to be a satisfactory number of tea-rooms, Gerry noticed, one of which abutted a narrow stone bridge with a trickle of running water beneath. All very 'Brigadoon', she thought approvingly, following in Maurice's footsteps and sheltering beneath his golf umbrella which he had handed to her on the carpark, since his hands were now fully occupied with her suitcase and overnight bag.

Then, abruptly veering left from the main street, he led the way unerringly through a maze of narrow passageways opening unexpectedly into small open areas hemmed about with tiny, two-up, two-down cottages with brightly-painted front doors and colourful window-boxes, grouped around miniature cobbled squares of Lilliputian dimensions.

A final right turn, then "Here we are," Maurice announced wearily, seemingly exhausted by the force of the storm and the weight of his oilskin clothing. Aghast, Gerry stared in horror at the door-knocker. A malevolent face crowned with horns. The face of a devil.

This was a building in decided contrast to the homely cottages seen so far. Of Georgian design, the flight of steps led to a door flanked by tall, twelve-paned windows, and the original russet brickwork wantonly daubed with layer on layers of bitumen, presumably as a safeguard against inclement weather. The neighbouring houses seemed dwarfed by its dimensions, its sheer ugliness, to Gerry's way of thinking.

Aware of a sinking feeling in the pit of her stomach, which she mentally likened to the way a cafétière must feel with its plunger depressed, she entered a panelled hall, feeling as if she had strayed into the pages of an Edgar Allan Poe novel. She stood there, shivering, dripping moisture on to rug-strewn floorboards, seeing, through intermittent flashes of lightning, a broad oak staircase rising to the upper landings, a long passageway leading presumably to the kitchen quarters, at the far end of which she discerned a faint glow of light from a slightly open door . . .

"For Christ's sake, where *is* everyone?" Maurice called out, stumbling forward to switch on a lamp on an oak chest at the foot of the stairs, wincing with pain as he did so. "Where's Lisl? I felt sure she'd be here to meet us!"

A figure emerged from the passage leading to the kitchen quarters, a thin-lipped woman with dyed brown hair, her eyes like steel behind her gold-framed glasses, as she glanced dismissively in Gerry's direction.

"Madam is upstairs in the studio, sir," Anita Temple said coolly, "do you wish me to call her?"

There was no need. Suddenly Lisl appeared at the head of the stairs, smiling, hands outspread in welcome, apologising profusely for her tardiness.

Descending swiftly to the hall, "Oh, Gerry darling," she cried, kissing her warmly on the cheek, "it's wonderful to see you again. Oh, but you must be dying to get out of those wet things. Why not come up to your room, then have a warm, relaxing bath before supper?"

"Sounds fine to me," Gerry said gratefully, following Lisl to the upper landing, and picking up her luggage which Maurice had dumped in the hall before heading towards a passage to the right of the stairs, taking with him the dripping golf umbrella.

As though reading Gerry's mind, Lisl said, "He'll be hanging up his oilskins in the conservatory to dry. I do hope the poor darling hasn't caught a chill. I offered to meet you myself, but he wouldn't hear of it. Well, you know what he's like."

Feeling guilty, Gerry murmured, "He told me he'd caught a tummy bug," hoping she hadn't added to his troubles in that department, following her hostess along a panelled passage to a door at the far end of it. "He certainly doesn't look well. What does the doctor say?"

"Doctor? My dear girl, he wouldn't hear of my sending for the local GP, whom he refers to as 'that quack'! He simply went to the chemist for some proprietary brand of medicine which hasn't so far done him an atom of good, the silly man," Lisl said impatiently. Then, "Well, here we are, this is your room," she continued, "I do hope you'll like it." She switched on the lights as she spoke. "I've had a fire lit for you, so you'll be able to dry your wet things and get thoroughly warmed through before supper. The bathroom's the second door on the right on the landing, next to Mrs Temple's room. Maurice and I are on the floor above."

"It's a very big house," Gerry ventured, staring about her, taking in at a glance the tester bed, the massive walnut wardrobe, matching dressing table and chest of drawers, the brightly glowing fire in the narrow Georgian fireplace, the tall sash-window occupying most of the wall space opposite the bed. "Much bigger than I'd imagined."

"Really?" Lisl appeared amused. "Rather too big for two people, you mean? But Maurice and I are people who need space, lots of it. The main reason why the house appealed to us so much in the first place, apart from its situation and the views from the rear windows."

Holding out her hand, "Come and look, Gerry dear, and you'll see what I mean," Lisl said persuasively. "Isn't it absolutely magnificent?"

Crossing obediently to the window, Gerry recoiled slightly at the sight of a heaving waste of water lit by a lurid sky beyond a rocky promontory on which the house seemed poised above a sheer drop, teetering on the edge of a precipice, to put it mildly.

What would happen, Gerry thought, if, one day, that precipice began to crumble? Cold beads of perspiration began to break out on her forehead.

Obviously, no such cataclysmic thought had entered

Lisl's mind, Gerry realised as, turning away from the window, she discerned an expression of intense and utter joy on the woman's face. She had never really seen Lisl this way before, as a kind of Valkyrie riding a storm with wings unfurled . . .

Oh God, she thought, there she went again, letting her imagination run riot, as usual.

Possibly she'd feel better after a nice hot bath, a change of clothing, and summat to eat inside her? Possibly, though she doubted it. For one thing, her London coiffure was ruined beyond redemption, and she'd forgotten to pack her styling mousse and can of firm hold lacquer.

Going downstairs at seven, hopefully in time for supper, Gerry thought that possibly it was the panelling that depressed her – there was so much of it. Or could it be the presence of Anita Temple in the house, the housekeeper's scarcely veiled hostility towards her when they had come face-to-face in the hall on her arrival – as if the ghost of Anna Gordino hovered between them, and that mysterious phonecall of Anna's to Mrs Temple on the night preceding her murder.

Drawn by the sound of voices, Gerry entered the drawing room to discover Lisl sitting near the fire, sipping a glass of wine. Maurice was standing on the hearthrug, with his back to it, nursing a glass of whisky, looking slightly better than he had done earlier.

"Ah, Gerry love," he smiled faintly, "what'll it be? G and T, whisky, brandy, sherry?"

"Brandy, please." She didn't care for the stuff, but it might just steady her nerves and, frankly, her nerves appeared to require a great deal of steadying at this moment in time, amidst so much panelling, and with rain beating steadily against the windowpanes, the odd growl of thunder now and then, accompanied by jagged flashes

146

of intermittent lightning, as if the storm was waiting in the wings to return, in full force, when its grumblings and mutterings were over and done with.

At seven thirty, Mrs Temple entered the room to announce that supper was ready.

The woman's presence in the house had come as an unpleasant surprise to Gerry, who had imagined her safely stowed away in Hampstead, which had been the initial suggestion that night on the terrace when Lisl said that Anna could stay with her housekeeper for the month of October.

But circumstances altered cases. Lisl may well have felt reluctant to leave Mrs Temple alone in the Hampstead house in view of what had befallen poor Anna, Gerry surmised. The odd thing was that so far no one had referred to Anna's untimely end. A word of sympathy from Lisl would not have come amiss when they were upstairs together, or was she being too sensitive? Obviously Lisl's thought had been centred on her husband's ill-health, with good reason. Despite Maurice's brave attempt to appear normal, Gerry knew, deep down, that he was a very sick man indeed: a fact betrayed by his thinness and pallor, the slight shaking of his hands as he had poured and handed her the glass of brandy.

Now he seemed reluctant to enter the dining room, and Gerry guessed why. In his state, the very thought of food would revolt him, let alone the smell of it. He should be in bed – preferably a hospital bed – undergoing tests to find out what was wrong with him.

Gerry also felt reluctant to enter the dining room. The previous owners, Georgians, sure had a penchant for panelling, she thought, and the olive green paintwork didn't do much to enliven the atmosphere. Green velvet curtains had been drawn against the darkness of the world outside. Unfortunately, the world inside was just as gloomy by candlelight. All very well in their way, candles, and in keeping with the age of the house, but strangely depressing just the same, in no way comparable to brass-chimneyed oil lamps of the Victorian era, with red glass shades and jingling cut glass lustres to enhance the scene. And this scene, in Gerry's opinion, needed some enhancing.

Despite her recent hot bath and the fire in her bedroom, she still felt far from relaxed; decidedly chilly if the truth were told. A stranger in the alien atmosphere of this frankly awful house, with its long, narrow passageways, inhibitingly tall windows, bitumen-larded façade, and its mind-boggling proximity to the cliff face beneath, on which it stood poised like a bird of ill-omen. But perhaps she was just 'seeing through a glass darkly' right now, she thought, taking her place at the dining table opposite Lisl, with Maurice, ashen-faced, in the carver chair at the head of table. He was about to open a bottle of claret to complement the beef-olives, tureens of potatoes and green vegetables the housekeeper had brought through from the kitchen and set before him to serve, as head of the household, apparently insensitive to the poor man's revulsion towards even the faintest whiff of hot, rich food in his present poorly condition.

Her dander beginning to rise, what the hell was Lisl thinking about, Gerry wondered, to even contemplate serving so rich a meal to a man with a stomach problem? Then Mrs Temple reappeared bearing a tiny portion of grilled plaice, parsley sauce, lemon wedges plus brown bread and butter to 'set before the king', and Lisl was advising him tenderly to eat as much of it as he could, and leave the rest.

"I'm not all that hungry," he protested mildly.

"Perhaps not, but you must eat something to keep your strength up," Lisl murmured concernedly. "Try just a mouthful or two, my darling. Then off to bed with you."

A slight pause, then, "We could all do with an early night, I'm sure; Gerry in particular after her long, exhausting journey, the storm and all. Isn't that so, Gerry dear?"

"Well, yes, now you come to mention it," Gerry concurred, having swallowed a mouthful or two of beef-olive, mashed potatoes and broccoli and thinking there was nothing she'd like better right now than to be alone in her room, to sleep till the cows came home. She felt so tired all of a sudden, far too tired to think clearly any more.

Now Lisl was saying, at the foot of the stairs, that she had switched on her electric blanket earlier that afternoon, to take the chill from her bed – one of those thermostatically-controlled blankets to provide an even temperature throughout the night. "After all," she added, bidding her guest a fond goodnight, "it's considerably colder up here than in London, and that wretched storm hasn't helped any to dispel the image of 'the frozen north', I imagine?"

Making ready for bed, she thought of Bill and wondered what he was doing right now? Better not to know the answer, perhaps?

Aware of a strange rushing and thundering sound in her ears, Oh Lord, she thought, not blood pressure at her age? She wouldn't be surprised, though, considering the stress factor of the past weeks, and the storm hadn't helped any. Then, with a sweet feeling of relief, she realised it was the sea she was hearing, an unaccustomed sound for a city girl. She hadn't seen much of the sea before, except on day excursions to Brighton, with her parents, as a child, when her ma and da had supped beer most of the time, and she had played the slot machines in a seafront arcade.

Lying in bed, watching the flickering dance of firelight on the ceiling, she thought about what a strange day this had been. At least her damp clothing – trousers, sweater and anorak, which she had placed in front of the fire before supper, making certain the fireguard was in place – would be dry by morning. Hopefully a fine morning.

Lisl had told her charmingly not to hurry down to breakfast if she didn't feel like it. Maurice would probably have his in bed, though they usually ate together in the conservatory adjacent to the kitchen, if he felt up to it.

Closing her eyes, drifting off to sleep, Gerry imagined poached eggs on toast, crisply fried bacon, sausages and mushrooms, the fragrant aroma of freshly-ground coffee . . .

In the early hours, she awoke suddenly to the feeling that she was being roasted alive. Sitting bolt upright, wet with perspiration, hurriedly switching on the bedside lamp, she saw, with horror, that the fireguard had been moved to one side and the garments she had spread out near the hearth to dry were now smouldering, filling the atmosphere with clouds of smoke.

Coughing and spluttering, eyes streaming, acting instinctively, she leapt out of bed, laid hold of a sheepskin rug and dragged it towards the fireplace to smother the incipient blaze, the tongues of fire already licking greedily at the fibre filling of her anorak.

But how could the fire have started? Who had moved the fireguard, and why were her pyjamas clinging to her like lost souls? Why had she awoken in a mucky sweat, when Lisl had assured her that she had set the thermostat of the electric blanket at low? Now the blanket control had been switched to high, Gerry registered bemusedly, by, presumably, the person who had removed the fireguard. But *who*, and *why*? Obviously someone insane, a pyromaniac whose actions might well have razed Black Gull House to the ground had she, Gerry, not woken up when she did, to bring the fire under control in its initial stages.

Shaken to the core, still suffering the effects of smoke

inhalation, she flung open the window to breathe in lungfuls of fresh sea air, wondering if she should alert the household. But what would be the point or purpose now that the trauma was over?

Too scared to go back to bed in case the fire flared up again, she spent the remaining hours till daylight in a chair near the open window, wishing like hell that her 'watchdog', Bill Bentine, was here with her now, to take care of her.

Fourteen

Lisl appeared shocked. Inspecting the damage, she asked incredulously, "My dear Gerry, how could such a dreadful thing have happened?"

"I'm sorry about your sheepskin rug," Gerry murmured apologetically.

"Forget about the rug! It's *you* I'm concerned about. What a blessing you woke up in time."

"I mightn't have done if I hadn't been so hot. Thank God the blanket was on at full blast, otherwise . . ."

"At full blast?" Lisl interrupted, frowning. "But it was on at low! It was meant to take the chill from the bed, not to roast you to death. I must have a word with Mrs Temple about this! I'll call her right away!"

"Please don't bother. It really isn't important," Gerry said. The last thing she needed right now was a confrontation with the steely-eyed housekeeper.

"Not important that the entire house might have gone up in smoke? You say that the fireguard had been moved to one side when you tackled the blaze?"

"Well, yes, but it wasn't a blaze exactly. There was more smoke than fire, and I could have moved the fireguard myself – in the heat of the moment. It all happened so fast, you see?"

"Even so, I mean to get to the bottom of the matter! Ah, there you are, Mrs Temple. Now I want you to tell me exactly what you did up here during supper, last night."

The woman's eyelids flickered momentarily, then, "I turned down the bed and mended the fire, as instructed," she said prissily.

"Did you touch the electric blanket?"

"Why yes, I did," the housekeeper admitted. "I switched it to high, the weather being so chilly on account of the storm."

"I see, and what about the fire? When you had mended it, what did you do then?"

"I tidied the hearth and replaced the fireguard," Mrs Temple said smoothly. "A natural precaution since Miss Frayling's damp clothing was drying out at the time."

"You are absolutely sure about that?" Lisl insisted.

The woman bridled slightly. "Absolutely sure," she said, studiously avoiding Gerry's eyes, not even wanting to know the reason for all the questions, which seemed decidedly odd to Gerry's way of thinking. But perhaps she didn't need to ask? Perhaps she already knew?

There had been four people beneath the roof of Black Gull House, last night. Herself, Lisl, Maurice, and Mrs Temple, so who was the obvious culprit, the mischief-maker among them? It didn't take a *Mastermind* finalist to work out the answer to that question, Gerry thought darkly.

Now Lisl was saying that she and Miss Frayling would be down soon for breakfast in the conservatory: just muesli, toast and coffee, unless Miss Frayling wanted something more substantial.

"No, muesli and toast will be just fine," Gerry lied through her teeth, thinking she could murder a gammon rasher and a couple of fried eggs, her stomach at half-mast with hunger.

At least the storm had grumbled itself away, thank God, the autumn sunshine had returned to lighten the atmosphere of Black Gull House, and the cluttered conservatory, overlooking the sea, was far more to her liking than the sombrely-panelled dining room with its plethora of candles. Quite a jolly little room, in fact, and the sea, beyond its windows, seemed almost friendly today.

Glancing about her, over breakfast, Gerry noticed that the sunny annexe contained several tins of emulsion paint, a paste-board and trestle, fishing tackle, a couple of unopened tea chests, and a clothes horse spread with tea towels, dish cloths and various items of underwear, newly washed, set in a corner of the room.

"Mrs Temple hangs the hand washing in here to dry," Lisl explained. "The door over there leads through to the kitchen."

"Oh? And where does that other door lead to?" Gerry enquired innocently, gazing in fascination at a solid iron-barred construction half hidden behind a welter of oilskins and anoraks, puzzled by the strength of the door and the size of its lock.

"Oh, *that*?" Lisl shrugged her shoulders dismissively. "The cellar. A no-go area as far as Maurice and I are concerned. It's quite horrid, really, with steep stone steps leading down to it. We decided to lock it up and forget about it. In any case, we have no use for it."

After breakfast, Lisl took Gerry upstairs to show her the studio, a long attic room occupying the entire upper area of the house, lit with an imposingly tall and handsome glass window overlooking the whole of Robin Hood's Bay to the far horizon, and the coast-line to the north and south as far as the eye could see.

Smiling indulgently at Gerry's expression of amazement as she looked about her, "It is a surprising room, isn't it?" Lisl asked. "Now you'll understand why Maurice and I wanted Black Gull House so much, not just as a short-stay holiday home but something more permanent?"

"Yes," Gerry said, suitably impressed at the sheer size of

the room and all it contained. Lisl's easel and canvases near the overpoweringly large area of glass panes overlooking the sea; a long, rough wooden workbench crowded with her painting gear; earthenware jars of paint brushes; bottles of turpentine; paint pots and palette knives; crayons and sticks of charcoal; various paint-rags, adjacent to a high stool festooned with a hastily cast aside artist's smock, facing the easel, on which rested a canvas, depicting a storm at sea, if Gerry was not much mistaken, judging by the dramatic whorls of colour.

So this was the reason why Lisl had been up here in the studio, last evening, Gerry surmised. Why she had flown down the stairs in such a hurry, discarding her smock as she hastened to the hall, hands outstretched, to bid her a belated welcome to Black Gull House?

"If you're thinking what I imagine you're thinking," Lisl said, tongue-in-cheek, "you are perfectly right. It was a temptation impossible to resist, I'm afraid, attempting to capture the might and majesty of a storm at sea by means of paint on canvas. That I failed so miserably to do so reflects my shortcomings as an artist, wouldn't you say, rather than any shortcoming on the part of Mother Nature?"

"I'm not really qualified to say one way or the other," Gerry said warily, not wanting to get into a discussion on art, about which she knew next to nothing. She was far more interested in the businesslike desk occupying centre stage, on which stood a word processor, a stack of reference books, folders and a colourful pottery jar containing a variety of pens and sticks of Stabilo Boss.

"Maurice is researching a new book," Lisl said, turning away from the easel. "He was working quite happily until he took ill, which reminds me, I must go down to him, find out if there's anything he wants. Then perhaps you'd like me to show you the sights, such as they are. I daresay Mrs Temple will want me to do some shopping."

"Yes, fine." It would be great to get away from the house for a while, Gerry thought, to get some fresh sea air into her lungs.

There was no harbour as such, just a coble landing at the foot of two parallel streets. The tide was out, the beach fairly deserted apart from a few fishermen, and people walking their dogs. It was, however, littered with the detritus of yesterday's storm: strangely convoluted items of driftwood, lobster pots cast adrift from their moorings, mounds of bladderwrack and long strands of ribbon-like seaweed, a dead seagull.

Black Gull House was clearly visible, poised on its lofty promontory, the cliffs beneath honeycombed with narrow inlets, reminders of the smuggling activity of old, Gerry thought, when contraband would be brought ashore under the cover of darkness and manhandled up the cliffs to secret and secure hiding places deep inside the caverns beyond those inlets.

How romantic it seemed, viewed from the safe distance of time, the wash of the waves against the sides of the boats rowing in the contraband from sailing ships anchored in the bay: 'Watch the wall, my darling, while the gentlemen go by', and all that jazz. 'Brandy for the parson, baccy for the clerk'; this was what came of reading *Doctor Syn* at an impressionable age, she reckoned to herself.

Walking along beside her, looking trim and self-contained in black slacks, sweater and a scarlet body-warmer, with not a hair out of place, Lisl said thoughtfully, "About what happened last night, I'm sure there's a straightforward explanation. Mrs Temple has been with us for some time now, and we've found her most reliable and trustworthy. By the way, we, Maurice and I, were devasted by the death of Mrs Gordino. I fully intended to contact you, but our phone was out of order at the time; we'd only just arrived here, and well, you know how it is? We were so busy unpacking, then the police arrived on the scene wanting to check up on your – alibi – which, thank God, I was able to confirm, not that it had even occurred to me that you would need an alibi in connection with poor Anna's . . . murder." She shivered slightly. "It all seemed so bizarre, so unreal, somehow."

"I know the feeling," Gerry said grimly. "I was there at the time, undergoing police questioning, being made to feel like a criminal."

"Oh, Gerry my dear, I'm so sorry," Lisl murmured bleakly. "What I fail to understand is why Mrs Gordino was murdered in so brutal a fashion."

Drawing in a deep breath, grasping the nettle danger, "Perhaps you'd better ask Mrs Temple that question," Gerry replied, sick and tired of beating about the bush. "Since Anna talked to her on the phone the night before her murder, telling her that she intended leaving for Paris early next morning!"

"I know all about that," Lisl replied quickly. "Mrs Temple was very upset. She rang me at once to express her disquiet at what had happened. That's when I decided that to leave her alone in the Hampstead house would be far too risky, and so I invited her here to take care of us until our return to London at the end of October."

Frowning slightly, clasping Gerry's arm, guiding her back to the coble landing, Lisl said quietly, disbelievingly, "Surely you don't think that Mrs Temple was involved in the murder of Anna Gordino?"

"Frankly, Lisl," Gerry confessed dejectedly, "I don't know what to believe any more!"

"You poor child," Lisl murmured sympathetically, "what you need is a hot cup of coffee. Let's find a café, shall we? We really need to talk."

They sat at a small table on a terrace overlooking the sea. The café Lisl had chosen comprised a gift department and bookstore, apart from the coffee shop, with a door leading on to the terrace.

Lisl had bought a quantity of fresh fish from a stall near the cobble landing, and meat and vegetables from shops en route to the café. Meanwhile, Gerry had nipped into an old-fashioned chemist's to purchase a bottle of shampoo, a can of styling mousse and a tin of hairspray.

When they were settled at their table, shopping bags beside them, and the waitress came to take their order, Lisl ordered a cafétiere of freshly-ground coffee for two.

When it arrived, doing the pouring, she said, "Maurice seemed a little better when I saw him after breakfast. In fact, he talked of joining us for lunch – hence the fish I bought earlier. Thankfully, he's fond of fish, the poor darling."

"Oh, I'm so glad he's better. But couldn't you persuade him to see a doctor?" Gerry asked, frowning. "Sorry, but it could be more than a tummy-bug. He's lost so much weight I scarcely recognised him when I saw him at the carpark."

"Do you imagine I haven't thought of that?" Lisl said impatiently. "The truth is, like most men, Maurice is scared stiff of illness. Afraid of finding out what really ails him. He's always been so fit and healthy till now; in control of his own mind and body, his own destiny, and we were working so happily together until the attacks started. We'd been sharing the studio, Maurice researching his new book, me painting to my heart's content, scarcely bothering to speak to one another, simply enjoying each other's company."

She paused, coffee cup in hand. "But I'm not the only one who's had a rough time of it recently. Please, I'd like you to tell me about it. I couldn't help noticing how uptight you were at dinner last night, as if you had something on your mind, and you scarcely ate a bite."

Chance would have been a fine thing, Gerry thought wistfully. She said, "I have had a lot on my mind recently. Being the prime suspect in three murder cases is no joke, believe me. Plus one attempted murder. *Mine!*" She shivered slightly.

"My dear girl! How ghastly for you! But – *three* murders? I knew about your gardener and housekeeper, of course, but nothing about the third, or that *you* had been attacked! Tell me, have the police no clues to the killer?"

Sensing danger, as she had done that day in the Portobello Road café, when she had rung Bill on Christian Sommer's mobile phone, Gerry said warily, "I doubt it, otherwise they'd have eliminated me from their list of suspects by now. All I know for certain is that my attacker was a man."

"I see. So it could have been anyone?" Lisl remarked, pouring more coffee.

"No, far from," Gerry said coolly. "It had to be a man worth blackmailing; a rich businessman, perhaps. The reason why Liam McEvoy was murdered: because he knew the name of that man and saw his chance to extort money from him.

"As for poor Anna, she also knew the identity of the man Liam intended to blackmail, the reason why she had to be silenced so abruptly. The third victim just happened to be old Mr Constantine who, I daresay, also knew the killer's identity. You remember Mr Constantine, don't you? I bought my house from him last April."

"Yes, of course," Lisl said bemusedly, "though I can't recall ever *seeing* him. One knew that he had been a famous archaelogist in his time, but he kept very much to himself. Maurice and I invited him to dine with us more than once, but he never so much as acknowledged our invitations. And you say he was murdered?"

"I'm surprised you didn't read about it in the Sunday papers," Gerry said mildly.

"No, we didn't, for the simple reason that we make a point of not reading newspapers on holiday," Lisl explained. "Also, in case you hadn't noticed, we don't even possess a television set. In short, Maurice and I come here to Robin Hood's Bay to forget about the outside world completely. Is that so difficult to understand?"

"Not to me it isn't," Gerry responded wistfully. "The same reason why I wanted to get away from London, to forget about the past for a while. I might have known it wouldn't work. I never stop thinking about what happened: finding Liam's body, identifying Anna's, the police questioning, the attempt on my own life, being half smothered to death in the middle of the night and finding out that Mr Constantine had been murdered by the same means – only *he* wasn't strong enough to fight off his attacker.

"Then something else happened. Something odd, in my opinion." Gerry paused dramatically.

"Go on," Lisl said hoarsely.

"Well, I was in the Portobello Road street market the following Sunday morning, browsing among the stalls, when I saw Christian Sommer and his fiancée . . ."

"His – *fiancée*?" Lisl looked shocked.

"Yes, Maurice's niece, Cassie Bowen. Leastways I supposed she must be his fiancée because of the ring on her engagement finger. I thought at first they hadn't noticed me, but they followed me into a café. I had the strongest feeling it was all a set-up, and that made me wonder what they were up to – why they had followed me, what they wanted."

"And what did you imagine they wanted?" Lisl asked in a low voice, moistening her lips with her tongue.

"To do away with me," Gerry said bluntly. "Well, you did ask!"

"*What*? But that's ridiculous! You're letting your imagination run away with you! Cassie is a member of our family, Christian Sommer a friend of long standing. I'm sorry, but I can't listen to any more of this." Lisl rose to her feet and picked up her belongings, ashen faced, obviously angry. "I must get this fish to Mrs Temple in time for lunch, if you'll excuse me. I take it you can find your own way back?"

An interesting reaction, Gerry thought, when she had gone. Not totally unexpected, the way Lisl had leapt to the defence of Sommer, though news of his engagement to Cassie appeared to have come as a shock to her. On the other hand, she had not meant to upset Lisl so deeply, and perhaps she had let her tongue run away with her. But Lisl had done the initial probing, had let slip that Mrs Temple had phoned her to impart the news of Anna's murder – when the phone was supposedly out of order.

Things didn't add up. The more she thought about it, the more convinced she was that the fire had been no accident but a deliberate attempt on her life, and the perpetrator Mrs Temple, who else?

The fire would not have been allowed to spread out of control. Mrs Temple would have seen to that. She would have relied on smoke inhalation to put paid to her, Gerry reckoned; would have entered the room, moving silently as a cat, to make sure she was deeply asleep before removing the fireguard and helping a few hot coals on to the clothing near the hearth.

What would she have done then? Waited on the landing for a while, most likely, to give the smoke time to thicken to suffocation point, armed with a fire extinguisher in the event of having to tackle a conflagration.

Easy enough to say afterwards, that she had smelt smoke and gone to investigate, and had found Miss Frayling dead in bed. The woman must have received one hell of a shock when she'd heard sounds of movement inside the room, the clattering of furniture as Gerry dragged the sheepskin rug from the floor, upending an occasional table in the process.

Leaving the café, walking slowly uphill, deep in thought,

there had to be some connection between Mrs Temple and Christian Sommer, Gerry pondered. Could they possibly be related to one another? Virginia Vale would find out the answer in two seconds flat via a quick visit to Somerset House. But she wasn't Virginia Vale, and she wasn't in London, just stuck away in a remote fishing village which, despite its picturesqueness, she was beginning to dislike intensely. In fact, the sooner she was away from it, the better, with a pyromaniac on one hand and an offended hostess on the other.

Lisl, she imagined, would not be entirely surprised or disappointed if she announced her intention to cut short her holiday and return to London tomorrow. No phoney excuses necessary. She would simply say she was leaving – and go. An end to a hitherto rewarding friendship, no doubt, but she would learn to live with that – or would she? No man is an island, she thought despondently. The last thing she wanted was to lose Maurice's friendship, or Lisl's, come to that.

Approaching Black Gull House, she came upon an antique shop, the door of which stood invitingly open. Gerry went in.

It was a dark little shop, with a twisting wooden staircase leading to the upstairs premises, crammed with tables of bric-a-brac, the inevitable assortment of small curios: Victorian paperweights, china candlesticks, brass spill-holders, shell-covered boxes and so on, placed there as soporifics to whet the appetites of end-of-season visitors wanting to take home with them reminders of Robin Hood's Bay. 'Genuine antiques, no less, bought for a song in the cutest little shop you ever saw in all your life,' according to the American fraternity, Gerry felt sure.

But it was a china egg-container, of Victorian vintage, that caught Gerry's eye, remarkably similar to the one she had seen in the Hampstead repository and in Christian

Sommer's collection of Victoriana at his arty-farty Chelsea galleries. She checked the price.

"May I help you?" The woman asking the question had appeared from nowhere, taking Gerry by surprise. At least Gerry supposed that she was a woman. She might just as easily have been a man by reason of her cropped, iron-grey hair, flat chestedness and the gruffness of her voice, her strong, knuckly fingers and the navy crew-neck sweater and corduroy slacks she was wearing.

"Yes, as a matter of fact I'd like to buy the egg-container," Gerry said. "I've been wanting one for ages."

"Of course. If you'll wait just a moment, I'll pack it for you."

"Thanks, but I'll pay for it now and collect it later, if you don't mind. Otherwise I'll be late for lunch. I'm staying at Black Gull House, by the way."

"Oh, then you must be Geraldine Frayling, the authoress? Mrs Berenger told me you were coming. I am Millicent Carslake."

"Really? How do you do? Pleased to meet you." Wanting to be friendly, Gerry continued, "I've heard your name mentioned, of course, in connection with the house. You were the original owner, weren't you?"

"Scarcely that," Miss Carslake said coolly, albeit grimly. "'Black Gull', to the best of my knowledge and belief, dates back to the early 1800s, during the reign of George the Fourth. It came into our possession much later than that. Our parents bought it just after World War One. When my father died in 1942, he willed it to my elder sister Phoebe. We were both quite young then, but we continued to live there until, quite frankly, we could no longer afford its upkeep."

"I'm so sorry. I didn't mean to pry."

"Not at all. As you have probably been told my sister has become something of a recluse in her declining years,

163

seldom if ever receiving visitors, the poor dear, ever since the fire at Black Gull House which scarred her face beyond recognition."

Millie Carslake turned away abruptly, with the air of one who has said too much and wishes she had not.

Leaving the shop without another word, Gerry thought, what a curious encounter, wondering about that fire that had robbed poor Phoebe Carslake of her beauty; whether there was some kind of jinx on Black Gull House, a poltergeist of some kind with pyromaniacal tendencies, who raised fire for the sheer hell of it?

To her surprise, entering Black Gull House, uncertain of her welcome, Lisl, who was in the hall at the time, said briskly but warmly, as if nothing untoward had happened between them, "Ah, here you are at last. Lunch is almost ready. Maurice is joining us, and we'll have it in the conservatory, if that's all right?"

So just what the hell was going on here? And why the gut feeling that Millie Carslake's poignantly recounted reminiscences had been a load of balls from beginning to end, Gerry wondered? She hadn't a clue, but she would dearly love to find out.

Fifteen

Dear Bill,
Don't want to worry you unduly, but if I fail to return home in one piece – I mean alive and kicking – don't bother about Westminster Abbey, just scatter my ashes on Hampstead Heath. Only kidding! More importantly, give this letter to Inspector Clooney to read.

The fact is, one attempt on my life has been made so far, and others may follow. The night I arrived here at Black Gull House, I woke up in the early hours to a smoke-filled bedroom. There had been a helluva storm and my damp clothing was spread near the fire to dry. The fireguard was in place when I went to bed, of that I'm certain. When I woke up, I noticed that the fireguard had been moved and my clothes were smouldering, hence the smoke. If hadn't woken up when I did, well, I'd have been a goner. I was already gasping for breath.

The person I hold responsible is Mrs Temple, who obviously hates my guts. Who else could it have been? There were only four people in the house that night: myself, the Berengers and the housekeeper.

Perhaps I'm being paranoid, but I still believe that Christian Sommer murdered Liam, Anna, and Mr Constantine. Now I also believe that he and Mrs Temple are connected in some way, that it was Sommer she rang on the night preceding Anna's murder, warning

165

him that Anna knew his identity – because she had said so on the telephone. In fact, Anna was not talking 'gibberish' at all. She was saying quite clearly that she knew the identity of Liam's killer.

Mr Constantine was murdered for the same reason. Liam, seeing a way to make some easy money, had attempted to blackmail Sommer – probably because he had caught Sommer in the act of stealing certain artefacts, worth a fortune, belonging to the poor old man.

I have no proof of this, but my guess is that Sommer agreed to meet Liam in a parked vehicle outside his usual pub, around closing time, ostensibly to stump up the blackmail money. Poor Liam was so naïve he wouldn't have suspected a trap until it was too late. Once inside the car, he'd have been too fuddled with drink anyway to realise what was happening.

My belief is that Sommer drove him to his galleries in Chelsea, where he bound his hands behind him and force fed him whisky and painkillers. It doesn't bear thinking about, but it all ties in. Perhaps Sommer intended to dump Liam's body in the garden shed in the early hours of next morning, but something happened to prevent him – the nightwatchman on his round, most likely. Whatever, Sommer was forced to leave the dumping of Liam's body till the next night. That's when Anna caught a glimpse of him replacing the padlock on the door of the garden shed. Scared out of her wits, she must have hurried back to the house to try to work out the significance of what she'd seen – not the dumping of Liam's body, which had already been done, but the padlocking of the door.

Later, realising his mistake, Sommer must have returned to the shed to unpadlock the door so as to create the impression that Liam's body had been there since the Wednesday – that he had committed suicide there a day earlier. Unfortunately – or fortunately as the case may be – he made two other mistakes in not leaving Liam's fingerprints on the empty whisky bottle, and forgetting to unscrew the cap of the painkilling tablets.

Look, Bill, I'm really sorry to burden you with all this. The fact is – it's difficult to explain – but I have the gut feeling that something awful is about to happen. So why don't I just get the hell out of here? It's not that simple. There's something going on which I don't fully understand as yet, and can't get to grips with, which is linked to the London murders. Also, dear Maurice is far from well, in need of my help and support in some way, and Lisl, as you can imagine, is worried sick about him, so I feel it would be mean and cowardly to simply turn tail and run away. What would Virginia Vale think of me if I did? More to the point, what would *you* think of me?

She signed the letter, 'Yours till hell freezes over, Gerry', and posted it that afternoon on her way to the beach.

"Please don't worry about me, I'll be perfectly all right on my own," Gerry had told the Berengers over lunch – needing desperately to be alone for a while – trying hard not to sound too eager. "After all, I'm not going far, just along the beach and back for a breath of sea air."

"Don't venture too far, that's all," Maurice said warningly. "Keep an eye on the tide. It comes in so rapidly."

"Thanks, Maurice, I will." She'd smiled at him across the table, pleased that he seemed a little better today, that he had obviously enjoyed his portion of fish pie, and a small helping of lemon meringue mousse.

The morning sunshine had begun to fade a little as Gerry stepped on to the beach near the coble landing. She wondered

167

if she had done right to post the letter, to even say what she had?

Trying to keep a sense of perspective and objectivity, she realised that Mrs Temple's presence here had thrown her. Arriving tired, wet and hungry, in the teeth of a violent storm, shaken by Maurice's changed appearance and the strangeness of Black Gull House, the last person she had expected to see was Anita Temple.

She had felt like a schoolgirl, on vacation, arriving at a seaside hotel to find a dreaded headmistress staying at the same hotel. And so, in a sense, it seemed that the events of the past weeks from which she had longed to escape, had not been left behind after all – more disconcertingly, they had come on ahead of her. Moreover, alarmingly, Maurice's strength and protectiveness had been missing, his usual bonhomie, keen sense of humour and intellectual capacity overshadowed by his illness.

Lisl too had seemed different, less charming, more brittle, edgy and ill-at-ease, probably by reason of her husband's state of health. And yet, over morning coffee, she had revealed a morbid interest in the London murders. 'We need to talk,' she'd said. But why on the topic of murder in particular? And why her angry reaction to the fact that she, Gerry, believed Christian Sommer capable of murder? It just didn't add up, especially in view of Lisl's curious mood swing before lunch when, her white heat anger apparently forgotten, she had reverted to her usual charming self.

Inevitably, dawdling along the beach, less serious thoughts occurred. She must not forget to pick up her egg container from Millie Carslake's antique shop on her return to Black Gull House, and to visit the carpark to make sure that her Mini was still there, not feeling too lonely or neglected. Her beloved Mini, her means of escape from Robin Hood's Bay if the going got too tough to handle.

Deep in thought, Gerry had not noticed the swift oncoming

of the tide swallowing up the sand. Then, staring in horror at the savage onrush of the sea, she realised, with a sinking feeling of despair, that a return to the coble landing was an impossibility.

How could she have been so stupid? Maurice had warned her not to venture too far, that the tide would be on the turn. Now it was racing towards her like a cavalry charge of white horses, and she was stranded on a mound of boulders at the base of the cliffs towering above her, panic stricken, not knowing which way to turn to escape from the maelstrom of water boiling about her, rising higher by the minute.

No use calling for help, there wasn't a soul in sight. Now the tide was lapping her feet. The mound of boulders on which she had sought refuge seconds earlier were fast disappearing beneath the devastating onrush of the sea.

Glancing upwards, she noticed a ledge of rock protruding from the cliff face. With grim determination to reach that ledge, pausing momentarily to drape her shoulder-bag about her neck, standing on tiptoe, with self-preservation upmost in her mind, albeit painfully, arm and neck muscles aching abominably, she just managed to reach it. She lay there for a while, exhausted, praying to God that she was now out of reach of the tide. If not, she might just as well commend her soul to its Maker here and now.

Feeling the benison of gentle rain on her face, she sat up and, looking down, saw to her infinite relief, that she was home, if not entirely dry. The rain, no longer so gentle and welcome, was also chilly and insistent, but the racing tide, to her infinite relief, appeared to be on the turn once more. The rain was now, however, reaching downpour dimensions, soaking her to the skin.

She was tempted to squeeze into an aperture in the rock face. Commonsense told her that she would have at least an hour to wait until the tide receded enough to allow her return to the coble landing – maybe even longer. No way

169

could she sit on the ledge getting wetter by the minute. She was already shivering from cold and shock, teeth chattering, hair soaking wet.

The aperture was a tight fit, a bit like a sentry-box, but once inside she saw that it led to a wider opening, the entrance to a sizeable cave into which she scrambled inelegantly, like a hermit crab trying to get back into its shell. At least she could now sit down, her back against the wall of the cave and her legs spread out in front of her, to massage her aching shoulder muscles and give some thought to her predicament. She had managed to pull herself up to the ledge, but the thought of lowering herself from it filled her with a nervous dread.

What if she crashed down on to the boulders beneath, breaking a leg? With her luck, both legs? Better not think of that. What would Virginia Vale do in these circumstances? Limbering up exercises, most likely – lumbering up exercises in her case. A sound idea at any rate to keep her circulation going, she thought, beginning a series of kneebends and clapping her hands smartly above her head. One thing for certain, if she returned home in one piece, she would not breathe a word of this escapade to the Berengers. If she did, they would never let her out of their sight again, and the last thing she wanted was an escort wherever she went.

Feeling marginally warmer from the exercises, she fiddled in her shoulder bag for a block of nut milk chocolate, which she nibbled ecstatically, savouring each nut to the full, looking about her as she did so, not that she could see much, the interior of the cave was far too dark for that – a smugglers' cave, she felt certain, one of the many honeycombing the cliffs.

Then the thought occurred that the cave she was in must be almost directly below Black Gull House, probably connected to it by a labyrinth of tunnels and passageways, and that had she had the nous to bring with her a torch – as Virginia would have done – she might well have found her way eventually to the cellar of Black Gull, and from thence to the conservatory. Ha! There she went again, letting her imagination run riot! No, there was no easy option in this dilemma. Virginia would have scaled the cliff face by now, as lithe as a mountain lion in her tartan trews and camouflage jacket, wearing her baseball cap back to front. She, Gerry Mudd, would end up dangling from a ledge, eyes closed in terror, feet scrabbling for toeholds as she descended dizzily to the piled up boulders on the beach below.

And, in the event, she was right. Well at least she'd made it without breaking both legs, although they appeared to have taken on the characteristics of half-set strawberry blancmange when they finally landed on terra firma, where, swaying like a drunken sailor, she stepped thankfully on to the stones of the coble landing once more.

Resisting the strong temptation to kiss, in turn, a group of fishermen gathered on the landing, she wobbled towards the nearest café where, sinking down at the nearest table, she ordered a pot of tea, ham sandwiches and a jam doughnut.

"Bin fishing?" the waitress enquired briefly. "Catch anything?"

"Just flu," Gerry replied mildly. The waitress laughed. Gerry joined in.

Later, in the ladies' cloakroom, having spent a penny, and washed her hands, Gerry recoiled slightly at her reflection in the washbasin mirror. 'The Wreck of the Hesperus' wasn't in it! Her nose was red, and shining like a beacon, her hair hung down like spaniels' ears on either side of her face, in which her eyes resembled organ stops – and that was just the top half of her. What she looked like from the waist down, she dreaded to think. Waterlogged, to put it mildly, she imagined. Certainly her feet were sopping wet and so were her slacks.

Seeing her in this state, no way would the Berengers

believe that she had been for a stroll along the beach and back, besides which she'd been gone for hours.

Repairing the damage as best she could, dragging a comb through her hair, powdering her nose and applying lipstick, squeezing the excess moisture from her trouser bottoms, emptying the water from her shoes and drying her feet as best as she could with a hand-towel, she prayed to heaven that she would gain entry to Black Gull House without being seen.

For once, luck was on her side. The front door was unlocked. Feeling like a Disney cat, Gerry crept up the stairs to her room, where, heaving deep sighs of relief, she stripped off her wet things, put on her dressing gown and slippers, picked up her bottle of shampoo, bath soap, sponge-bag and towels, and hurried along the landing to the bathroom to lower herself blissfully into a steaming tub full of hot, scented water.

Warm and relaxed from her ablutions, returning to her room she put on clean dry clothes and put her wet garments to dry in front of the fire, making certain the fireguard was well and truly in place. Towel drying and moussing her sagging hairstyle, she finger-combed it till it stood up like a hayrick about her face, to which she applied more than her usual amount of makeup – especially in the nose area.

Glancing at her watch, she saw that the time was fast approaching seven o'clock. Time to go downstairs to the drawing room before supper – possibly to answer questions about where she had been that afternoon. If so, she'd say quite simply that she had walked along the beach for a while until the rain started, when she'd taken shelter until it had stopped, after which she'd had tea in a café near the coble landing. As simple as that. She wouldn't lie, just bend the truth a little, as writers were wont to do now and again, in order to earn a living.

Entering the drawing room, Gerry saw to her surprise

that Lisl was alone in the room, sitting near the fire, looking worried. She seemed suddenly much older than usual, robbed completely of her normal buoyancy and self-confidence.

"Lisl, what is it? What's wrong?" Gerry asked concernedly. "Where's Maurice?"

"In bed, I'm afraid." Lisl drew in a deep breath of despair. "He seemed so much better this morning, then suddenly, after lunch, the stomach pains started again. Mrs Temple and I helped him up to his room, the poor darling." She paused. "He's resting more quietly now, thank God, but I'm terribly worried about him, and he utterly refuses to seek medical help."

"Oh, sod that for a game of darts," Gerry said in her forthright fashion. "There comes a time when you have to decide what's best for someone you love when they are incapable of deciding for themselves."

"You don't understand," Lisl said sadly. "Maurice would never forgive me if I went against his wishes. You see, his trust in me is absolute, and I cannot possibly betray that trust."

"Then let *me* send for a doctor," Gerry suggested anxiously. "Let *me* take the blame!"

"No, I'm sorry, that is out of the question."

Mrs Temple entered the room at that moment. "Supper is ready when you are, madam," she said coolly.

"Thank you. We'll be along directly." Lisl rose to her feet. Tucking her hand into the crook of Gerry's elbow, "You must be starving after all the fresh air you've had today," she said charmingly. "Come, let's eat, shall we?"

As a guest in someone else's home, Gerry could scarcely refuse the invitation, and yet, for the first time ever, she felt that to eat a mouthful of food would choke her. Especially food cooked and served by a potential murderess.

Sixteen

Lisl apologised profusely next morning that she felt unable to accompany Gerry on a walk round the village. Maurice had passed a reasonably comfortable night, but she felt loath to leave him. There was a divan bed in the studio in which Maurice could rest while she painted.

"No need to apologise," Gerry said warmly, relieved to know that Maurice was feeling better.

"It just seems so unkind, having invited you, to leave you to your own devices." She paused. "Unless, of course, you would care to spend time with Maurice and me in the studio?"

"Thanks, but presence of a third party may prevent his resting completely."

Lisl smiled. "What a kind, thoughtful person you are. But won't you feel bored on your own all day?"

"Heavens, no. I'm used to being on my own. Besides, I'd like to explore the area more fully." A thought occurred. "I'll drive along the coast road to Whitby, have lunch there, take a look at the shops – especially the antique shops. Which reminds me, I have a parcel to pick up from Miss Carslake's, a china egg-container which I – er – forgot to collect yesterday, as promised."

"Really? So you've met Miss Millie? I had no idea. What did she say to you?"

"Say to me?" What a curious question, Gerry thought. "Well, we had quite an interesting conversation as a matter

174

of fact. She sketched in a brief history of Black Gull House, and told me about the fire that scarred her sister for life. When did that happen, by the way?"

"I haven't the faintest idea," Lisl said vaguely. "A very long time ago, I imagine. Why not ask Miss Millie?"

Why not, indeed?

Picking up her parcel from Millie Carslake's before heading towards the carpark, Gerry rejoiced in the sight of her Mini patiently awaiting her reappearance to pat its bonnet and boot – rather like an old dog accustomed to kindness. She had surmised, correctly, that Miss Carslake would not be overjoyed to see her again, having said far too much at their first encounter, for whatever reasons best known to herself. A tissue of lies from beginning to end, Gerry felt sure, accepting the parcel, her Victorian egg-container, neatly boxed and wrapped in brown paper and sellotape.

Scarcely two sentences had passed between them, and yet, leaving the shop, Gerry retained the strong impression that they had met somewhere else. Glancing back over her shoulder at Millie Carslake's rear view, glimpsed leaning forward to write in her desk diary, slipping on a pair of reading glasses as she did so, suddenly, shockingly, Gerry felt that she was looking at a distorting mirror reflection of – Anita Temple!

Walking towards the carpark, she thought, *How utterly ridiculous*. And yet – the two women bore strikingly similar characteristics. Both were thin, flat-chested, of the same height. True, Mrs Temple's hairstyle was different, worn slightly longer, curled and tinted, and she wore glasses. Curiously, it was when Millie Carslake had slipped on a pair of reading glasses that Gerry had noticed the resemblance. But there was more to it than that. Their hands were identical. Both possessed strong hands with enlarged knuckles. Gerry had noticed Mrs Temple's hands in particular when she had served supper on the night of her arrival, thinking how at variance they were with her carefully cultivated feminine persona.

Driving towards Whitby, Gerry stopped at a garage to cater to the needs of her car – a good drink of petrol for starters, a windscreen wash, and a tyre check-up. This accomplished, on arrival in Whitby, Gerry cruised around for a while until she came across a long-stay carpark, before setting off to explore the town: a fascinating place as she quickly discovered, steeped in history.

The road north from Robin Hood's Bay had brought her in close proximity to Whitby Abbey and the Church of St Mary, overlooking the River Esk, the colourful harbour, red-roofed houses and the twin arms of the lighthouse piers held out to sea.

It was a delightful morning, clear and fresh. Breathing deeply, Gerry sensed freedom in the air, a feeling of relaxation long denied her as she walked down the incredibly long and ancient flight of steps leading to the town centre. Coming up them would prove a different matter entirely, she thought wryly, but she would cross that bridge when she came to it. Right now, she was about to cross a bridge over the river in search of a coffee shop, preferably an 'Olde Worlde' coffee shop with lots of atmosphere to complement her present need of security, for want of a better word.

She came upon them by chance: worn stone steps leading down to a basement café, dimly lit, with oak tables and chairs and a stone fireplace in which burned a real log fire. And the coffee was *real* coffee, freshly ground, served with either hot milk or cream.

Studying the luncheon menu on the table, Gerry decided that she would return later to eat a prawn salad sandwich with homemade mayonnaise. In the interim, she would make her way to the public library to research the area more fully, concentrating on smuggling activities during the last century, in particular.

*   *   *

The Chief Librarian had been most kind and helpful. Her name had obviously rung a bell with him right away. When she had given it as a matter of courtesy, he had invited her through to the innermost sanctum of the archives department, normally out of bounds except to members of staff and bona fide researchers such as college professors, accredited A level students and their ilk.

And so, at the drop of a name, she had been given access to a veritable wealth of information, not merely books, but ancient deeds and documents pertaining to the smuggling industry in general, throughout the last century to the present day. So it was still ongoing, apparently? No longer confined to 'Brandy for the parson, baccy for the clerk', but far more dangerous substances: Smack, Crack, Heroin and Ecstasy, for instance . . .

Of far more interest to Gerry was the book she discovered on notorious smugglers of the eighteenth century, including the name of one Franklyn Dogberry, a hitherto well respected magistrate and Justice of the Peace, residing at Black Gull House, Robin Hood's Bay, who, upon being denounced as the leader of a smugglers ring by a member of the gang intent on saving his own neck from a hangman's rope, had fled the country with his wife and family, never to be seen again on these shores, having sailed to France aboard a schooner anchored in the Bay.

No wonder the man had needed a house the size of Black Gull, Gerry thought, with a wife and seven kids to shelter, and a bit of extra income from smuggling to keep his magisterial cart on its wheels. The world hadn't changed all that much. In this day and age, he'd probably have been claiming housing benefit. Now France was probably overrun with succeeding generations of Dogberrys sprung from the loins of the reprobate Franklyn. And really, the wheezes the smuggling fraternity had got up to so as to divert the attention of superstitious, law-abiding citizens away from their nefarious nocturnal activities, had been nothing short of amazing. 'Ghost Riders' for example, daubed with phosphorescent paint, glowing in the dark, putting the fear of God into the hearts of ordinary, decent folk, who drew their curtains and said their prayers when the ghost riders were abroad.

Food for thought, which reminded Gerry of prawn salad sandwiches and coffee.

After lunch, she strolled towards the harbour to take a closer look at the fishing vessels anchored there. She relished the tang of the salt air in her nostrils, the crying of the seagulls clamouring for scraps of food thrown overboard from the trawlers hawsered alongside the quay. She was savouring to the full this new experience in the life of a Londoner born and bred: this scaled-down version of life, as it were, yet every bit as vital and exciting as the scaled-up version she was used to.

Perhaps it was time that she and Virginia went further afield in search of adventure? She must ask Bill about that the next time they met. Bill. She wondered what he was doing right now . . .

He had been waiting in an outer office for the past fifteen minutes, fairly champing at the bit, Gerry's letter burning a hole in his pocket.

"Inspector Clooney is free now," the desk sergeant called out to him. "The second door on the left down the passage."

Bill stood up. "Thanks, Sergeant," he said briefly, thinking it expedient not to add, "About time, too!"

Bookshops, as well as antique shops, had fascinated Gerry since childhood. *Real* bookshops, not book departments in soulless departmental stores, but the real McCoy, albeit dusty and dim, where people who really loved books were encouraged to browse, were not browbeaten into buying the latest, glossy bestsellers currently on offer. Her own included.

The woman behind the sales counter had merely smiled at her in a friendly fashion when Gerry entered the dim and dusty bookshop in a side street near the harbour, to browse among the shelves of the secondhand department, not knowing what she was looking for. But this, to her way of thinking, was the most exciting aspect of all – akin to living – not knowing what one really wanted until the discovery had been made beyond a shadow of doubt.

Riffling through the pages of a well-worn copy of the ninety-seventh edition of Pears Cyclopaedia, under the heading Classical Mythology, she came across Tantalus, the son of Zeus and the nymph Pluto – a bit of a bad lad, by all accounts, whose many crimes included murdering his own son, Pelops, whose flesh he'd cut up and served – presumably cooked – as a meal to the gods.

Yuck, how awful, Gerry thought. What kind of person would not only kill his own flesh and blood, but serve him barbecued into the bargain?

But Tantalus had got his comeuppance in the long run when, banished to the Underworld, he'd been placed in a lake the waters of which receded whenever he tried to drink, whilst above his head were boughs of fruit 'tantalisingly' beyond his reach, the poor devil.

At that point, Gerry recalled the definition of Tantalus in her Oxford dictionary, as a spirit stand containing decanters which can be seen but not withdrawn until the bar holding them is unlocked.

Paying the smiling lady behind the desk for the Pears, Gerry went in search of afternoon tea . . .

*   *   *

179

"Look here, Inspector Clooney," Bill said hoarsely, "you've read Miss Frayling's letter. What, if anything, are you going to do about it?"

Clooney sighed deeply. "There is nothing I *can* do about it at the moment, without substantiative evidence that would hold up in a court of law, in the case of an arrest at this stage of my investigations. Frankly, Mr Bentine, the evidence we have in respect of Mr Sommer is purely circumstantial. There are no witnesses to the murders . . ."

Bill broke in excitedly, "But if you could prove that some kind of relationship exists between Sommer and the Berengers' housekeeper, Mrs Temple? And what about DNA testing of the rope used to tie Liam McEvoy's hands behind him and the kind of rope used in the packing of crates at Sommer's galleries?"

Clooney shook his head. "Proof of a relationship between Sommer and Mrs Temple would be of little or no value unless the woman changed her testimony regarding the phonecall she received from Anna Gordino the night preceding her murder, in which she stated that Mrs Gordino was talking gibberish. You see what I'm up against, Mr Bentine? No way can I prove that Mrs Temple was lying. As for the DNA testing of the rope used to tie Liam McEvoy's hands, that will be long gone now – incinerated most likely – if it ever existed."

"I see." Getting up to leave the Inspector's office, "Sorry to have wasted your time," Bill said coolly, keeping his anger in check. "So where exactly does Miss Frayling fit in to the picture? That girl's been through a hell of a lot, through no fault of her own. Well, you've read her letter. Doesn't it strike you as sinister that a second attempt on her life occurred within hours of her arrival in Robin Hood's Bay, with Anita Temple under the same roof as herself?"

"Possibly," Clooney concurred, "but once again we come

up against the problem of proof. Think about it, Mr Bentine. Miss Frayling states quite clearly in her letter that all she says is merely guesswork. And guesswork is simply not good enough! Hard, irrefutable facts, not guesswork, is needed to bring a murderer to justice." His face hardened. "As we shall, in the long run, believe me."

Glancing at her watch, Gerry realised, albeit reluctantly, that it was time to think of returning to Black Gull House. En route to her car, she purchased two hefty bars of nut milk chocolate, a man size torch complete with batteries, and a sizeable bunch of flowers – chrysanthemums, dahlias, carnations and gypsophila – wrapped in cellophane and tied with a red and gold ribbon.

How she managed the one hundred and ninety-nine steps or so to the carpark near the Abbey, lumbered down with her various carrier bags and the bouquet, she would never know. Mind over matter, she supposed, born of her sheer determination to reach her destination, allied to her reluctance to go back to all that black bitumen and panelling. But this had been a lovely day – a day to remember – filled with sunshine and fresh air, good food, and new ideas: hope for the future . . .

Reaching Black Gull around six o'clock, finding the front door open once more, first she went upstairs to her room to ditch her carrier bags, to comb her hair and powder her nose, after which she went up two more flights of stairs to the studio, carrying the bouquet of flowers.

She knocked twice on the door before, receiving no response to her knocking, she entered the room, unbidden, to find Maurice there on his own, in the divan bed, ashen faced, propped up with pillows.

Laying down the flowers on his desk, kneeling beside him, not bothering to ask how he felt, wasting no time on trivialities, she said intently, "Look, Maurice, no way can you *must* see a doctor!"

"*No!*" Placing an unsteady hand on hers, he whispered, "I'm afraid."

"Afraid of finding out what's wrong with you?" Gerry asked gently.

"Yes."

"That's understandable. Anyone would feel the same." Holding his hand, she continued, "But it could be a bug of some kind. There's been a lot of such cases in Scotland recently. A strain of food poisoning. You must have eaten something that disagreed with you, and the bug's still in your system."

"Yes."

"Yes? What do you mean, yes?" She looked at him doubtfully.

"I agree with your diagnosis." He smiled faintly, a mere upturning of the mouth, a touch of the old Maurice glimpsed through a mask of pain.

"Then why not see a doctor? Have treatment? I'm sorry, I don't get this. You need antibiotics! Injections! I don't know what, but there must be something they can give you when they've found out what's swimming about inside you."

"Maybe I don't want them to find out."

"Not *want*? Why ever not, for God's sake?"

"Listen, Gerry. Lisl will be back any minute and I don't want her to hear this, but I want you to leave here. The sooner the better. Promise you will? *Promise!*"

A frisson of fear ran through her, a dreadful possibility forming in her mind. Something so shocking, so unbelievable that she could scarcely credit the thought even entering her head.

"No," she said hoarsely. "No way am I leaving you alone in this state! The only way you'll get rid of me is the hard way. I'm not leaving this house until you are safely in hospital, and you'd better believe it!" Tears filled her eyes.

"You don't understand." He was speaking fretfully, clinging to her hand, fighting against a fresh onslaught of pain. "There are things you know nothing about. Dreadful things hidden away . . . Ahhhh!" His body jerked convulsively as the pain took it. Perspiration poured from him, soaking his hair, beard and the bedclothes. Flecks of blood appeared at the corners of his mouth, then he vomited violently – blood-stained vomit. His eyes were closed now, face contorted. Quickly, she handed him a towel.

Fearful that he might choke on the vomit, Gerry leaned him forward against her shoulder, cradling him as a mother would cradle a sick child and bunching up the pillows behind him. Glancing quickly about the room, she noticed a mobile phone on his desk. Rising swiftly to her feet, picking up the phone, she dialled 999.

Lisl entered the studio at that moment. "What the hell's going on?" she uttered hoarsely. "I demand an explanation!"

Putting down the phone, confronting Lisl, Gerry said defiantly, "I've phoned for an ambulance, something you should have done yourself, ages ago!"

"How dare you have done such a thing without my permission?" Lisl flung at her. "By what right have you . . ."

"Oh spare me the self-righteous indignation," Gerry interrupted impatiently, "the ambulance will be here at any minute, and unless you want a dead man on your hands, Maurice had better be in it when it departs! Do I make myself clear?"

"I shall never forgive you for this," Lisl said angrily.

"Fair enough. I can live with that," Gerry responded. "The question is, if Maurice dies, will you be able to forgive yourself?"

Later, alone in her room, an imperfect end to an otherwise perfect day, Gerry thought wryly. But at least Maurice would be safe for the time being, receiving the care and attention he so richly deserved.

Lisl had gone with him in the ambulance to Whitby Hospital. The least she could do in the circumstances. Now, doubtless she'd be playing the role of the dutiful, distraught wife.

Deep in thought, Gerry recalled her conversation with Maurice, trying to make sense of it. His words, 'There are things you know nothing about. Dreadful things hidden away!' What 'things', for heaven's sake? And why his insistence that she should leave Black Gull House, the sooner the better?

No prizes for working out the answer to that one, Gerry realised – because her life was in danger. She had said as much in her letter to Bill.

Bill. Her watchdog, her guardian angel, her knight in shining armour. Not for the first time, she wondered where he was, what he was doing right now?

Around nine o'clock, Anita Temple knocked at her door.

"Yes, what is it?" Gerry asked cagily, opening the door a crack. "What do you want?"

"Simply to tell you that madam – Mrs Berenger – is spending the night at the hospital with her husband, and I'm on my way to bed now."

"Let us hope your conscience won't keep you awake," Gerry said recklessly, determined to speak her mind. "I imagine it won't take the doctors long to find out what kind of poison you used in the poor man's food!"

The housekeeper's eyes narrowed, then, uttering a brittle, unmirthful laugh, she said coolly, "You have a vivid imagination, Miss Mudd. That *is* your real name, isn't it? Maurice – Mr Berenger – has a virus of some kind, nothing more serious than that, easily cured, I daresay, with antibiotics. To suggest otherwise is monstrous! So think carefully, Miss

Mudd, if you are capable of thought, that is, to beware your habit of unsubstantiated accusations pointed in *my* direction in particular. Take the case of Anna Gordino's phonecall to me on the eve of her death, for instance. I told you and the police that the woman was talking gibberish, and nothing can or ever will be proved otherwise."

Turning away, the woman walked along the passage to her room on the landing.

Seventeen

There was something terribly wrong here, Gerry thought. Something reeking of evil to do with this house, with Maurice's illness, linked in some way with the London murders, she felt certain. But what?

Unable to sleep, not bothering to undress, in a chair near the window, she stared out at the blackness beyond, hearing the sullen crump of the sea on the rocks beneath, her thoughts in a turmoil, trying to make sense of the muddled images that flashed through her mind like the coloured pieces of a kaleidoscope. She recalled that night on the Berengers' terrace following her discovery of Liam's body in her garden shed, that first reference to Black Gull House, the way Lisl had reacted to the mention of their meeting with its owner, Pheobe Carslake: that nervous laugh of hers, the slight shudder that had hunched her shoulder blades, that momentary deviation from her normally cool and collected air of sophistication, which had puzzled Gerry at the time, and continued to do so.

What she could not fathom was the reason why Lisl had even thought of buying the house in the first place. Surely not because of the view from an attic window? A woman of discernment, surely to heaven she had realised the impossibility of turning such a plug-ugly house into a home? So she and Maurice needed space? But surely to God not a house built to accommodate a man and his wife and seven children, plus servants? There must have been some other, underlying reason why she had wanted this house so much.

Knowing Lisl, she would have been the prime mover in the purchase, the adoring Maurice easily persuaded to accede to his wife's wishes, as usual. Of this, Gerry entertained no doubt whatever. Lisl, despite her air of fragile femininity, her slender, youthful-looking body, and her distinctive French perfume, created especially for her in Paris, was by far the stronger partner in the marriage, psychologically speaking – the iron hand in the velvet glove, Gerry realised.

So what? What possible conclusions could she draw from a besotted husband's desire to please his wife to the extent of holing up here away from London, his natural milieu containing his publishers, agent, and his vast circle of friends and acquaintances? Maurice belonged in the thick of things. An extrovert personality, he thrived on contact with his fellow human beings. Impossible to imagine him ever facing retirement in a backwater fishing village far removed from his natural environment.

A holiday cottage in Robin Hood's Bay, she could have well understood, a kind of bolt-hole as a means of a temporary escape and mental and physical refreshment when necessary, away from the flesh-pots of London, but not Black Gull House with its preponderance of panelling, tall, rattling windows and long corridors, teetering on a cliff honeycombed with caves, the former home of a notorious smuggler, Franklyn Dogberry.

Of one thing, Gerry was entirely certain. She had not mistaken the resemblance between Mrs Temple and Millie Carslake. A coincidence, perhaps? After all, what possible connection could there be between the Berengers' housekeeper, the owner of an antiques' shop, and her reclusive, fire-scarred sister, Phoebe Carslake, the former owner of Black Gull House?

The more she thought about it, the less sense she made of it, Gerry thought wearily, unable to fit together the whirling kaleidoscope images in her mind's eye to form a composite pattern. Akin to attempting a jigsaw puzzle of which the vital component parts were missing.

Rising stiffly from her chair, thinking in terms of sleep, glancing out of the window at the inky darkness beyond, she noticed intermittent flashes of light, presumably from some vessel anchored in the bay. What other explanation was possible?

Then, fully alert and aware, she heard footsteps on the landing, the creaking of the stairs as someone descended to the hall below. Mrs Temple! Who else? It *had* to be Mrs Temple, since they were alone together in Black Gull House.

When the footsteps had died away, carrying the torch she had bought earlier, Gerry quietly opened her door and trod softly along the panelled corridor to the landing where an edge of light shone from the open door of Mrs Temple's bedroom. Leaning over the banister, scarcely daring to breathe, she saw a faint glimmer of light from the conservatory. So what was the woman doing down there? Watering the plants? Folding her laundry? Or had she gone through the connecting door to the kitchen to make herself a cup of cocoa? In which case, why pussyfoot downstairs like a Disney cat, in almost total darkness?

No. There was more to it than that. There had to be. Putting two and two together, the likelihood was that the woman had gone down to the cellar, that her nocturnal meanderings had to do with the vessel anchored offshore. Only one way to find out. Drawing in a deep breath and switching on her torch, Gerry made her way downstairs to the conservatory . . .

Advising his secretary that he would be out of town for

a few days, Bill Bentine had slung an overnight bag on the back seat of his car and set off on his long journey north as daylight was fading over the great City of London. Gerry's life was certainly in danger: he had therefore to go as quickly as possible to her, and to hell with Inspector Clooney's insistence on irrefutable proof of her suspicions before taking positive action on her behalf.

Bill's painstaking perusal of certain documents stored in the archives of Somerset House had proved an eye-opener, proof positive of Gerry's present predicament. Names and dates had suddenly slotted together to provide a possible, if bizarre solution to the London murders, closely linked to the happenings at Black Gull House.

He'd be late arriving in Robin Hood's Bay, and what he'd do when he got there, he hadn't the faintest idea. He'd have to play it by ear. At least, before leaving the office, he'd had the nous to fax Clooney about his findings in the archives of Somerset House. He simply prayed to God that the thick-headed Inspector would act on that information without further prevarication or delay . . .

The cellar door had been unlocked and opened. There was no sign of Mrs Temple, but the woman could not have simply disappeared into thin air, Gerry surmised, shining her torch on the flight of stone steps confronting her.

According to Lisl, the cellar was a no-go area, quite horrid, suggestive of a slimy cavern with moss covered steps and dripping stalactites hanging from the ceiling. But the cellar was surprisingly dry and well ventilated, sans moss or stalactites, and completely empty. So where the hell was Mrs Temple?

It was then that she glimpsed a flicker of light from a narrow opening in the wall opposite, of the kind she had squeezed through the day she had very nearly met her death by drowning. So what to do about it?

189

Common sense warned her that she'd be better off making
her way back to bed. On the other hand, common sense had
never been Gerry's strong point. Like her alter ego, Virginia
Vale, she preferred to live dangerously, otherwise she might
as well switch to writing romantic fiction from henceforth,
a la Clarinda Clarkson. With this thought in mind, she
squeezed herself into the aperture, and remained there,
motionless, witnessing a scene beyond belief – a present
day version of Franklyn Dogberry's days – the landing of
contraband from the vessel at anchor in Robin Hood's Bay,
with Mrs Temple and Millie Carslake seemingly in charge
of the operation.

Efficiency was the name of the game. The cave beyond
the aperture was well lit and air conditioned in respect of
the works of art, paintings and icons stored there, smuggled
treasures worth a fortune to collectors of fine works of art
both here and abroad, later sold on, presumably, through
some central agency or other. A London-based agency?
But no, not an agency as such, simply an agent. One man
– Christian Sommer – the undoubted head of a smuggling
racket which, Gerry strongly suspected, would include far
more than works of art. Drugs, more than likely, worth
millions at street value.

There was little talk, a great deal of action. The men
heaving and rolling the casks and boxes had obviously done
this work many times before. A grim looking lot, they wore
dark clothing, sailor-caps and sea-boots, speaking as and
when necessary in low, gutteral accents, German, Russian
or Scandanavian – Gerry could not be sure which.

Visions arose of another age, long gone, of Dogberry the
magistrate supervising the operation. The cave would have
been lit then with flickering torches and candles, casting
dancing shadows on walls and ceiling. The presence of the
two women surprised her, and yet Millie in dark slacks and
a thick-knit fisherman's jersey, with her cropped hair and

flat chest, seemed less out of place than Mrs Temple, whom she associated more with cooking and flowered pinnies, than with smuggling.

She now knew that she had been right in assuming some kind of link between Christian Sommer and the Berengers' housekeeper. Now she was equally convinced that the relationship included Millie Carslake. The resemblance between Anita and Millie was too strong to be coincidental. They had to be sisters.

Had Maurice found out what was going on in the warren beneath Black Gull? Was that what he meant by 'dreadful things, hidden away'? Could that be the reason why Anita Temple had tried to poison him? And where did Lisl fit into the picture? Impossible to believe that she had any connection with – evil. Lisl was a well balanced woman of the world, happily married to a rich, successful man she adored. She was self assured, talented in her own right, lovely to look at, a charming hostess who enjoyed entertaining her own and Maurice's wide coterie of friends, including herself, Gerry thought, remembering that first dinner party she'd attended chez Berenger, when she had sat opposite – *Christian Sommer*!

Suddenly, Gerry recalled Lisl's look of shocked disbelief that morning on the coffee shop terrace when she had referred to Cassie Bowen as Sommer's fiancée, her angry reaction to the news of the engagement. The reaction of a jealous woman, perhaps? Strange, she had not thought of that possibility at the time. And now was neither the time nor place to work out the ramifications of that possibility. The heist was nearing its end. The smugglers' work completed, they were on the point of departure to their mother vessel at anchor in the bay.

If the two women came this way to discover her presence in her narrow hiding place, her goose would be well and truly cooked, Gerry thought. Adhering to the adage that discretion is the better part of valour, the sooner she got the hell out of there and back to her room, the better, she realised. But Anita and Millie were heading in the opposite direction, and Gerry guessed why. There must be a passageway leading to Millie's antique shop – the obvious outlet for the gradual dispersal of smuggled works of art by a reputable local shopkeeper, loaded into a van parked on the clifftop by a woman often seen to be ferrying boxes and packages, items of secondhand furniture, and the like, to and from that van. Inured to the sight, no one would even stop to wonder what those boxes and packages contained. Millie Carslake was an inhabitant of long standing in the local community, therefore above suspicion.

The passage continued for a while in an upward direction, Gerry discovered, emerging warily from her hiding place when the coast was clear. There were rough-hewn steps here and there, and intersecting passages leading presumably to other caves – reminiscent of a subterranean Hampton Court Maze.

The sea could be heard as muffled drumbeats at an execution on Tower Hill in the days of Good Queen Bess. Thump, thump, crump, crump, and yet the sound was comforting inasmuch as it impinged on the eerie silence of this underground world, imparting an awareness of streets and shops, lamplight, stars, sand and sky.

If she came out of this mess alive, she would fly back to London as a homing pigeon to its loft, then walk the streets till the pavements wore holes in her shoes. *If* she came out of this mess alive!

So far, the passage had been dimly lit by a series of electric light bulbs dependent on an overhead cable. Suddenly, shockingly, the lights went out, leaving Gerry in total darkness, feeling strangely vulnerable and disorientated. Entombed, to put it mildly. Thank God for the torch she had with her, brand new, and with good solid batteries. Ah yes, that was better, much better. Now she could see where she was going once more, yet, curiously, the character of the passageway had changed dramatically. The stones beneath her feet were no longer dry but moss-grown and slippery, leading downwards, not up, and the sound of the sea on the rocks seemed much closer than before.

Obviously she was no longer heading towards the cellar beneath Millie Carslake's antique shop. In that moment of disorientation when the lights failed, she had lost her sense of direction and ended up in a narrow tunnel leading to an inlet in the cliff face. So what was wrong with that? With luck, she would soon be out of this rabbit warren, feeling fresh air on her face, looking up at the stars. A consummation devoutly to be wished, in her present state of mind, dog-tired and hungry into the bargain.

She must have been mad to even consider following Anita and Millie to their ultimate destination. She had simply been eager to discover if their scarred sister Phoebe Carslake was their partner in crime or, more importantly, the mysterious, shadowy figure who had masterminded the racket in the first place?

There was something infinitely sinister about a reclusive old woman in a darkened room, dressed all in black, who had put the fear of God into the Berengers, of all people, suggestive of a Black Widow spider in its web, spinning evil, rejoicing in it as a means of retribution against an unkind fate which had robbed her of her youth and beauty.

But even a recluse with a fire-damaged face could not possibly sit in a darkened room all day long, Gerry thought commonsensically. In the nature of things, she must need to spend a penny now and then, to make herself a cup of tea, to bathe and clean her teeth, to change her clothes, wash her yashmak and knickers at the kitchen sink, potter about the apartment in general, as women were wont to do in the privacy of their own home.

193

And yes, Gerry thought, she would dearly wish to meet Phoebe Carslake face-to-face one of these days . . .

The torchbeam caught a slight movement and Gerry's eyes followed its movement upwards before her body convulsed in uncontrolled vomiting.

The skeleton of a woman, discerned by the torchlight, had been suspended by the wrists above a bubbling pool of seawater seeping into the cave, her clothing reduced to mere rags by the relentless incursion of the tide about the island of rock which had been her last resting place on earth.

What Phoebe Carslake had suffered before death claimed her, Gerry could scarcely imagine. She had, quite literally, been crucified, chained up alive and left alone to rot, with no hope of escape from her bondage, simply the knowledge of the certain death confronting her without food or water to sustain her in her hopeless struggle for survival.

Deeply shocked, retching feebly, Gerry crawled on hands and knees towards the narrow entrance of the cave where, thanks be to God, she felt the night wind blowing on her face, and looked up to see the stars shining down on her.

But the night wind was not all she felt. The tide was rising. Kneeling, she felt the seepage of water, saw, with horror, the first rivulets washing into the mouth of the cave, heard the snakelike hiss of the sea, as Phoebe Carslake must have heard it in her agonising death throes.

Scrambling to her feet, Gerry now knew what Maurice had meant by 'dreadful things, hidden away'. He too must have chanced upon the pathetic, rag-draped skeleton and realised its identity, as she had done, by the scrap of material covering the lower jaw of the victim.

How long Phoebe Carslake had been dead was a matter of speculation which only expert forensic scientists could decide with any degree of certainty. Years, in all probability, which meant that the woman the Berengers had seen in that darkened room above the antiques shop had been an imposter. The self and same imposter who had dreamed up and promoted the fable of reclusive sister living in a darkened room, in a shadowland of warped imagination, a sick woman eternally repining the loss of her youth and beauty.

But now was neither the time nor the place to dwell on the subject. The sea was bubbling into the cave with the force of an express train, almost up to her knees, Gerry realised, wading towards the exit passage of the cave, intent on finding her way back to the one she had been in when the lights went out, before she had lost her way in the dark.

Shining her torch, breathless with exertion, bathed in perspiration, legs and feet sopping wet, at last she gained her objective: dry ground above sea level.

Back to the wall, she stood still for a while to regain her breath and decide which way to turn to find her way back to the cellar of Black Gull House.

Suddenly, the ceiling lights came on again as swiftly as they had gone out. Gerry's heart sank like a stone. Coming towards her were the last people on earth she wanted to see: the sisters from hell, Anita Temple and Millie Carslake. The latter holding a revolver.

Eighteen

M illie's low, mindless laugh sent a chill down Gerry's
spine. "I take it you've met Phoebe?" she chuckled.
"Looking remarkably well preserved for her age, don't
you think?"

"That's enough, Millie," Mrs Temple said warningly.
"Let's just get on with it, shall we? There are questions
to be answered, and time's moving on. The sooner we get
this over and done with, the better."

"Get what over and done with?" Gerry asked, but she
could hazard a guess: a spell of mental torture followed by
a bullet through the brain, if she was lucky. If not, death
by starvation in an underground cavern with a skeleton for
company. Given the choice, she'd prefer the bullet through
the brain.

"You'll find out soon enough," Millie assured her. "Now,
drop that torch, put your hands up and start walking!"

For a brief moment, Gerry considered the possibility of
a left hook to Mrs Temple's jaw, a well-aimed kick in the
region of Millie's midriff, a courageous dash for freedom.

As if reading her mind, "Don't even think about it," Millie
advised her. "You'd be dead within seconds!"

Gerry felt inclined to believe her. Obviously the woman
was as mad as a hatter, betrayed by her fiercely burning eyes
in the evil mask of her face. A woman who had already killed
and would not hesitate to do so again.

As for her sister, Anita Temple, her murderous attempts

had been just as evil, if less successful – that fire in her room on the night of her arrival at Black Gull House, the slow, systematic poisoning of Maurice Berenger, her collusion in the death of Phoebe Carslake. Whether or not she had been present at the time of her sister's rough crucifixion in that underground cavern, she must have known about it and turned a blind eye to it – an act of cruelty against any human being, unimaginable against a member of her own family. And so, presumably, Anita Temple too, was mad?

Walking ahead of the two women, Gerry thought of Pelops, killed and eaten by Tantalus, his own father who, like poor Phoebe Carslake, had ended up chained in an underground cavern.

Classical mythology was one thing, reality a different kettle of fish entirely. This feeling of helplessness in the hands of the enemy, a theme touched upon often in her novels in imaginary situations dreamed up to thrill the readers. She said, "You don't think you'll get away with this, do you? The police know my whereabouts. They'll come looking for me."

Millie chuckled. "Not to worry. They'll find you!"

As Gerry had suspected, the passage led to the cellar beneath the antiques shop, a flight of stone steps leading to the interior of the shop. "This will do," Millie said shortly. "You, sit down over there," indicating a high-backed chair. "Now, about the police. How much do they know?"

Thinking quickly, drawing her bow at a venture, taking a calculated risk, she said, "About Christian Sommer, you mean? Pretty well everything, I imagine. It's just a matter of time before his arrest for the London murders. He may well be in custody right now, helping the police with their enquiries, as the saying goes."

The effect on Mrs Temple was electrifying. Eyes blazing, face contorted with anger, "You're lying," she uttered

197

hoarsely. "There is no proof against him whatsoever! He saw to that!"

"That's where you're wrong," Gerry said coolly, despite her fast-beating heart and racing pulse, "he made several mistakes. That bottle of sleeping tablets, for instance, found beside Liam McEvoy's body. He left fingerprints. He really should have worn gloves."

"He *did* wear gloves! I told him to wear gloves, and he always did as he was told . . ."

"For God's sake, Phyllis, if that precious son of yours has blown it, that's his bad luck. What we need to know is the whereabouts of the eggs. We can't afford to go without them. She *has* to know where they are hidden, what that bloody gardener of hers did with them after he stole them." The truth suddenly dawned on Gerry – Anita Temple and Phyllis Constantine were one and the same person!

Millie had interrupted her sister impatiently. Now she was standing within inches of Gerry, the revolver pressed against her ribs. "Well, come on," she hissed. "We know they weren't in the shed, so where are they?"

"*Eggs?*" Gerry frowned. She felt inclined to laugh. Here she was, a gun to her ribs, in peril of her life, being questioned about eggs, of all things. "What eggs are you on about?"

"Don't pretend you don't know. Charlie Constantine's collection of Fabergé eggs. Half a million pounds worth! Perhaps more! I want them, and I intend having them!"

"*You* want them?" Mrs Temple burst forth. "*You* intend having them? But they're *mine*! Charles was *my* husband, and in case you've forgotten, it was *I* who spotted them in the first place, *I* who persuaded him to buy them, *I* who smuggled them through Customs!"

"Yes, and it was you who lost track of them, remember?" Millie said scathingly, "and serve you damn well right, you stupid fool! You should have known better than to rush off the way you did!"

"I *had* to! I was *desperate*!" Anita Temple's voice had risen along with her temper.

Millie interrupted contemptuously, "And you knew exactly where to come running to for help. You owe me plenty, Phyllis Constantine, and don't you forget it! You could have kidded Charlie into believing that he was the father, but oh no! Well, I told you all along that that bloody Dane wouldn't marry you, so *I* got lumbered with you all those years – not Phoebe. Phoebe didn't want to know, the selfish cow! All she cared about was money, holding on to the purse strings."

"She deserved what she got in that nice little fire I arranged for her." Millie chuckled evilly. "That put paid to her vanity once and for all. No wonder she couldn't bear to look in a mirror when I was through with her! A stroke of genius on my part, I'd say!"

Gerry listened intently, slotting together the missing pieces of the jigsaw puzzle in her mind, realising the truth of the saying, 'A house divided against itself, cannot stand', sensing the enmity between the sisters, beginning to understand the train of events leading to a series of brutal murders. Murders based on greed, hatred, and a wicked desire for revenge on Millie's part, greed and an unhealthy kind of mother love, on her sister's . . .

Now everything pointed quite clearly to the guilt of Phyllis Constantine, AKA Anita Temple's, illegitimate son, Christian Sommer, in the London murders, and at last she had grasped the full meaning of that 'shopping list' which she, Gerry, had discovered in the Hampstead repository: a poor old man's obsession with eggs. Not 'hen fruit', as she had imagined, but golden eggs, jewel-studded, fashioned by a master craftsman whose name had become synonymous with the fruit of his dedicated workmanship, with diamonds, sapphires, rubies and emeralds.

But even if her life depended on it, she had no more idea than the man in the moon as to what had become of Mr Constantine's eggs, unless . . . A thought occurred. Something Maggie Bowler had said to her that weekend at the Hamburger Joint – 'The best place to hide a banana is in a fruit bowl!' By the same token, Gerry figured, the best place to hide eggs would be inside a Victorian egg-holder, of the kind she had purchased from Millie Carslake, of the kind she had noticed in the Hampstead repository with its lid sellotaped securely in place.

Dear Maggie Bowler, Gerry thought fondly, wishing she was here with her now, muscles flexed, ready, willing and able to go into battle on her behalf. The Carslake siblings wouldn't stand an earthly chance of survival against a fifteen-stone, ex-lady-mud-wrestler with her dander up. But there was no one here in this second-rate antiques shop, dimly lit by candlelight, with shadowy corners, and the slow, sonorous ticking of a grandfather clock in the background, apart from herself and her captors. The hands of the clock were solemnly ticking away the minutes of her time left on earth. Tick, tock, tick, tock.

It had been a good life, all told, Gerry reckoned. All too short, but sweet while it lasted, thanks mainly to Bill Bentine, her knight in shining armour, and her friends, Maggie and Barney Bowler. Lisl and Maurice Berenger, too. Especially Maurice, whom she regarded as a father figure, far more dear to her than her own father had ever been.

But what the hell was the matter with her? She was still alive and kicking, for God's sake, and she'd better believe it, otherwise she risked having her ashes scattered on Hampstead Heath, and no way did she intend ending up on that 'Blasted Heath'!

Suddenly, all hell broke loose. First came the wailing of police sirens from the carpark, then the sound of a rocket fired from the sea, a distress signal of some kind, she imagined.

Whatever, with a well-aimed blow at Millie's revolver which sent it skittering across the floor, along with its owner, springing up from the chair she was sitting in, picking it up, and taking aim, she hefted it against the shop window, shattering the glass with an explosion of sound in the quiet air of the street beyond, yelling like a banshee as she did so, pausing momentarily to deal with the woman she would always think of as Mrs Temple, who had her hands about her throat, intent on adding yet another murder to her list of crimes so far.

In time to come, Gerry would feel deeply ashamed of kneeing an elderly woman in the groin, as she had done her son, but there was really no other option, under the circumstances, during that brief life or death struggle by candlelight, with blood flowing freely from both protagonists, given the broken glass surrounding them, so that neither would emerge unscarred by the ordeal.

Half fainting from shock and blood loss as she climbed from the shattered window into the street beyond, bemusedly, Gerry heard a familiar voice in her ear. "Thank God I reached you in time!" Bill Bentine murmured, holding her in his arms.

Smiling faintly, she whispered, "What the hell took you so long?" seconds before lapsing into unconsciousness.

The sleeping village had suddenly come alive to the awareness of something untoward and dramatic happening in their midst. There were uniformed figures in the street near Millie Carslake's shop, which looked as if a bomb had hit it, with all the broken glass and a hefty chair on the pavement, along with blood and scattered *objets d'art*.

There were glo-coated paramedics, two women receiving attention, a third being led away in handcuffs, coastguard cutters heading out to sea, flashing blue lights on the carpark, people emerging from doorways to find out what was going on at four o'clock in the morning.

Gerry's hands, arms and face had been badly cut in the glass explosion. Beside her in the ambulance on the way to Whitby Hospital, Bill remembered his drive from London as a nightmare episode, seemingly endless miles of motorways, oncoming headlights from the opposite carriageways, rain hitting the windscreen, the monotonous rhythm of the wipers, the relentless drumming of the tyres. There had been much nervous tension, the gut feeling of something awful about to happen, a strong premonition that Gerry was in danger, badly in need of help, allied to the frustration of not being able to get to her quickly enough.

Then had come the added frustration of minor roads in what appeared to be the back of beyond, of losing his way not once but three times before he virtually hit the Robin Hood's Bay signpost. Not a swearing man by nature, he had surprised himself by his previously unsuspected command of obscenities uttered at that juncture.

Reaching the carpark, stumbling from the driving seat of the Golf, he had found his way almost instinctively to Black Gull House, at which point he had heard the wailing of the police car sirens in the distance, and witnessed the explosion of glass from the antiques shop window a few yards away, including the landing on the pavement of what appeared to be a hefty Jacobean armchair. By which time the police had arrived on the scene to find him holding Gerry in his arms, to the sound of a rocket or distress signal of some kind fired from the sea.

Gerry had been put to bed in a private room adjacent to the women's ward. Bill elected to stay at the hospital for as long as necessary, at least until she recovered consciousness from the morphine injection she'd been given to dull the pain of her injuries. The police were in evidence in the foyer where Bill was sitting – two young male constables and a WPC. The less badly-injured woman, who had been with them in the ambulance under the charge of a WPC, had been taken to Casualty for further treatment.

Desperately hungry, and in dire need of a bath and a shave, Bill wondered how come the police had appeared at the scene of the antiques shop incident so promptly? When he asked, he was told that they had acted on information received, leaving him none the wiser. Information from whom, for God's sake? About what? A gang of terrorists, the planting of a bomb? Darned if he could make head or tail of it. Moreover, he'd been asked for proof of identity and his relationship to Gerry before being allowed to accompany her to hospital. At which point he had dragged the name of Detective Inspector Clooney into the catechism, had given them his phone number and requested an urgent, immediate call to Hampstead Police Station in corroboration of the fact that he had alerted Clooney to the possibility of a life-threatening attack on Geraldine Frayling, which had actually taken place, as he had predicted.

Hardly likely that DI Clooney would be on duty at that hour of the morning, had come the reply.

"Then have them ring his home address! Well, don't just *stand* there! *Do* it! This is an emergency!" he'd shouted. Seldom had Bill felt so masterful before as he had done then, kneeling on a pavement, holding Gerry in his arms, his clothing stained with her blood, faced with the dreadful possibility of losing her – his star performer who had brought fun and laughter into his life, his Pearl Beyond Price. His wonderful, brave, amazing Gerry.

Yet even now, in this place of seeming safety, with police on guard in the hospital foyer, Bill retained the gut feeling that something was terribly wrong somewhere, that Gerry was not yet out of danger. To do with tiredness, he supposed, an empty stomach, and the irritation of his chin in need of a razor.

*　　　*　　　*

The initial sensation was that of a soft, billowy cloud settling delicately on her face, nothing to be afraid of, nothing to worry about. Gerry had always loved clouds floating gently above the world, like swan's down . . .

But this cloud was becoming increasingly heavy and insistent, no longer gentle but demanding, making it difficult for her to breathe.

Struggling for breath, too weak to fight off the attack, she caught the unmistakable scent of a well-known perfume, an individual perfume, created in Paris, for only one person on earth – Lisl Berenger.

The voice, heard from afar, as if in a dream, was also familiar, that of Maurice Berenger, hoarse with emotion, crying out to Lisl to let go of the pillow, that it was all over now. All over now . . .

Then came a stronger, more decisive voice, a scuffling sound as, grasping Lisl's wrists, Bill forced her backward from the bed, at the same time calling out for someone to come quickly to help Maurice and herself.

Gasping for breath, emerging from darkness into light, Gerry heard the sound of running footsteps, saw Bill engaged in a desperate struggle to subdue Lisl, flurries of white and navy blue as nurses and police crowded into the room, Maurice weeping openly, covering his face with his hands, being led back to bed by a ward sister, and Lisl, her face a mask of fury, trying desperately to free herself from Bill's restraining grip on her wrists, to no avail. She heard her sharp cry of terror as the police took charge of her.

Then Bill was beside her bed, speaking softly, telling her not to worry, that she was safe now. Quite safe.

Nineteen

Nothing in the world was more frightening or disturbing than the realisation that someone regarded as a friend was nothing of the kind after all, but a deadly enemy, a demon face hidden behind a smiling mask. A potential killer. Gerry had been right about that supposition.

Even now, with Christmas fast approaching, Gerry could not bring herself to believe that Lisl, of all people, had tried to murder her, and might well have succeeded had it not been for Maurice.

What it must have cost him, in terms of mental suffering, to blow the whistle on the evil happenings at Black Gull House, in which his wife was deeply involved, she could scarcely imagine.

Knowing how much Lisl meant to him, it must have come as a bitter blow that the woman he adored had long been engaged in a passionate love affair with another man – Christian Sommer.

A highly sensitive, astute human being, he must have pondered long and hard his wife's obsessive desire to purchase Black Gull House from its reclusive owner, Phoebe Carslake.

He could not possibly have known, at the time, that Phoebe, Millie Carslake, and the woman he knew as Anita Temple, were related to Christian Sommer, or that the veiled recluse who had signed the deeds of the property was an imposter, that the real Phoebe Carslake had been chained up alive, and left to rot in a cavern beneath the house which had once, legitimately, belonged to her.

But Lisl must have known. Oh yes, assuredly, Lisl must have known, and turned a blind eye in her obsessive desire to please her lover, who was desperately in need of an ally, a new, bona fide owner of Black Gull to ensure the continuation of his smuggling activities, in view of his Aunt Phoebe's stubborn refusal to 'play ball' any longer.

Making preparations for Christmas, Gerry deeply regretted all that had happened in the past few weeks, particularly the loss of Maurice Berenger from her life. Lisl too, now await-ing trial alongside Christian Sommer, Phyllis Constantine and Mildred Carslake, all of whom faced charges of murder, attempted murder, collusion in the act of murder, and the smuggling of illegal substances and works of art.

Acting on information received from Maurice Berenger, Customs officials had boarded a Norwegian fishing vessel within the three mile exclusion zone, to discover a hoard of heroin stashed away in the hold. The captain and crew had been placed under arrest, the vessel impounded and escorted to Whitby Harbour, where the captain and his crew were bundled into police vehicles and taken to Police Head-quarters to spend what was left of the night in prison cells.

Next day, well enough to answer questions put to her by a Detective Inspector Brambell, and despite her admission that Lisl Berenger had held a pillow to her face, Gerry had refused to press charges against her. Poor Lisl, she reckoned, had suffered enough; a basically kind, warm-hearted human being, who had had the misfortune to fall desperately in love with a man much younger than herself, who had misused her shamefully to gain his own ends. No way was Gerry prepared to add to her distress, to the shame of knowing that her lover had cared far less for her than she had for him.

Later, Maurice had come to her room to thank her for her kindness.

"Lisl was kind to me," Gerry said simply. "You both were. And we all make mistakes." She paused. "How are you feeling now?" She meant physically.

"Guilty," he said slowly, his eyes filling with tears. "The way Judas Iscariot must have felt when he betrayed Jesus. But what else could I possibly have done? I knew what was happening at Black Gull. I'd seen that wretched skeleton, begun to put two and two together in my mind. But I still couldn't bring myself to believe that – Lisl was involved. I thought she loved me, you see?" He buried his face in his hands, his shoulders shaking with sobs wrung from the depths of his body.

"Please don't, Maurice," Gerry said tenderly. "None of this was your fault. You *must* believe that!"

"I wish I could, but I can't!" he wailed, lifting his face from his hands. "The last thing on earth I wanted was to hurt Lisl! She's my wife, for Christ's sake! Even when I started feeling ill, I couldn't bring myself to believe that she was responsible, yet I knew all along that I was being slowly and systematically poisoned, the reason why I refused medical help: I was so afraid of finding out the truth! Afraid the doctors would find traces of arsenic in my guts. Sorry, but that's the plain and simple truth. I'd sooner have died than have Lisl accused of attempted murder!"

Back on form, "You weren't thinking straight then, were you?" Gerry reminded him. "If you'd – popped your clogs – so to speak, there'd have been an inquest. Whatever poison you'd been fed would have been discovered as surely as eggs is eggs! But, wait for it, my belief is that there was no recognisable poison as such. You were simply being fed meals prepared well in advance and insufficiently heated to kill the bacteria.

"Take chicken, for example, removed from the deep-freeze, not thawed-out as per instruction, just given a couple of whirls in the microwave, and hey presto! Bugs galore!

207

As long as it was reasonably tender and tasty, would you have known, would anyone, that it hadn't been thawed out properly in the first place? As for fish, would you have known that it was probably days old, not even refrigerated, just left on a work-surface to gather more germs?"

"Thanks, Gerry dear," Maurice said gratefully, "but Lisl must have known what was happening, and given her consent. That is what I can't come to terms with, the reason why, when all this is over, I shall put the Hampstead house on the market and go abroad somewhere, to live. America, most probably. You see, my dear, Lisl has made it perfectly clear that she no longer wants to live with me, and I couldn't bear to go on living in our old home, without her. You – understand?"

"Yes," Gerry said bleakly. "I understand, but nothing will ever be the same again, without you."

Now, here she was, tucking sprigs of holly behind picture frames, pausing now and then to make shopping lists for food enough to feed an army – including eggs.

Eggs!

Mr Constantine's gold, jewelled clutch, had been discovered at the Hampstead repository, in a Victorian egg-holder similar to the one she had bought from Millie Carslake's shop, the lid of which had been stuck on with masking tape.

At first glance, she'd been told by Detective Inspector Clooney, those Fabergé eggs had appeared to be worthless junk, resembling egg-shaped stones, dirt encrusted, the reason why Constantine had picked them up for a song on that fateful trip to Russia when his wife, Phyllis, had met and fallen in love with a Danish sea captain, the man destined to father their son, Christian.

Clooney, Gerry recalled, had been quite charming to her the day he had called at The Eyrie to thank her for the tip-off which had led to the discovery of Charles Constantine's treasure trove. In fact, she had warmed to him on that occasion and, being a kindhearted girl, never one to hold grudges, she had made him a cup of coffee and a bacon butty, and congratulated him on his handling of the case of what the Press were pleased to refer to as 'The Antiques Murders'. She had felt pleased, for his sake, that he would quit the Force in a blaze of glory, come Christmas.

Christmas! Good lord, she really must get on with things: airing beds, shopping, buying and decorating the trees she had planned for the hall and the drawing room, purchasing lots of surprise presents for her guests, Bill and Maggie and Barney Bowler, making sure there was plenty of booze, having her hair done, treating herself to some new clothes to accentuate her new, slimmed down silhouette, a bottle of exotic perfume.

Perfume! Lisl! She now realised that Lisl's attempt to put paid to her had stemmed from a bitter, rejected woman's feelings of hatred and resentment towards someone who had reduced the frail edifice of her life to ruins, shattering her faith in her lover when she had heard of Sommer's engagement to Cassie Bowen, her hatred centring on the person who had broken the news to her so glibly, so unthinkingly. Gerry would never forgive herself for that, but how could she have known how deeply that news would affect Lisl?

Then, to add more fuel to the fire, she had taken matters into her own hands concerning Maurice's illness.

Useless to dwell on the past, Gerry told herself severely, and yet – how could she possibly forget it? She couldn't, nor would she wish to. The best she could do was learn how to live with it, the way Zoe Smith had done.

Zoe's Christmas card, posted from Ireland, contained the brief message that she and Mick were getting married in the new year, in a proper church. She had written in her sloping, childish handwriting, 'Mick and Liam's Ma has been ever so good to me. Marrying Mick don't mean I've forgot Liam, or ever could, but life goes on. Well, it has to, don't it?'

Smiling, Zoe had hit the nail squarely on the head, Gerry thought wistfully, propping up the card on her drawing room mantelpiece.

Bill's father had died ten years ago, since then his mother had remarried, and was now living in San Francisco. His sister, Marguerite, also lived abroad – in the south of France with her current boyfriend – whom she refused to refer to as her 'partner', this being 'no business deal', she'd explained to her brother.

When he knew that Maggie and Barney were spending Christmas at The Eyrie, Bill said he'd better bring a couple of ducks, to be on the safe side, and possibly a turkey and a sirloin of beef as standbys.

Gerry said he could bring what he liked, as long as he brought himself as well. Christmas wouldn't be Christmas without him. She thanked her lucky stars that she was still here to make plans and preparations for the festive season after all the attempts that had been made to separate her from her breath. At least she hadn't ended up blowing in the wind on the Blasted Heath!

Maggie and Barney were chuffed to bits to have been invited to spend Christmas 'up market', as Maggie put it. Normally, they opened the Caff on Boxing Day. This year, their clients could do without their cuppas and bacon butties, she'd decided, rushing 'up west' to buy presents for all and sundry, and to have her hair tinted a becoming shade of mahogany.

Bill was the first to arrive on Christmas Eve, having closed the office early in order to do some last minute shopping, including the comestibles. Mustn't forget the green peas, he thought, remembering that he and Gerry had jokingly agreed on duck and green peas for Christmas dinner, after the Clarinda Clarkson incident.

Waitrose was packed to the doors. Standing in the checkout queue, he recalled the fun they'd had that night at the Caff, their shared laughter when he'd regaled her with the saga of poor Clarinda's flying peas. But he and Gerry had shared far more than laughter these past months, deepening the bond between them. Never would he forget that moment when, holding her in his arms on the pavement near Millie Carslake's antiques shop, he had known, beyond doubt, how much she meant to him, how poor a place the world would be without her, that people like Gerry Mudd were irreplaceable.

People like Gerry Mudd? But there were no people *like* Gerry Mudd. She was a state of the art original!

He arrived on her doorstep hefting his overnight bag, an assortment of bulky carrier bags, and a binliner stuffed with gift-wrapped presents to stash away under the drawing room tree.

"Come in if you can get in," Gerry commented drily. "What have you done with the reindeer?"

"Here," he said, lumbering across the threshold, "you'd best put the peas in the deep-freeze, before they start swimming for shore!"

"Oh, Bill. How did you guess? How could you have known that all I really wanted for Christmas was a bag of frozen peas?"

"Call it intuition." He grinned amiably. "And while you're on about it, you might as well put the ducks, turkey and beef in the fridge before the weight of them pulls my arms from their sockets. Meanwhile, I'll just nip back to the car to bring in the rest of the gear."

"You mean there's more? Don't tell me you've brought along a Palm Court orchestra?"

"Now why didn't *I* think of that?"

He reappeared, minutes later, bearing a holly wreath for the front door, another binliner stuffed with presents, and a bouquet of red roses. "For you, Gerry," he said. "Merry Christmas, my love!"

Maggie and Barney put in their appearance much later, after they had closed the Caff for the night, bringing with them more presents, several bottles of wine, and a couple of hefty suitcases, to find the dining room table set with green candles in silver candelabra, a centrepiece of holly and Christmas roses, and a collation of cold food including smoked salmon, green and fresh fruit salads, prawn cocktails, chicken and mushroom vol-au-vents, cold roast beef and ham, cheeses, pickles, and a Black Forest gateau alongside a jug of thick Jersey cream.

"Eee, this is summat like," Maggie murmured admiringly. "If you only knew how sick and tired I am of bloody hamburgers and bacon butties!"

Christmas had got off to a flying start, Gerry thought gratefully, as pleased as Punch that Maggie and Barney had enjoyed their first meal under her roof, and looking forward to tomorrow, to cooking them a late breakfast, if they felt like it. Later, roast duck and all the trimmings, the opening of their presents to one another on Christmas morning, in an atmosphere of warmth, conviviality – and love. Above all – love. A thought uppermost in Gerry's mind, at the moment, knowing that she had fallen deeply and permanently in love with Bill Bentine, whether or not he had fallen in love with her, which seemed highly unlikely.

Ah well, returning to her memories of Bette Davis in *Now, Voyager*: "Why ask for the moon? We have the stars!"

After supper, they gathered in the drawing room for drinks, before bedtime.

"You've really made something of this place," Maggie said. "It feels like a proper home, all warm and cosy an', well, solid, if you get my meaning? I can't tell you how long it is since I sat near a real log fire. Beats all them syndicated whirligigs into a cocked hat. All fuss an' bustle an' no heat."

"What would you like to drink?" Gerry asked as she crossed to the sideboard.

"A drop of whisky would be nice," Maggie said.

"What about you, Barney?"

"The same for me, please."

"Bill?"

"Yes. Great."

"That's a nice-looking set of decanters you have there," Maggie remarked. "Does the lock fasten, by the way?"

"Yes. At least I suppose so. The key's here somewhere. I'll give it a try, shall I?" She fitted the key into the lock, and turned it.

"Gerry! Is anything the matter?" Quickly, Bill rose to his feet. She had turned pale, and her hands were trembling. "Here, let me help." He hurried towards her. "What happened?"

"Nothing, I . . ." She bit her lip. "It's just that, turning the key reminded me of . . . I'm sorry. I was just being daft. I couldn't help thinking of those three women, Lisl, Millie, and Phyllis Constantine, under lock and key – bound together like these three decanters in a tantalus."

"Shall I do the pouring?" Bill asked quietly.

"Thanks, Bill. If you wouldn't mind." Gerry returned to her chair.

Maggie said sympathetically, "I know how you feel. It's a bad job, isn't it? I feel sorry for anyone banged up, especially at Christmas, whether they deserve it or not. But try not to let it spoil your Christmas."

"Thanks, Maggie. I'm fine now."

"You're worn out, that's your trouble," Maggie said tenderly, leaning forward to squeeze Gerry's hand. "And no wonder, after all you've been through lately."

"Aye well, she don't need reminding of that," Barney said, accepting his glass of whisky, "not tonight of all nights. What I think is, let's make this a night-cap, shall we? Let the lass have an early night?"

"Yeah, you're right, as usual," Maggie conceded, "except I'd like to know how the new book's coming along."

Bill stepped into the breach. "It's coming along just fine," he said cheerfully, smiling at Gerry. "The girl has another bestseller in the pipeline. I'm already inundated with television and film offers, wheeling and dealing on her behalf. So congratulations, Gerry."

"I'll drink to that," Barney said solemnly, draining his glass. "Now, come on, my girl," he nodded to Maggie, "time for bed."

Gerry went up with them to make sure they had everything they wanted. Maggie hugged her warmly, and kissed her goodnight. "You don't know how much it means to us, being here," she said.

"You don't know how much it means to me, having you here."

Bill was standing near the fire when she returned to the drawing room, staring into the flames.

"A penny for your thoughts," Gerry asked.

"I was just thinking over what you said about the tantalus, the aptness of the simile: the three decanters, the restraining hasp, the lock and key. About this house, and the strange events that have taken place here. Sorry, am I upsetting you?"

"No. It's at the back of my mind most of the time. I often think about old Mr Constantine, living alone here, in squalor." She hunched her shoulders. "Perhaps it was here, in this very room, that he discovered the letter his wife had left him, saying she'd met someone else who cared for her far more than he ever had."

"Perhaps you'd rather not talk about it?"

214

"No, not at all. I'd like to talk about it, to get things straight in my mind, if you don't mind listening, that is?"

"Of course not. I'd like to get things clear in my mind, too. There's still a lot I don't know. How Lisl Berenger became involved in the smuggling racket, for instance, and how Mrs Temple fitted into the picture?"

"It all started a long time ago," Gerry said, sitting down to nurse the drink Bill had poured for her earlier. "When Mrs Temple – Phyllis Constantine – knew she was pregnant with another man's child, she sought sanctuary with her sisters in Robin Hood's Bay, believing it was there that she would meet up with her child's father again. Who knows what she thought? More than likely that he would take her to Denmark with him on his next trip abroad.

"No such luck, apparently! The dashing Dane didn't want to know, so Phyllis stayed on with her sisters until her son, Christian, was old enough for boarding school, when, so far as I can gather, Phyllis returned to London, with her son, to set up in what can best be described as a secondhand furniture shop, in the Mile End Road, with money provided by her sisters' smuggling activities. Except, of course, that the secondhand furniture shop was, in reality, a front for stolen goods, worth a small fortune to the buyers, hand-picked by Millie, to ensure the success of the business.

"Meanwhile, I suspect, Millie and Phoebe Carslake had begun to quarrel violently over the nefarious activities at Black Gull House. Phoebe wanted out and, in the long term, the poor soul's wish was granted, in the most horrible way imaginable."

"Please don't go on, if you'd rather not," Bill interrupted gently.

Gerry smiled wanly. "No, in the words of a well-known Quiz Master, 'I've started, so I'll finish'. There's not much left to tell, anyway. Where was I? Oh yes, well, by the time Christian Sommer's education was complete, his mother had amassed enough money to set him up in a small but lucrative antiques business of his own. But never had she forgotten that cache of Fabergé eggs belonging to her ex-husband, Charles Constantine, which rightly belonged to her, or so she imagined, since she had been instrumental in persuading him to buy them in the first place, and had smuggled them into England under the noses of the Customs and Excise Officers. Don't ask me how, but she succeeded. The mistake she made lay in leaving her husband so suddenly, when she knew she was pregnant, so distraught that she neglected to take with her a cool half a million's worth of merchandise, which she fully intended to get back, one day, by fair means or by foul.

"Then, when Lisl Berenger appeared, one day, in Christian Sommer's newly established fine art galleries in Chelsea, knowing who she was and where she lived – in the house next door to Charles Constantine's, *this* house, to be exact – and realising that Lisl had fallen head-over-heels in love with her son and would do anything to please him, Phyllis persuaded the besotted Lisl to hire her as a housekeeper, for the purpose of keeping a watchful eye on her ex-husband, for his own good, no doubt.

"Well, there you have it in a nutshell. Poor Lisl so madly in love that she couldn't see straight, a mother so bound up in her son that she induced him to commit three murders, at her behest, to ensure his safety against a blackmailer, Liam McEvoy, who had himself witnessed Sommer's theft of certain priceless artefacts discovered by Charles Constantine in the heyday of his world-wide renown as an archaeologist.

"But the murder syndrome, once started, didn't end there! Next on the list of victims came Anna Gordino, simply because she had had the misfortune to recognise Christian Sommer the night he padlocked the door of the garden shed, in which he had already hidden the body of Liam McEvoy.

"Not that poor Anna could have known that, at the time. She simply rang up someone she thought she could trust –

namely, the woman she knew as Anita Temple – for help and advice, in her dreadful dilemma.

"Of course, Mrs Temple advised her to leave London – this house – as quickly as possible, by the first train from Hampstead Station at eight o'clock next morning. She then rang up her son, from a public phonebox in the village, to incite him into committing a second murder. The third, that of Charles Constantine, was, I imagine, committed when the poor old man refused to reveal the whereabouts of his cache of Fabergé eggs. Perhaps the poor old soul was too far gone by that time, too ill to even remember what he had done with them. But he might well have remembered, had he been allowed to live, the identity of the man who had entered his room to wrest from him that vital information.

"Meanwhile, all that time, Lisl Berenger was becoming more and more involved in the affairs of Sommer and his scheming, cold-blooded mother, to the extent of agreeing to the purchase of a holiday home in a remote fishing village called Robin Hood's Bay, though she possibly scarcely knew why, at the time. Poor Lisl. By the time she found out why, she was as helpless as a fly in a spider's web to know which way to turn to get out of the mess she was in. A mess for which she was not entirely to blame. There," Gerry sighed deeply, "but for the Grace of God, go I."

"I see," Bill said gently, "thanks for telling me." He paused awhile. "So am I right in thinking that you have a poor opinion of the male gender, as a whole?"

Pondering the question, "Well no, not as a whole," Gerry confessed. "Why do you ask?"

"Hmmm? Oh, no reason in particular." Then, changing the subject adroitly, he asked. "So what's to become of Cassie Bowen, who also loved not wisely but too well? It was she, I imagine, who stole Mr Constantine's shopping list and opened your mail?"

"No, that was Mrs Temple." Gerry frowned. "Look, Bill, I can tell there's something up with you, so what is it?"

Bill prevaricated. "You haven't answered my question."

"*What* question?"

"About Cassie Bowen."

"Well, *I* don't know, do I? Knowing that daft ha'porth, she'll probably stand by her man till he comes out of clink thirty years hence, as bald as a coot and sporting a brand new set of dentures! Why ask me? After all, love's a funny thing, isn't it? No telling how it begins or how it will end."

"Well, maybe yes, maybe no," Bill conceded thoughtfully. "But not in my case, thank God. You see, Gerry, I know exactly how my own love affair began, and I really do need your advice on how it might end. The trouble is, the girl I'm in love with hasn't a clue how I feel about her."

Gerry's heart sank like a stone. So the thing she had dreaded all along, had finally happened? Imagining some slender, long-haired bimbo with a penchant for Italian swimwear, heading towards the door, she flung over her shoulder, "Then why don't you stop pratting about and ask her? For your information, Bill Bentine, I happen to be a crime novelist, not a bloody Agony Aunt!"

"Right, then, I'll take your advice, stop 'pratting about' and come straight to the point. So *you* stop 'pratting about' too, and answer one simple question: will you marry me?"

"Huh?"

"You heard!"

"Who? *Me*?"

"Yes! *You!*"

"You mean you really *want* me?"

"More than anything else in the world," Bill murmured tenderly, gathering her into his arms, his precious, one and only Gerry Mudd.